Going Too Far

'I suppose it's all about power,' I said defiantly, almost condescendingly, as Carlos slipped his hand up and down the wet satin.

He laughed in genuine amusement. 'Sure it's about power. But more than that, Bliss. I take part of my pleasure from giving it to you, as well as from seeing you unable to help responding to me.'

'Why? Do you take pleasure from humiliating me in public?'

'No, Bliss. You were getting pleasure from that. Weren't you?'

Of course I was. Don't we all like that element of danger in misbehaving in public, even if it's only as a teenager, snogging in your bedroom when your mum might burst in at any minute, or being felt up in the back row of the cinema.

'If what I'm feeling now isn't a sign that you're getting pleasure,' he said smugly, 'then I can only assume you've wet yourself.'

Other books by the author:

ON THE EDGE
FIRE AND ICE

Going Too Far

LAURA HAMILTON

BLACK
lace

Black Lace novels contain sexual fantasies.
In real life, make sure you practise safe sex.

First published in 2001 by
Black Lace
Thames Wharf Studios,
Rainville Road, London W6 9HA

Typeset by SetSystems Ltd, Saffron Walden, Essex
Printed and bound by Mackays of Chatham PLC

ISBN 0 352 33657 9

Chapter One

I don't like safety nets. Life should be a journey of adventure, not a trip through the maze of savings schemes and endowment policies with a nice pension waiting at the end, giving you the illusion that whatever happens, you're protected. When I booked my ticket for three months in South America my idea of taking sensible precautions was making an appointment to have my eyelashes dyed and my hair cut to avoid unnecessary grooming while on the road, not to mention the Inca Trail. However, in one of his occasional, guilt-provoked and sometimes unwelcome acts of financial generosity, Dad insisted on paying for me to have what he called a 'sound insurance policy'.

What I said about safety nets being an illusion: here's the perfect example. Thanks to Dad I was insured against flight delays, luggage losses, missing money, robbery, sickness, injury, death and disease. The only thing he hadn't protected me against was something neither of us could have foreseen: the fact that my friend and travelling companion would break her leg ten days before we were due to go.

1

Rachel put up with my scathing fury for at least five minutes before she put the phone down on me. While I couldn't blame her – after all, how many times do you want someone to call you a stupid selfish thoughtless cow? – I don't think it was out of order to express my contempt for her choice of that particular weekend to try out downhill mountain biking in Ingleborough, particularly on the wheelie version of off-piste.

Having done the shouting – at least for now – I turned to practicalities, which meant first of all an anaesthetic in the form of a large lemon vodka from the freezer – special offer at the Co-op – and secondly a trawl through my mental address book. While I could easily have found someone to step in at the last minute for a week in Turkey or Cephalonia, a three-month trip around South America was going to be a problem. The only people I knew who could take three months off work, or who had no work to take three months off, couldn't afford it.

Maybe an ad in *Time Out*? That seemed like the best bet:

THELMA SEEKS LOUISE! Smart, intelligent designer, F, 30, n/s, suddenly let down due to illness, seeks companion for three-month trip to South America, starting in Peru in ten days' time, ending in Argentina, including walking, camping, sightseeing, wine drinking. Only solvent, personable fit applicants please, with photo.

I wrote it on the back of an envelope, crossed it out and started again, then crumpled it up and chucked it. This was a three-month trip, not just a few drinks in All Bar One. What if I got a psychopath? Someone who seemed fine in London but turned into a nutter once we were tucked up in the specially purchased light-

2

weight tent in the middle of the Atacama Desert? I'd be better off on my own.

Besides, people never take me seriously at first. Well, how many people do you know called Bliss? My mother, lovely as she is, was a drippy hippy when I was conceived on Plumpton Racecourse though in fairness to her I should point out that at the time there was a pop festival going on rather than a horse race. It could have been worse: she could have named me after one of the bands there. I don't much fancy Fairport, Sabbath or Purple. Or Plum, after the location. Anyway she's probably got it wrong about the bands that actually did play; after all it was only months after the end of the 60s, and going by the state of her memory Mum was definitely there.

Dad was – and still is – a Dutchman called Willem van Bon. They'd met two days before and got together in a haze of peace, love and marijuana, and I was conceived under canvas or, as Mum usually claims, in the woods on the edge of the field as Deep Purple closed the concert. I've always felt a bit miffed that they didn't make it the Isle of Wight festival; it's the one everyone's heard of. I wonder what difference it might have made to me if I'd been conceived to the strains of Leonard Cohen or Bob Dylan rather than Deep Purple.

You might think after Plumpton Mum and Dad would go their separate ways before they even knew I was in the pipeline, but in fact they fell in love and she went to live in Holland with him. She goes misty-eyed when she tells me about how cool it was in Amsterdam, where Dad was a student. Unfortunately laid-back life in the communal house by the canal where they took turns to cook the lentils and buy the dope came to an end once he graduated and moved to Rotterdam, bought a suit and got a job. Within a couple of years, thanks to the Arabs raising oil prices, he was making loads of money in the new business of oil trading, but the suit had been enough for Mum and she'd already taken me back to England to get her head together, leaving me cheated of any memory of the land of my father and fumbling in the dark of the three-day week that was making him rich.

Having rejected the material world of Rotterdam Mum was content with making macramé potholders in a tatty flat in Stoke Newington, not that the tattiness impinged on me. The area was happily multicultural and when I went to school a year later I mixed naturally and joyfully with friends such as Earl and Yasmin and Elvena and Hassan as well as Emma and Susan and Robert. It wasn't until I went to comprehensive school that I realised that Bliss van Bon was a bit of a strange label to be saddled with.

I digress. The third thing I had to do was phone Kip and bawl him out. He's my second best friend, occasional fuck and unfortunately the little shit who'd taken Rachel down Ingleborough the hard way.

'Don't say a word, Bliss. I'm coming round.'

Then the bastard put the phone down.

I suppose he guessed that I wouldn't be able to sit fuming for half an hour until he got here and hoped I'd have recovered a bit of my cool in the meantime. He should know me better by now; I'm good at doing angry. To reinforce it I rifled through the guide books, picking out all the places where they suggested you didn't go alone, where you were likely to get mugged, pickpocketed or even murdered. South America did most emphatically not seem the sort of continent where a girl wanted to be on her own. Kip had some explaining to do. What made him decide to introduce Rachel to mountain biking at this particular moment in her life? I couldn't even force him into taking her place. Well, I suppose I could try, but after serving years of

4

his apprenticeship in journalism, starting with the *Hackney Gazette* and working his way up through the lifestyle pages of different newspapers and magazines, he's recently landed a job at *Slice* magazine. Yes, that one, the style bible of the seriously cool and achingly rich. I can't even afford the magazine, never mind the stuff in it. Unless he could convince his editor that South America was where it was at, cutting-edge-wise, and he needed three months to research it, I was on my own.

The phone rang; Vicki wanted to drop off some stuff at the flat while she had the use of her brother's car. I had to agree, despite the fact that it would interrupt whatever revenge I was going to exact on Kip, as I wanted to make sure nothing went wrong with our little arrangement. She's moving in while I'm away, paying the full rent, as she's just split up with her partner and needs some breathing space. The timing couldn't have been better. It's not a great flat, I have to say, but Stratford's quite convenient and I've been too busy trying to learn Spanish and practise my non-existent camping skills in Epping Forest to want to pack up my stuff and trek over to Mum's with it. It's a shame Vicki's gay otherwise I could enlist her help in some special revenge game, but there you go.

Kip beat her to it. I pulled him through the door and into the sitting room by his tie – didn't know they were back in fashion – and threw him into the middle of the room, where he landed quite gracefully on the sofa. I hadn't meant to do that – I had intended him to hit the deck – but, seeing as Kip actually enjoys pain, maybe it was better not to indulge him when I was out to punish him. But sometimes it gets confusing thinking of everything the opposite way round to the norm.

'Thanks, Bliss. Does that mean I'm forgiven?' He was smiling in his wolfish, sharp-toothed, wild-man way.

'Like buggery,' I replied, rather compounding my earlier error, as he licked his lips at the prospect of painful, unlubricated anal penetration. 'Let's start again, Kip.'

I planted myself in front of him, hands on hips and looking down on his jet black Razor Razor haircut. 'Your role is to play Mr Sorry. You are contrite and you want to try to compensate me in any way you can for potentially ruining my trip. I want you humble.'

'Oh, I am,' he assured me, pulling off the tie and starting to unbutton his shirt. 'I am so sorry, mistress. I'll do anything you want, anything at all, to make up for what I've done.'

'Yes, you bloody well will, but I don't know why you think you can take your clothes off. Your compensation to me is to do exactly what I want you to do but without me punishing you. Get it?'

A snarl replaced his smile. 'All right, spoilsport.'

'That's you, not me. Do your shirt up; Vicki's coming round in a minute with some of her gear.'

'God forbid she should see a man's naked chest,' he said sullenly, but still not rebuttoning. 'So you're going to punish me by making me watch you two make out and then send me home untouched, I suppose?'

'Wrong. She's not the type to enjoy an audience, though if she was it'd be a start. As you didn't give me a chance to get a word in on the phone you can hardly complain that I'm going to have to give some time to somebody else. For all you know I had the whole local Territorial Army coming round to give me lessons in naked square bashing. Whatever that is.'

'I should be so lucky. What time's she coming? Let me give you a quick hand job as phase one of my compensation package.'

I looked at my watch. 'Ten minutes. OK, then. I need to release some tension.'

Lifting my skirt and slipping down my knickers I moved closer. The restraint of knicker elastic against parted thighs turns me on usually but I decided I wanted maximum input and so stepped out of them and spread my legs wide. 'Actually, I don't want to hear your voice for a couple of minutes. Get your tongue moving, and do it fast.'

His head went obediently towards his target and his tongue connected, making me aware that anger is a real turn on. But I was still furious with him, and decided that not only did I not want to hear his voice but I didn't want to see his face either. So I dropped my skirt over his head and imagined he was Gabriel Byrne. I've always had a thing for older men and, as you may have gathered, for men with black hair. Of course Kip's half Irish as well, but he wasn't in my mind at the time. Gabriel's tongue was going up and down my slit and then fastening urgently on my clit, and I bucked my hips back and forth, thinking of what I could do for him given half the chance. The tongue wasn't quite hard enough though.

'Your tongue's fantastic, but can you leave it and finger me?' I instructed breathily, talking to Gabriel. Encouraged, Kip's head emerged from my skirt as his right hand moved into place. 'Not you, prat,' I snapped, exasperated. 'Get back under the skirt, I don't want to see you. And shut up.'

He did as he was told, maybe a bit confused as to who exactly I had been talking to, and I resumed my conversation with Gabriel as he pressed down on my mons at the same time as rubbing the fiery tip of my clit. 'That's brilliant; that's perfect; I'm nearly there; you're fantastic; oh my God . . .'

Gabriel brought me to a shuddering, knee-trembling climax and gripped me with just the right amount of pressure as my muscles clenched and unclenched against his hand. If only I could repay him. Briefly I lost myself in a reverie of how I could do just that but then realised there was a head up my skirt.

'Christ, get out, Kip. You've done your bit for now.'

His head came back into view and I smoothed my skirt down, inspecting it critically. It's a new fabric, a polymer-enhanced linen and silk mix that is going to be everywhere next year, take my word for it. It was printed in one of my own designs, a dizzy black and white spiralling print with fluorescent pink and yellow blobs, just like Liquorice Allsorts, born of op art out of Jackson Pollock, which is going to be everywhere, etc. I'm very pleased with my skirt; the odd sample coming my way is the only perk of fabric design, but at least it means that I'm not totally dressed by Oxfam or George.

'Bloody big head, you've stretched my skirt.'

'That's it, moan. You were talking nicely enough to me just now.'

'No I wasn't: I was talking to Gabriel Byrne. He was there in spirit; you were just the right hand.'

'What does that mean? I don't get any credit for it?' He licked his fingers, his big tongue curling in what I presume he thought was a suggestive manner, but I could have assured him it was not.

I looked down. 'You've got a stiffie; what more do you want?'

'You know . . .' He pouted suggestively and licked again in a travesty of a top-shelf mag. It's hard to know whether to laugh or cry at him sometimes.

The bell rang and he stopped licking and wiped his hand round his mouth as I answered the door.

Vicki seemed to have forgotten my flat was already furnished. A stereo, lampstand, TV, two large but sickly-looking plants and four heavy boxes were decanted from the back of her brother's estate. His painting and decorating gear was still in the car.

'And this is without your clothes,' I observed. 'Going to be a tight squeeze.'

'Not many of those,' she retorted gloomily.

We embraced, with an extra long hug as I feel sorry for her. Correction: I felt sorry for her because she was living with Jo, but now she's getting out I think things can only get better. Jo is a totally self-absorbed bitch, neurotically obsessed about getting older, and she's been taking it out on Vicki. The poor girl has really suffered; it's been like living with Sister George. Vicki's actually quite attractive but thanks to jealous Jo she's spent the last year making herself more and more frumpy so that Jo could be the attractive one. Still, with a bit of luck, let loose in my flat with my extensive pre-owned wardrobe and makeup at her disposal she might pull herself together.

'You know Kip, don't you?'

'We've met,' she said, nodding disinterestedly at him. 'Your shirt's undone.'

'I was just doing a Gabriel Byrne impersonation,' he explained. If Vicki was confused she didn't remark on it.

'Where shall I put this stuff for now?'

'There's plenty of room in the bedroom.' She followed me in and I put the first box down near the window and turned on the light. I only go in there to sleep and dress so I keep the curtains drawn. Sex in bed really turns me off and I never let anyone stay the night, so I think of the bedroom as my nun's cell.

We traipsed in and out with the stuff while Kip watched from the settee. It's not that he's lazy: he just likes being ordered to do things, so I disappointed him. Vicki likes to keep men fairly arm's-length as well as being shy, so she wasn't going to ask him either.

'Get the beers in, Kip,' I finally ordered, as his desire

to be told what to do became palpable. He went towards the kitchen.

'No, you tosser, from the off-licence.'

He nodded resignedly and I heard his old beloved Volkswagen Karmann Ghia rev up as I put the TV at the foot of the bed. The off-licence is two hundred yards away but Kip doesn't believe in walking. His car, his Suzuki Bandit and his mountain bike are equal in his affection, so it's not that he doesn't like exercise. It's just that he thinks that feet are for being whacked with a ruler from time to time rather than for motion.

'You still screwing him, Bliss?' asked Vicki, almost incredulously.

'Only now and then,' I answered. 'You don't like him, do you?'

She shrugged. 'He's all right, I suppose, once you get past the trendy hair and clothes. He'd be better if he admitted to himself he's gay.'

'He's not,' I assured her. 'He's a masochist. Well, mainly. It's not that he hasn't been with men, it's more that he doesn't mind too much who's doing the hurting.'

'Oh, right. So why are your knickers on the floor?'

I winked at her. 'He owed me one. Actually he still owes me several. Jealous?'

'Don't be daft. I'm not interested in straight women. It's time you learned to take no for an answer.'

It amuses me to tease Vicki. I don't really fancy her at all, but I think she quite likes me pestering her from time to time, especially lately when her confidence has been so knocked by Jo. To bolster it I told her about Kip's idea of watching me and her together.

'If he's a masochist he wouldn't enjoy it, would he? Most men are pathetically keen to know what lesbians get up to, and the thought of watching two women should be a treat.'

'Yes, but then the scenario was that I send him home without any contact.'

She continued trying to work out whether that wouldn't still be a treat for a masochist while I put my knickers back on, taking my time over it as though I was trying to get her going. Her cheeks were quite pink and I think she took it as the compliment it was intended to be. It has to be said that I do have nice long legs – my calves enhanced by the cheap black stilettos I bought to go with the posh skirt – and fairly muscular but shapely thighs, crowned by a nice blonde bush and lovely pink lips, plumped and moistened of course by Kip's attentions. The knickers were pretty good too: a rather pricy cream satin thong, only mine thanks to Dad's last cheque. As I pulled them up I turned round as though unconsciously to show her my back view, just so she could see what she was missing. Smoothing my skirt down for the second time I gave her a lecture about the material and the role of polymers in twenty-first-century fabric technology, inviting her to feel the texture of the skirt. She felt my arse, laughing, and I wondered if one day I might persuade her that the odd straight woman wouldn't hurt, personally or politically.

Kip came back with a case of Beck's and I made him confess the enormity of his crime in conspiring to put Rachel out of action. Of course as Vicki was having the flat it hadn't occurred to me to ask her if she might take Rachel's place. She's only a social worker so I don't suppose anyone would mind if she didn't turn up for work for three months. In fact if I told you which borough she worked for, you'd probably bet they wouldn't even notice. Anyway she looked almost offended at the idea that she could possibly give up her case-load for more than a long weekend, so that was that.

She left after just one beer, which is probably just as

well when you know what a terrible driver she is, leaving me and Kip cracking open the second bottle and looking at each other challengingly. I was still slightly confused as to whether I should punish him, or whether not punishing him would be the greater punishment.

'Phase two of compensation package,' he offered. Having had a large vodka and a beer I was feeling mellow and tempted to agree and get him to give me a nice lazy screw but he was pulling a piece of paper out of his pocket.

'I have a friend –' he announced, leaving the sentence hanging. As it was I was fairly impressed; I thought Rachel and I were the only ones he had.

'I have a friend,' he repeated, 'in South America.'

'What?' Astonishment would be too mild a word for my reaction. 'Why didn't you say so before? Where is she?'

'He,' he corrected. 'Charlie, or Carlos as he now calls himself, is at this very minute –' looking at his watch he made mental calculations '– eating his lunch in a seafood restaurant in downtown Miraflores – and in case you don't know, that's in Lima.'

Stupefied, I looked at him vacantly. 'Which Lima?'

'How many Limas are there? Lima in Peru. The one you are flying to in a few days' time. I managed to get in touch with him and he says –' he scrutinised the piece of paper '– that he would love to meet any friend of mine and show her round the city.'

I snatched the paper out of his hand. 'Oh yeah? Let me see.'

It was an e-mail from Lima, all right, or so it said. Carlos started off with 'hey buddy long time no hear' stuff and then went on to say he'd been in Peru for a couple of months as a representative of a development agency and, yes, he would be delighted to meet me.

12

He'd be in the office all day apart from lunch at a seafood restaurant, etc.

'If this is kosher, how come you didn't tell me before? Even if Rachel had been coming, it would have been nice to know someone in Lima.'

Kip had the smug look of a magician who'd pulled off the perfect sleight of hand.

'Because last time I heard from him he was in the States. However, he just happens to be originally from Peru, so when it turned out that Rachel was going to be in plaster for six weeks I phoned him at work to see if he had any old aunties or mates in South America and, amazingly, they told me he'd been working there himself for the last six months, moving around a bit, and was actually at this moment in time in Peru. They gave me the e-mail address and *voilà*, or *hola*, if that's more appropriate.'

Studying the e-mail I tried in vain to think of the Spanish for 'there you go', but could only come up with *ecco!*, which is most definitely Italian. Half of me decided I should kick Kip out now that he'd atoned in some way, though not completely, for his part in Rachel's downfall and get back to the language tapes but the other half was so pleased to have a contact in the one city I had been feeling slightly intimidated by that the least I could offer was a reciprocal wank.

'That's hello,' I said absently. 'It's – *ecco* – bollocks, I keep thinking of that one – it's *voilà*, no it's . . . oh sod it. Where do you know him from? And what did you mean, Charlie who now calls himself Carlos? If he's from Peru, how come he used to be a Charlie?'

'Because he's half English and half Peruvian, a bit of a donkey like you.'

'Watch it. Now I've got his e-mail address you've got nothing to trade with. Insults are out, except in the

13

me-to-you direction. And I presume you didn't mean he's hung like one.'

'Sorry, just clarification. And I don't know how he sizes up. Anyway, we met at university, same college, different class of degree. I did journalism after while he went to Harvard, then our paths crossed again briefly when I was on the *Evening Standard* and he was working for some high-flying management consultant in London. Then he got some job in Madrid and I went into mags. He moved to the States a couple of years ago. Don't you remember I stayed with a friend in New York when I went over on assignment last year?'

'Strangely enough I don't remember every detail of your itineraries,' I said drily.

'I bet,' said Kip complacently. 'Anyway I've always thought of him as half Spanish but, believe it or not, Bliss, I have been agonising over the predicament I've put you in and it came to me that in fact his father was Peruvian. There was a bit of a left-wing coup before Charlie was born and the family left when he was a kid. I vaguely remember him talking about it; they were quite well off but the government gave the land to the peasants and they were kicked off the estate, *estancia* or whatever they call it. Charlie spent the first ten years or so of life in Spain, then came here to school.'

'So what's he like, apart from the biographical details? Looks, personality?'

'Quiet, reflective, strong, muscly; quite a bit like me, actually.'

Bless.

'Sounds a great improvement on you,' I observed archly, getting fonder of mouthy, dissolute Kip by the minute. 'Don't tell me he's got the same predilections.'

I fixed his eyes and kneeled between his legs. My fingers pushed his shirt further apart and fastened

14

gently round his nipples and then squeezed, just a little firmly, then harder. His breath quickened in anticipation.

'So?' I demanded, pinching meanly. I let go with my right hand and pushed it up to pull his head back hard. His angular face was pale under the raven black hair.

'No, he hasn't. I don't know exactly, and that's the truth. But a girl I know who went out with him said he was . . . he was weird.'

My breath was coming harder too. 'How?'

He narrowed his eyes as I unzipped him and curled my hand round his hard-on. 'He made her dress up, corsets and so on.'

'I like doing that; it's normal.'

'And he had handcuffs but she wasn't into it.'

My interest was definitely piqued now, and a pulse beat between my legs. Kip was big and solid and I swept my hands up and down him hard, the way he likes. 'Did he make her do anything she didn't want?'

'Christ, no, this is a friend of mine; he obviously just likes a little rôle play. Don't tell me you're worried?'

'Just excited. Get your kit off.'

He stood to take off his trousers, and as always he turned his back so that I could see the faint scars, white even against Kip's luminously pale body, where he was whipped once, too hard, which made him realise that his pleasure in a little pain didn't extend to real masochism. For my part I like to imagine being whipped while crying out for mercy, but if it came to it I'd wimp out. Still, looking at Kip's scars and imagining myself in his place gives me a little thrill. Discarding my skirt and black top I stood tall in my high heels, still in my expensive cream satin bra and knickers, but in my mind I was wearing a black basque and suspenders for Carlos, alias Charlie.

'What does he look like?'

15

'Oh don't mind me, the one who's actually here. Dark, long hair, short body, muscular, nice face, big nose, like a Spaniard, you know? Can we fuck?'

'Not yet.' I kneeled on the floor and took his cock in my mouth and gave him plenty of spit and a mixture of little licks and big sucks. Then, when he started to get comfortable, I dug my nails into the cheeks of his arse, both sides, and rotated my hands while still gouging away. He made guttural noises in his throat but didn't say a word as I ran my hands slowly down the back of his thighs, still digging in.

'Vicki thinks you're a repressed homosexual,' I told him after I removed my mouth to make way for my hands. 'But I told her you didn't care who you fucked as long as they dug in their nails.'

'There's a guy at work,' he gasped as I circled my left hand round the root of his prick and swept my right up and down the smooth, saliva-wet length of him. Compared to the paleness of his body his cock stood out pinkly from the smooth black pubic thatch. I wanted more about the guy at work and I wanted Kip to enjoy telling me, so I reached over to my desk and pulled out my little box of tricks. He sighed with satisfaction as he saw me fit the slim finger-sized attachment on to the vibrator and I gave his balls a nasty little squeeze as I told him to rubber up and get down on all fours like the dog he was, both of which intensified his excitement. Lubeing his arse and the vibrator, I pushed the vibrator slowly but firmly inside him and wriggled it around a bit until I was sure he was loving it even before I switched it on. Leaving it hanging out of him I took my knickers off, then got Kip's arse buzzing as I lowered myself directly under him for face-to-face, cock-to-cunt contact. I wrapped my legs around his back and levered myself up so I could slide wetly over him. He was even bigger than

16

he had been before and I pushed hard against him, my legs gripping and my hands moving back to the vibrator, which I started moving slowly in and out.

'This guy?' I queried.

His voice was coming in little jerks. 'Photographer, called Stevenson. Long hair, tied back. Wears black, great body; he's got presence, you know? Likes to talk sex, almost made me come in the bar just by talking.'

'What? The man who likes hands-on viciousness nearly came without even a stroke?'

'Yeah, once we established a sort of connection I told him what I liked and he said it reminded him of a story about a woman he knew who had two guys who both wanted her but before they could have her she made them submit to hurting each other while she watched. It wasn't anything too weird at first: a little light whipping, pinching, gouging, that sort of thing, just enough so they'd scream a bit and beg her to let them stop, then she'd reward them with a shag. But things got harder and meaner and when she said they could stop they asked to carry on for longer before fucking her.'

'Sounds like she might have got her come-uppance.' Clamped hard around Kip's cock I moved my legs so that I could dig my heels in his sides. His breath was fast and I guessed he was almost there.

'Yeah, but then she thought she'd teach them a lesson and she made them fuck each other. At least, she thought she was making them, but maybe they wanted to. It progressed slowly at first, a finger or two then the slim end of the vibrator, but before too long they were just giving it to each other up the arse. She got off on watching them and then let them take it in turns to fuck her and finger her, but after a while they were so turned on they came with each other.'

'So they did without her?' My clit was connecting

like an electric point with the plug of Kip's bone and spreading a nice warm current through me but I needed more. Leaving the vibrator buzzing inside him I eased off my shoes without breaking rhythm. As Kip confirmed that the guys turned the tables and gave her a quick hand job after she'd watched them I stuck one stiletto in Kip's mouth, to his joy, and used the toe of the other on my clit. He bowed his head in shame and excitement and came just a second after I did.

I detached myself from his cock and lay back on my elbows. With the shoe in his mouth, the johnny on his fast-shrivelling prick and the vibrator up his arse, he looked as ridiculous as even he could wish. I got him with the Polaroid; although he'd messed up my travelling plans, I was sated and felt generous enough to give him a special treat.

The going-away party was a blast, full of people who had absolutely nothing in common. Rachel's leg arrived plastered and that's how everyone left, apart from Kip's object of desire, the man in black who was attractive but too self-contained. Kip was welcome to him. Daily phone calls had kept me aware of the progress of their relationship, which was tantalisingly slow. While pretending to do a line or two in a toilet – Stevenson was pretending, that is; Kip has never said no to an illegal substance in his life – the man gave Kip 'the most amazing blow job I've ever had in my entire life' (thanks a bunch, pal) except he didn't let him come. Well, if he had a pain in his balls for the rest of the night, I guess that suited him just fine.

Mum came with Terry, her new guy who I've met once or twice and who gives me the creeps. While he's never blatantly groped me, he uses any excuse to get his hands on my body and I can just see it reflected in his nasty little John Lennon glasses that he's not going

18

to let go of his sordid little mother and daughter fantasy. Dream on, sunshine.

The crowd from work was miffed to be out-hipped by Kip and Stevenson and made up for it by swanning around me as though I were their bestest friend. OK, I admit I did say I'd probably be back after my travels, but it's like a sort of maternity leave in that there's nothing to stop me telling them to shove it, which is probably exactly what I'll do. A few eyebrows were raised by the blow-up of the Kip Polaroid I'd put on the wall, but everyone else loved it. I wasn't sure about exhibiting it in front of Mum, but at her age and vanity level she can't see that well without the glasses she never wears, so I'm not sure she even knew what it was. Anyway, photography could be the next project for me so, despite my reflex antipathy to Stevenson, his approval of the picture led me to be nice to him in an abrasive way, which seemed to go down quite well.

The lesbian contingent, headed by Vicki and without Jo, had a great time and it was brilliant to see her relaxed and happy. It was even more brilliant to see the looks I was getting from her friend Sally, which improved as the evening wore on and more booze went down.

'Your hair's terrific; why didn't you do it before?' she said as she ran her hand over my newly cropped head. 'Hey, have you seen the light? I mean, planning to go away with Rachel, cutting your hair; are you making some kind of statement here?'

'What, an outing? No, but I'm very flexible,' I told her, trapping her hand on the nape of my neck. 'Are you?'

She laughed and raised her eyebrows. 'What time are you expecting this to break up?'

'I don't know, but you look like you've got staying power.' I fluttered my newly dyed eyelashes a couple

19

of times and gave her the narrow-eyed, parted-lips look and hoped for the best, though if my new highlighted deep fringe and feathered nape didn't do the trick I didn't know what would. I've been thinking about short hair for a while but needed the impetus of the trip to get it organised. With my healthy-looking complexion and freckles it gave me a gamine look that seemed to be appealing, if only to lesbians and pain-hungry wannabe gay guys.

As it turned out Sally couldn't stay the distance, as Mum and Terry seemed to have set in for the night and Rachel was rambling on about the trip of a lifetime she'd had to forgo while Unity and Franco, the two I do like from work, were engaged in landscaping her cast.

'So you're going camping? On your own?' asked Mum anxiously.

I shook my head. 'Nah, seemed like it was asking for trouble, apart from which we had enough grief trying to put up the tent with two of us, let alone sticking pegs in and stretching guys out on my own.'

'Stretching guys, sounds right up your street,' said Rachel defensively but obviously feeling guilty.

'I am taking a sleeping bag and mat, though, as I'll probably have to do the Inca Trail in an organised group, and I'd rather have my own than hire. Can you imagine, a sleeping bag that tons of dirty travellers have slept in.'

Rachel looked even more remorseful, as well she might. One of the impetuses that had propelled us into going now, this year, was that soon the authorities are going to stop people hiking the Inca Trail on their own, and force them to go on organised tours. I do not like tours in any form and so we booked our flight to get to Cuzco in time to beat the new rule. Now, of course, that was irrelevant.

'I'm so sorry,' she said for the zillionth time, but this time there were tears in her eyes and I realised she'd had enough booze to blub all night. Franco tried to wipe away her tears and Unity turned to me.

'Are you coming back to work?' she asked quietly.

I shrugged. 'Only if all else fails. I want to do something a bit more me, you know? This was only supposed to be a temporary job for some experience, and it's been five years now. Just because I did that textile project at college doesn't mean I want to spend my life designing dress material.'

'You're good at it,' she observed.

'Yeah, well, I'm good at screwing but I don't want to spend my life as a whore either.'

'Oh, Bliss,' sighed Mum. 'I am going to worry about you. Peru can be dangerous, you know. What about those revolutionaries?'

'It's all died a death, Mum. Don't worry, honestly. Kip's old college friend lives there. He's going to meet my flight.'

She beamed. 'Oh, that's marvellous; I'll stop worrying then, I promise.' She ruffled my hair as though I was still ten years old. 'You do look like your dad with your hair short.'

Frowning, I moved her hand. 'Mum, I thought when you lived with Dad he had hair halfway down his back.'

'Yes, he did, until he got that job. Such a shame. But you look like him now.'

'You mean I look like he did when he reached thirty and decided to be sensible.'

'He deceived me,' she said solemnly. 'Changing so drastically . . . still, it worked out all right in the end.'

Briefly I wondered why Mum couldn't have fallen for someone who looked more like Willem Dafoe than Willem van Bon. Sculpted cheekbones and a wide

21

mouth would suit a girl far more than Dad's snub nose and round face. Still, can't have everything.

I finally stopped dropping hints and threw them all out. Common sense had kicked in for once and I hadn't held the party on the eve of my departure, so I had the whole of the next day to clear up. The only thing I had to get done in order to get to bed was move the sitting-room furniture out of the bedroom. I piled my leaving presents on the sofa: guide books, condoms – amazing how many people thought that was original – a couple of decent paperbacks, which was thoughtful considering the long flight, and a watch that lit up in the dark, which would have been perfect in the tent, but Mum had bought it before the Rachel disaster.

That out of the way I poured a last glass of wine and sulkily reflected on the irony of finally meeting one of Vicki's friends who doesn't make the sign of the cross and eat garlic at the thought of shagging a straight woman, only to have my chances scuppered by so-called friends and my mum. But maybe I was too tired anyway.

The phone rang; I expected Mum telling me they'd got back all right, as though she was the errant child. But it wasn't.

'Have they gone?'

'At last. Wish you'd stayed.'

'Sorry. Your mum's boyfriend was giving me the creeps.'

'Me too. I suppose there's no chance of seeing you before I go?'

'Not unless you're sober enough to drive to Peckham now.'

'I doubt I'll be sober enough to drive to the end of the road tomorrow. But seeing as I don't have a car, that's no big deal.'

She giggled. 'Well, I'll still be here when you get back.'

'I'll send you a postcard.'

'See you.'

I went to bed with Sally in my head but also a little tingle at the thought of Carlos 'Charlie' Garcia, who liked women to dress up. As I drifted off to sleep I was in a black leather catsuit kneeling in front of Sally, who was dressed in red lace and PVC and chained to the wall. Carlos, who looked like Che Guevara, was got up in a military uniform like a South American dictator and directing my tongue action with barked instructions. My hand moved down into my slipperiness and just a few strokes later I tensed and came, and the next thing I knew it was morning.

Chapter Two

*F*lying has got to be the most mind-numbing way to pass the time apart from prancing up and down on a Stairmaster – though at least you can think that's doing you good. I know, flying doesn't have to be harmful unless you get a blood clot, and as long as you follow the no-booze and not-much-food rules, but while I always like to imagine myself as a disciple of health, fitness and asceticism, it is of course a complete lie. I can't do the common sense stuff in life and the bit about drinking nothing but water and not eating on a plane always strikes me as the first step to catatonia. So although I resisted breakfast en route to Amsterdam – a bizarre route but it was cheap – I was more than ready for a little sustenance, especially of the alcoholic variety, by the time I got on the next plane.

The woman who had sat next to me had obligingly moved to the aisle seat when no one else appeared after takeoff, so I had contentedly spread out my sweatshirt, mags, books and diary when the stewardess appeared. Ready to order a large anything I was more than irritated that instead of taking the drinks orders she was guiding someone else into the empty seat. I picked up my things resignedly.

'I'm sorry. It's just that I was at the front with a load of kids, and –'

Smiling politely I stowed my stuff in the sickbag pouch. 'Don't blame you. No problem.'

Still I was a bit annoyed to have had space and to have lost it. However he was a nice-looking guy, Dutch, but dark and fine featured, not the homely farmer type like yours truly. I could have flirted with him but in view of his *Wall Street Journal* I put my nose back in *Marie Claire* and began the countdown for the drinks trolley.

At last I got my miniature vodka followed shortly by one of those quarter bottles of wine with my 'lunch' and felt a bit better. I'd managed to prop the Peru hiking book by the window so I could pretend I had no neighbours but I wasn't going to be allowed to get away with a long flight like that without conversation.

'Looks like you're planning an adventurous trip.'

I couldn't blame him for wanting to chat; he had no room to read and the woman in the aisle seat looked like Nana out of *The Royle Family*.

'Yeah. I guess.'

'Have you been before?'

'No.'

Maybe it would be entertaining to see how long I could keep the conversation going by answering only in monosyllables.

'Are you alone?'

Even better, I looked round as if startled at having lost my pal. 'Yes.'

He laughed. Nice deep chuckle.

'You don't have to talk to me. Are you afraid of flying?'

'No.'

25

'It's just the way you're going through the booze . . . maybe you're just an alcoholic?'

'Cheek.'

'OK, you're just bored. So I'll carry on talking to you. My name's Peter, what's yours?'

'Bliss.'

He really burst out laughing at that one.

'Seriously?'

'Yep.'

'Peter Verhoeven.'

'Bliss van Bon.'

We shook hands. His face was grave but his mouth was dimpling rather nicely at the corners. I wondered if he believed me or thought I'd invented my name as part of the monosyllable game.

'You're Dutch?'

'Half.'

'Which half?'

I shrugged. Like Mum, I like the Dutch. It always seems to me that they're very similar to the English; they have the same sense of humour and practicality; their idea of a good meal is Indonesian food while ours is Chinese, and we've got Soho and they've got their red light district. The only difference is that we're more buttoned up about sex and drugs than they are. I like to think the broadness of my mind is Dutch rather than English, though Kip would tease me that the broadness of my brow is ditto.

Peter Verhoeven had turned his attention away from me and managed to flag down the stewardess for another bottle of wine for each of us, for which I was duly, monosyllabically grateful.

'It's brave of you to travel to Lima alone. Do you know anyone there?'

'Yep.'

'Will they be meeting you at the airport?'

'Sure.'

'Good, because it's quite intimidating. Your friend: male or female?'

'Male.'

'Uh-huh.'

He looked slightly disappointed and I started to feel just a bit interested. After all, should Carlos prove to be a pain, or gay, or even a masochist – I'd had enough of Kip for a while – it would be nice to know a decent-looking Dutchman in the city. But it was a hell of a long flight and I didn't want to end my game just yet, so I knocked back the wine and put my seat into recline and my sweatshirt behind my head.

'Sleep.'

I closed my eyes and astonishingly drifted off.

I awoke to find Peter Verhoeven immersed in my *Marie Claire*.

'Hey, Bliss van Bon. Good sleep?'

'OK.'

He put the magazine down. 'Oh no, are you going to carry on with that stupid game?'

'No, give me a chance; I've just woken up.'

'Good. I'm just reading about what women really want, and I was hoping you'd tell me if it was true.'

I glanced at the article and then along the row to the woman next to him.

'She's Dutch. She doesn't speak English,' he explained.

'Hope she speaks Spanish if she's going to Lima.'

'No, she's getting off in Aruba to visit her son, who works there.'

'OK. What do women really want? Right now, a gallon of water and a mouthwash. Any offers?'

Bless, he produced a big bottle of Vichy. That got me looking at him with new respect. If there's one brand

27

of mineral water that tastes different to me, that's it. It's got that sort of salinity that tastes, frankly, like cunt juice. I told him.

'Oh, Bliss,' he said intimately, moving slightly closer. 'What a lovely thought. Even nicer to see you drinking it.'

I immediately put my mouth firmly round the neck of the bottle and tipped it down. Not all at once, so I could lift it from my lips just a trifle carelessly and spill some down my T-shirt. As if rehearsed he produced a clean white handkerchief and after hesitating while I nodded approval touched it delicately to my wet throat. I closed my eyes to savour the progress of his hand wrapped in fine cotton as it caressed my collarbones and slowly moved down the front of my top, carefully and gently 'drying' me. I hadn't realised I had spilled so much water but he had to go as far as the satin of my cream bra before he was satisfied.

'Silly girl,' he reproved me. I opened my eyes. He was leaning over me, his handkerchief now on the magazine he had put in my lap while he did the wiping-up operation, his fingers trailing across the swell of my breasts above the T-shirt. 'I think you're dry now.'

'Oh no, I'm not. But you've mopped up the water I spilt, thanks. I'll be more careful this time.'

I took another slow swig of the water then handed it to him. He put his mouth where mine had just been and swallowed.

'I'm not sure if you're quite right about the taste of this water. I need a comparison.'

'That's a shame. It's too public here, and if you think I'm following you into the toilet for a fuck over someone else's pee you've got another think coming. I grew out of that sort of thing a long time ago.'

He laughed. 'I can imagine, and I wouldn't dream of

asking you to. Who I had in mind was the stewardess with long blonde hair. Think I stand a chance?'

Oh yes, that's more like it. 'Do I get to watch?'

'Why not?'

I could think of one or two reasons, like arriving in Lima so wired I'd want to sit on Carlos's face before I even saw it, or the effects of a dramatic increase in blood pressure a mile and a half up in the air, but the thought of a private sex show was too much to turn down. I crossed my legs, not easy in a 747, and squeezed my sex muscles and my thighs. With the seam of my jeans pressing into my crotch I was just a finger's breadth away from an orgasm. Peter watched me and I had absolutely no doubt he knew exactly what I was doing.

He replaced the magazine on my lap and wordlessly offered me his empty wine bottle.

'No, tacky. Let's just continue our little chat for a bit, if that's all right with you. Then maybe after we leave Aruba you can try out the taste test – if you can set it up.'

'Fine. Actually I'm in marketing and it's just the sort of thing I'm going to Peru for.'

'What, oral sex?' I laughed out loud.

'No, setting up tastings. We're test-marketing a new soft drink.'

'Really? I thought they had their own. Inca Kola, isn't it?'

Peter made a disgusted face. 'Wait till you taste it; it's like bubble gum. This one's going to be a winner, though possibly not in the South American market. It's a cross between fizz and milkshake. Did you ever have ice-cream floats when you were a kid?'

'Mmm, delicious. But how can you export from Holland to Peru? Surely it'd cost a fortune to get it there?'

He laughed delightedly. 'Oh, Bliss, you're not very

up in the ways of business, are you? Of course we wouldn't export it; we'd get a factory to make it there and just send the secret concentrate, like everyone else does. After all, there's no reason why the Americans should hog the whole of the market with Coke and Pepsi.'

I digested that information. He was right, I wasn't up in the ways of business at all. My job was to design fabric, and that was as near to the material world as I wanted to get.

'Great. Can we go back to talking about sex?'

By the time we had to fasten our seat belts to land in Aruba I felt like I was sitting in a pool of melted ice-cream myself. Seizing my hand and guiding it under his *Wall Street Journal* Peter quickly demonstrated that he too was ready for action.

Only a handful of people were ending their journey in Aruba but after they'd gone the stewardess announced that anyone who wanted to stretch their legs could get off for half an hour. I immediately stood up but Peter pulled me down.

'See how many are getting off,' he said quietly. 'It might be nice and quiet on here.'

Sure enough nearly everybody left the plane. The stewardess with the blonde ponytail came round telling everyone the doors would soon be closing. As she leaned over our row Peter said something to her in Dutch and she shook her head. Quietly he said something else, looking at me briefly and back, and she burst out laughing and answered him with another shake of the head. He persisted and an exchange I couldn't even begin to follow ensued. Finally she walked to the front of the plane and Peter immediately pulled me up and went to the back.

As he slid open the toilet door the stewardess finished the announcement she had made in Dutch and began in English: 'Ladies and gentlemen, we would remind you that the toilets are not to be used while the plane is in the airport. Thank you.'

Two minutes later she joined us, Peter having in the meantime done another pretty efficient mopping-up operation on the washbasin and spread paper towels over the floor.

'Marjo, Bliss,' he introduced. 'Bliss doesn't speak Dutch, Marjo, despite being a van Bon. Do you mind English?'

'You want to lick me out, Peter; I don't care what language you do it in,' she answered, winking at me. 'I don't think I ever had an audience before, Bliss. You do this sort of thing a lot?'

'First time for me too.' I almost felt like a gawky virgin as Marjo casually unzipped her skirt and wriggled out of it. She was wearing stockings and suspenders, so don't tell me she wasn't in the habit of screwing someone during the course of a long haul. Folding the skirt, she put it neatly on the toilet lid and pulled her knickers down and placed them on top.

'I've had more propositions than I can remember on flights but it's the first time a man's ever said, "I want to lick you out and this girl here wants to watch,"' she confided as she perched on the edge of the washbasin and opened her legs. 'Hat on or off?'

'Oh, definitely on,' said Peter gravely. He undid her blouse and exposed quite startlingly big tits in black lace to match the rest of her underwear.

'You said no first off,' I guessed as Peter kneeled on the paper towels and ran his hands up her stockinged legs to the creamy flesh above. I was almost tempted to elbow him to one side and have my second taste of Vichy water but instead was transfixed as his thumbs

31

moved gently up to her light brown thatch – her hair was dyed – and pulled her lips apart.

'Sure I did. Then he told me you said Vichy water tasted like – like sex juices and I thought, how does she know? And when he said he didn't want any payback I thought, why not? That's another first.'

Her eyes closed and I saw Peter's tongue brush lightly over her clit. It looked like a pink opal, hard and gleaming, set in lush pink moistness, and I heard her breathe in sharply.

'Nice, Marjo?'

She laughed deep in her throat. 'I've never had a tongue on my clit that wasn't. Have you?'

'Our Alsatian used to be a bit rough, but – no, sorry, only joking.'

Marjo laughed again but I could see that just for a minute she'd believed me and despite being shocked was sinfully turned on. At the same time Peter's tongue delved deep inside her and she moaned and I saw her hands tighten around the taps behind her. It was tempting to thrust my own hand down my jeans but I decided to gamble on something better later.

Peter's tongue was brushing broadly from clit to arsehole and back and I was slightly jealous.

'Are you near to coming, Marjo?'

She opened her eyes. 'Not far off. Has he already done this to you?'

'No, we've just talked, apart from when he wiped up some water I'd spilled.'

'Really?' her eyes widened. 'So are you next?'

I deliberated. 'I don't think so. What if I wanted to be next with you?'

'Shit!' Her breath was harder. 'I don't know; I've never done that sort of thing before.'

'But you like the idea of it.'

'Sure, the idea . . .'

32

I moved towards her and rubbed her nipples under the lace bra. My crotch made contact with the back of Peter's head, which was moving up and down rhythmically and I knew he was lapping hard at her clit and she'd be coming before too long. I wanted to make it nice for her and pulled her bra cups down and scuffed her nipples harder. Her lips were swollen and lipsticked and I moved my mouth slowly towards them, not wanting to spoil it and waiting for her to shake her head or move away. Instead she closed her eyes and moved her head towards me. As she parted her lips I caught a glimpse of her pink tongue before my mouth closed over hers. I moved purposefully towards her so that Peter's head was dragging the seam of my jeans over my own clit as he tongued her. As her tongue sought mine greedily and my hands luxuriated in the lushness of her breasts I thrust closer towards her and as we kissed and came Peter was forgotten, an impersonal instrument of our mutual orgasms. I wondered briefly and triumphantly if he felt used as I pressed my mons on to the crown of his head and wondered if he could feel the violent contractions of my muscles.

'Good work, Verhoeven,' I observed coolly as I detached my mouth and hands from Marjo and my crotch from the back of his head. 'So what's the result of the taste test?'

He stood up and turned towards me, then without speaking kissed me with a tongue full of Marjo's juices. She was watching but mindful of the time we'd been in there. I handed her knickers to her while responding to Peter's tongue.

'Definitely Vichy, but stronger and creamier,' he admitted when we disengaged. 'I've never fucked anyone with the crown of my head before.'

'Don't think I've ever rubbed off on the back of

someone's head before either,' I countered. 'Not to mention kissed a woman in a bowler hat.'

Marjo tucked her blouse into her skirt. 'Nice timing. Thank you both.'

'Yeah, we'll fly with you again,' I said, winking as she left the toilet. I locked it behind her. After squashing Peter's head between us like a double-ended vibrator I felt he deserved a bit of reciprocity. 'You want a little tonguing too? Or a hand job?'

'No chance of a shag?'

What the hell, as long as it was quick and impersonal. Kissing Marjo and fondling her tits had been enough excitement for one day. As I nodded OK he pulled a rubber from his pocket and I dropped my jeans and knickers and bent over the toilet. He was big and slid satisfyingly into my wetness and with a bit of drawling obscene verbal encouragement he came in no time.

Lovely people, the Dutch.

Almost twenty-four hours later I woke up with the usual, hell, where am I, before remembering. I was in Lima, I had just slept off jet lag – hopefully – and I was on Carlos Garcia's sofa bed absolutely desperate for some water.

Groggily getting off the couch – they are just not comfortable, those things – I managed to get my brain into first gear while trying to find the kitchen. No hangover, thank God, because after my exuberant meeting with Carlos, who looked not at all like Gabriel Byrne (bad) but more like a black-haired David Ginola (good) and babbling like an idiot in the car back to his flat, I had almost instantly folded like an over-excited child. My mind was telling me that he seemed pleased and amused by my enthusiasm, though I was prepared to believe it lied and he would turn out to be totally pissed off by being landed with an impressionable unsophisticate. However, I would soon put him right.

I found loads of bottled water in the kitchen, plus coffee, bread and a note.

> Good morning, Bliss! I'm at work till around five, won't call in case I wake you. There's some sausage and stuff in the fridge or plenty of cafés down the road (see map). Help yourself to anything you want. *A las tardes.*

That must be Spanish for catch you later; it's incredible what the phrasebooks don't tell you. After drinking a litre of water I did a time check. I hadn't changed my watch but both the video and the radio alarm told me it was almost two in the afternoon. Great, we must have got back at about eight the evening before, so I'd had plenty of sleep.

The bread looked good and fresh but I wanted to explore so, after a hiccup with the shower, which finally produced hot water but not after I'd been accidentally soaked in cold, I picked up my *South American Handbook* and Carlos's map and headed into downtown Miraflores.

Rachel and I had given each other a severe talking to about our usual careless expenditure – neither of us earns a fortune but we're used to spending what we like and running out by the end of the month – and vowed to budget carefully on our trip. However I reasoned that as I'd saved loads of money by staying for a couple of nights with Carlos and getting a lift to and from the airport, a decent lunch wouldn't hurt. I changed a couple of travellers' cheques into Peruvian sols – nice name – and contemplated menus. The open-air café faced a flowerbed and after calculating that the

35

two-course lunch was less than a fiver I got myself a table.

After tucking into a stuffed avocado followed by pasta with meatballs, washed down with local beer, I felt extremely pleased with myself. The feeling was only bolstered when I unfolded the piece of paper I'd shoved unread in my purse the night before.

Peter Verhoeven, Hotel Arequipa, until Friday.
Thanks for making the flight so enjoyable.

Central Lima might prove to be a tad overwhelming, I thought, but this was just like civilisation. Young people walked purposefully or romantically through the square, while the lunching ladies at the next table wore expensive tweed suits, despite the fact that it was quite warm. The sun shone weakly through the sea mist that lies over Lima and I suspected it might be stronger than it seemed and made a mental note to use sun block the next day. A couple of girls who looked American were sitting by the railings in front of the flowerbed with their guidebooks propped on their rucksacks and I smiled indulgently. Already I felt at home and kidded myself that in my anonymous jeans, T-shirt and shades I could pass for a local out for lunch. Amused by the idea I hid the guidebook under *Aunt Julia and the Scriptwriter* and, despite my Nordic rather than Latin looks, imagined I was a moneyed Peruvian trying to improve her English before Daddy paid for her to visit the UK.

Back at the flat I had a good look round – after all, Carlos had given me carte blanche to help myself to anything. He had told me the previous night he only had a short lease on the flat as he moved around a lot, so I wasn't surprised it was a bit impersonal. Still I was able to check his taste in books, at least the English ones – a reasonable selection of contemporary American fiction – and music, which was mainly salsa and other South American and Caribbean stuff. I put a CD on and danced round the sitting-room. Despite the flight – not just the length of it and the time change but also the fun I'd had on it – I was feeling decidedly energetic, or what Kip disdainfully calls frisky.

Before going out to lunch I'd put the sofa bed back together and now thought I'd better unload my backpack. There was plenty of room in the wardrobe so I hung up my one skirt, one blouse, one dress and one pair of trousers and rearranged the rest of the contents of the pack. I slid back the other side of the wardrobe door to find a space for my sleeping bag and mat and as I moved some shoes out to make more room was not surprised, though almost triumphantly pleased, to find that far from being sensible black office brogues or trainers there were two pairs of stilettos and a pair of black thigh-high boots. Kip hadn't been leading me on after all.

His note had said help yourself, so without compunction I rifled through the second half of the wardrobe: bingo. A couple of basques, one black, one red, a proper lace-up black corset – bit too serious, that – and a black leather bra and shorts set.

The question was, though, did he intend me to find them? I went through the what-ifs. Did he assume Kip would have told me about his penchant for accessories, in which case he would be pleased to come home and find me corseted and high heeled? And if not, why hadn't he hidden his little outfits? Or would he think I had a nerve poking round in his wardrobe? Not to mention, who else wore these? For all I knew, he was a cross-dresser himself.

I decided to go with my instinct and put on the red

basque. It had suspenders and I had brought with me a pair of black holdups – OK, I know this was supposed to be an adventurous trekking holiday, but a girl never knows and they don't take up much room – and little black knickers so I dressed up. Pretty good, I thought, a little bit tight, but then I'm a wide-boned woman. The boots were a good fit but disappointingly hid the stockings so I tried the shoes. I couldn't believe how high they were. I thought I was taking high heels to the limit when I bought my cheapies but these were amazing. Unfortunately they were also too big. Seeing as my feet are pretty huge – six and a half on a good day – I started to think that maybe Carlos was indeed the wearer of the fancy dress. I didn't want to give up too easily though and, with a flash of inspiration, put a pair of white cotton ankle socks over my stockings, then slipped into the shoes. Not a bad fit, and in my view at least a bit of a turn on, the hint of St Trinian's making the rest look even more decadent. The heels were so high that my feet in the socks seemed to flow vertically down into the shoes, as though I was on points. If he didn't like it perhaps I could get a cab over to the Hotel Arequipa, where I was pretty sure somebody would. One thing was for sure, somebody had to, because I'd got myself pretty excited by the get-up.

It was just after five. Not knowing how far away Carlos worked I couldn't guess when he'd be back but satisfied with what he would find I put my one skirt (the polymer Liquorice Allsorts one) and my one good top (long sleeves, low necked and stretchy jersey) over the rest and made some coffee while waiting to ask if he'd had a nice day at the office.

Despite my tiredness the night before I'd registered that Carlos looked pretty good in black jeans and turtleneck, but in a cream linen suit and collarless white shirt he was as inviting as a double vanilla ice cream and I could have licked him all over. I know, the cream linen suit is such a Latin cliché, but give a girl a break. I'm sick of hip Kip and the fashionistas at work and was happy to wallow in Carlos's conventional and quite frankly stunning look. He smelled faintly of a musky aftershave or cologne, and though usually I like men to smell of nothing but men it suited him and I even quite liked it.

I poured him some coffee and he raised his eyebrows at the shoes. 'Did you find everything you want?'

It was going to take time to get used to the fact that despite looking Spanish and having decidedly American cultural leanings his accent is as English as mine. Or did he speak with an American accent when in the US? I liked the thought that he could become three completely different people.

'I hope you don't mind,' I said innocently. 'You said to help myself.'

'Sure, I meant you to.' He smiled, and what a brilliant smile. Slightly dark skin, like a very good tan, so that his teeth were really white against it. Mouth wide with thin lips. Nose long and broad but straight, horizontal lines across it at the top, surprising for someone his age, forehead also slightly lined. Eyes such a dark brown they looked almost black, Tia Maria mixing into a Black Russian, as he sat with his back to the light. Hair black and thick, shoulder length, pulled back in a ponytail, though it was loose last night. Oh yes. I wanted to tell him he could help himself as well but I guessed that as I was wearing his shoes and obviously a bit more of his besides he'd take it as read.

He did. After the small talk about my day and night he gestured towards me. 'So you dressed up for me?'

'Well, Kip said you liked it, and after I found the stuff I thought you'd left it there for me . . . is it OK?'

A smile played round the corners of his mouth. He had a faint outline of stubble, just enough to be sexy and not too much to be George Michael-y.

'Maybe, depends what you've got on. I was actually planning to dress you myself . . . well, never mind. Kip told me you're headstrong.'

I wished I'd waited for him to dress me.

'Oh did he? I suppose he told you he's into gay masochism?'

'Wasn't he always? So, you want to show me what's under the skirt and top?'

Did I ever. Without even explaining the miracle fabric I whipped the skirt off and pulled the top over my head before he could change his mind.

He walked round me as though I was a live gallery exhibit, his eyes moving up and down, assessing me. I liked it. Just occasionally I enjoy being treated like a sex object.

'I can do better,' he pronounced finally. 'Red and black; a bit tacky, don't you think?'

'Your red basque,' I pointed out. 'Shall I take it off – or will you?'

He smiled, his lips not quite meeting, giving me just a tantalising flash of those white teeth.

'You. There's something slightly unappealing about pulling elasticated garments off flesh.'

That told me. As appealingly as I could I rolled the basque down and off after making the most of undoing the suspenders.

'What about the rest?'

He nodded. 'Not bad. I like the socks. And your legs; long legs, longer in those heels. Don't you feel sexy?'

'Yeah, but is this it?'

I felt decidedly disappointed. He was supposed to

like dressing up and I wanted to comply but quite frankly black pants and holdups, even when propped up by massively high heels, didn't seem too outrageous.

'Bliss, I've let you down.' He circled me again then put his hand down the waistband of my knickers. 'Of course not. But these must come off first, then I'll show you what you ought to look like.'

I wriggled as suggestively as I could out of my knickers but he wasn't watching, instead pulling a box from the back of the wardrobe. I hoped it wasn't going to be whips and crops; I'm not into pain. Inflicting it on Kip is one thing but, as I said before, as far as I'm concerned being whacked is for fantasy purposes only.

But first the black corset came out of the wardrobe. It was a real old-fashioned type, satin with bones at the front and a tangle of laces at the back. He pushed me round with my back to him and got me to hold it at the front.

'The romance of the lace, pulled tight, is a million times more exciting than the synthetic appeal of lycra, don't you think?'

'I think, Carlos, that the fact that these bra cups fall just short of my nipples is rather nice. As for the back view, I'll let you know.'

I smiled at him over my shoulder. The view I'd just had in the full-length mirror was pretty good. Apart from the obvious appeal of the minimal cups, one of my arms was holding the corset just under my breasts, pushing them upwards, while the other smoothed down the tummy panel and disappeared between my thighs. Narcissism is, I'm afraid, one of my weaknesses. And as Carlos pulled the first of the laces tight, I wondered if bondage might be one too.

By the time he had silently and methodically pulled and squeezed my body into the corset I was breathless.

The constriction was a turn-on I hadn't anticipated and the way my hips swelled out after he had pulled in the waist of the corset made me look like a 50s film star. My short breaths meant my breasts rose and fell quickly and the slope of the boning under them made my cleavage absolutely astonishing. The corset came down almost to my pubes, and I wished it could be longer; I tried to imagine the effect of tight lacing over my pubic mound.

'Pretty good.' I wanted to break his silence, but he only smiled and pulled up my holdups further so they were almost at the top of my legs. My blonde curls were emphasised by the stark black satin above them and the black stockings below them, and I guessed I wasn't going to get any knickers.

Out of the box came something else in black satin and gold. Expecting knickers after all I drew in my breath, but it turned out to be a wide choker decorated with gold chains. He fastened it round my neck – it wasn't tight, thank God – and then pulled out long black satin gloves also adorned with chains. Raising his eyebrows he offered them to me.

'What do you think, Bliss? Do you like yourself like this? How about the gloves? I'm not going to do anything against your will.'

'I love myself like this, and I love long gloves. I'll tell you if you're going too far, Carlos.'

It was the first time anyone had put a pair of gloves on me since I was four years old and I was unprepared for the electricity that shot through me as Carlos slid each finger into the satin. I've always found men entranced by the sight of me fitting gloves over my fingers, and having a man do it for me hinted tantalisingly at role reversal. He took his time over it, smoothing down each finger and fitting the gloves over my hands then pulling them up right above the elbow, to midway up my upper arm. The gold chains brushed against my tits as he manoeuvred the gloves. I couldn't see why they were there until both gloves were on.

'Tell me if you don't want me to do this,' he repeated, standing behind me and showing me myself in the mirror. For a moment I expected him to get a camera out and photograph me, and I certainly wouldn't have minded a souvenir of how I looked, not to mention enjoying posing for him however he wanted. But it was better than that. No camera, no more accessories, he just – if I had seen it coming I suppose my sex muscles wouldn't have reacted the way they did – he just pulled my gloved arms behind me and started fastening the chains, and my arms, together.

'Oh boy.'

Absorbed in his task of lacing the chains through each other he didn't look up. 'Oh boy good or oh boy bad?' he asked quietly.

'Oh boy fantastic,' I breathed. He pulled tighter.

'Still fantastic?'

It wasn't what you'd call comfortable but my tits, which were already high and full from the corset, were gently but definitely expanding even further as he teased my arms back a little more, and my shoulders were pulled back and down. I suppose it was similar to being on the pec deck in the gym, though I had never felt like this while sweating in lycra. I nodded and then, while I was getting over the shock of looking like an advert for a bondage video, another megavolt ran through me as suddenly my head was pulled back sharply. The chains from the gloves had been fastened round the chain on the choker.

'You're beautiful.' He turned me slowly, so I could see myself from the side. I was: he was right. I was beautiful and totally helpless, my hands tied, my head not able to move far, and practically hobbled in the

43

high heels. Like most capable women I sometimes put on the little girl act – you do it for me; you choose; look after me, and so on – but this was taking the game on to a higher level. And I liked it.

'Is Lima ready for this?' I asked him with a self-satisfied smile.

'I don't think so. After your long flight, I thought tonight we could stay in and chill out – if that's all right with you.'

Chilling was approximately the reverse of what I was feeling, feverish being a more appropriate description, but I nodded. Apart from anything else I liked the constriction of my head on the chain as I moved slightly.

'Just one more thing.' He bent down to my feet. 'If you don't mind?'

Did I mind? I should mind, I told myself. Although I felt as though I couldn't walk in the heels anyway, he reinforced it by clipping a short chain, no more than nine inches long, on the loop at the back of each shoe. Oh yes, Bliss the feminist thought she ought to mind, but Bliss the sex goddess luxuriated in her rôle.

I tentatively put one foot forward. By taking short steps and putting one foot straight in front of the other I coped. And I have to admit it made my walk as sexy as hell.

'But now what, Carlos?'

The smile that played round his mouth was broader now, happier than the enigmatic smile he had had on his face before. Had he been nervous?

'Whatever we decide, Bliss.'

'Well, while I like the outfit, it does occur to me that this chain on the shoes . . . it's not very practical as far as access is concerned, is it?'

He laughed and reached out a hand towards my sex, brushing it over my pubes and downwards. Instinc-

44

tively I opened my legs as far as they could go, and demonstrated that it wasn't indeed very far. With his eyes on my face his fingers trailed along the length of my slit, putting the thousands of nerve endings in my clit on red alert and sending my muscles into overdrive as he slipped into the almost embarrassing wetness.

'You mean for fucking? I don't always think that's necessary, do you? Seeing you like that, it's almost its own reward, Bliss.'

His fingers were moving up and down in the musky heat of my cunt and I had to admit that fucking wasn't necessary, thinking that it wouldn't take long for me to come anyway, but then, disconcertingly, he moved his hand and turned me round again. Facing the mirror once more what I could see of him behind me seemed to be lost in contemplating the sight of the chains and laces that bound me. His hands caressed my shoulders and moved downwards, tracing the curve of my exaggeratedly small waist and the swell of my hips, until they were on the bare flesh of my arse. He circled my buns gently, then harder and more suggestively, his powerful free hands brushing against my bound immobile ones, and I felt suddenly disappointed, guessing that maybe, like Kip, he too had as much interest in the arse as the cunt. God knows I've tried but I don't like anal sex. I gave it up for Lent last year and have kept off it ever since. Still I would have no choice but to submit if Carlos bent me over.

Instead he said, 'How about dinner?'

The tradition of cooking meat impaled on skewers has got to have its roots in sexual symbolism. Holding a kebab and tearing the meat from it with the teeth has always seemed to me the perfect way of demonstrating that you're willing to get down and dirty and back to the primitive. Having a strong dark man holding a kebab slightly above your supplicatingly raised breasts while your arms are bound behind you so you have to reach your constrained head up as far as you can to tease the meat with your teeth is the perfect way of trying to have a hands-free orgasm. Not that I did – do they exist outside the pages of bestsellers? – but I came as near as I ever have to the female equivalent of the waking wet dream.

The meat was savoury, with an oddly smooth texture, spiced and a little tart. The juice dripped on to my tits and Carlos licked it off.

'Not guinea pig, I hope?' I asked suspiciously. You may be disgusted but Peruvians do eat the poor little pets.

'God, no. They're far too small and bony. It's heart.'

'Heart. Human?'

'Ox. It's a traditional speciality. They cook it at the takeaway alongside the chicken. Don't you like it?'

'It's great.'

Of course I remembered it from the guidebooks, *anticuchos*, skewered ox heart, and I have to say it was one item I wouldn't have ordered for myself. But I'm not a squeamish sort of girl and when he held the skewer up again I bit down hard on a particularly succulent-looking chunk and chewed with enjoyment. After I had a couple more mouthfuls of meat he held up a piece of sweetcorn.

'I read a story once about a woman who was fucked in some ritual ceremony with corn on the cob. Or was it up the arse? The texture would be interesting, better than a ridged johnny.'

'It's a shame they only come in pieces at the takeaway, but thanks for the hint.' Carlos forked up half a dozen chips and offered them to me, but I was happy with my meat and veg. The corset was tight enough to

46

suppress my appetite as well as my waist. His dark eyes were glowing with, I hoped, desire.

'You're very horny, Bliss. Are you always like this? Or is it a while since you had sex?'

That was a good chance to tell him about the newly inaugurated on the ground in Aruba club. Well, I've done the mile high thing before. He nodded slowly.

'So you're not desperate for sex.'

'You're the one who's setting the agenda here – you mean you don't fuck?'

He poured some wine into a glass and held it to my lips. I tilted my head even further backwards than the chain held it and swallowed, feeling some trickle down my throat on to my exposed breasts. Despite spilling it he gave me more until I shook my head and made a noise in my throat. As he put down the glass he once again licked the spillage from my breast, but this time took each nipple in his mouth in turn, sucking gently, then harder. If he wasn't going to let me come I was going to explode.

I didn't explode, of course. But it wasn't easy to believe that, after the dressing up, the fondling, the nipple sucking, etc. Carlos simply undressed me and put me to bed. Though for simply undressing me, read slowly, sensually and regretfully. The last thing he took off was the gloves but as he moved my arms forward to a more usual position in their sockets he asked me if I always slept on my back.

'Yeah, I think so . . . why?'

'Why? Because I want to give you the most forceful climax you've ever had in your life. But not tonight and, I'm afraid, Bliss, that as you've already lived up to Kip's description of headstrong, I don't trust you not to do it for yourself.'

He propelled me to the sofa bed and laid me down.

As he tied each wrist to the top of the opposite arm I felt almost like a corpse.

'I won't be able to sleep like this.'

The last thing I remembered was his disbelieving smile then the jet lag kicked in again and I fell asleep.

Chapter Three

'Your tour guide's ready and waiting.'

I came to. Carlos was back in casual gear and holding a huge cup of coffee. I sat up and wriggled back to prop myself against the wall. It was hard to believe I'd slept with my hands tied but he assured me I'd had a good ten hours.

He untied me so I could hold the cup, rather than risk scalding me.

'I need a shower.'

'Sure. Breakfast? Bread, toast?'

'How can you trust me while you're getting my toast?'

In black again, and with his hair loose and brushing his shoulders, Carlos looked more like a man who preferred his women in chains than the persona he'd presented in his work suit.

'In my experience it's men who wake up raring to go with one thought on their minds. You'd rather warm up slowly . . . wouldn't you?'

'If I get as warm as I was last night I'll self-combust.'

He did have a nice laugh. I wondered whether to stay a few extra days in Lima.

'You shower and I'll do the toast.' He moved towards the kitchenette. 'Bliss, you looked wonderful last night. Can I dress you for sightseeing?'

Immediately the warm-up started, and not that slowly either.

After my shower I put on the towelling robe he'd given me and ate my toast and had another cup of coffee while Carlos made a few calls in rapid Spanish. I realised that my language lessons were going to be of limited use in the real Spanish-speaking world.

'Which charity do you work for?' I asked as he put the phone away.

He looked puzzled. 'Charity?'

'Kip said you worked for a development agency.'

His brow cleared and he nodded, a smile at the corners of his mouth. 'Oh yes, but it's not charity funded. It's more along the lines of encouraging industry to set up here, you know, bringing in more work and so on. I've got a couple of projects on the go at the moment, but I think the big one's going to be on Chiloe, an island off the coast of Chile, so I'm probably moving down there soon. It's crying out for development.'

'Oh, right. I'm planning to go over there too.' I nodded with polite interest though my mind was engaged with the prospect of dressing up. Despite trying to travel light I had put a small aromatherapy body lotion in my bag and had smoothed it on after my shower. My skin felt soft and supple and I guessed Carlos would like to handle it.

'I hope you're not expecting anything too different from last night,' he said softly. 'That corset is stunning on you. Your waist looks so much better in it . . . and I want you to be aware of wearing it with every breath.'

It was fine by me, despite his remark reminding me

of a meditation class I took once where you had to be aware of each breath. Maybe bondage would do wonders for my spirituality. Once again I was laced up, though I could swear it was tighter than before. Carlos directed me to put on my black knickers and the skirt and top I'd been wearing when he came home, and then got the boots from the wardrobe.

'I'm not going to be able to walk far in those,' I complained.

'We'll go slowly.' Carlos crouched down to ease my foot into the boots and then pulled the butter-soft leather up to mid-thigh, followed by the other. My skirt came just above the top of them. Having practised with the shoes I managed to walk quite well in the boots, adopting the same procedure as I had for the shoes chained together, a model-girl walk that made me look even more like a Parisian hooker than I already did, with my breasts swelling above the low-necked top and my nipples clearly outlined through the thin stretchy fabric.

'More goth than hooker,' he assured me, clasping a black velvet choker round my neck. It was only half as deep as the collar I had worn last night but the resemblance was enough to shift my sexual warming-up process into a higher gear. I was surprised that the goth revival had reached Peru but felt slightly better about going out as Countess Dracula and with Carlos's approval did my eyes moody dark and my lips crimson, with a tinted sunscreen over the freckles. Finally he handed me a pair of black gloves.

'If you think I'm going to walk through the streets of Lima with my hands tied behind my back –'

'No. But I might just want to fasten them, if it's appropriate. Trust me, Bliss. No one will know.'

Just a little longer than wrist-length, they had an innocent-looking trimming of braided loops and beads, but he demonstrated how the loops on one interlocked with the beads on the other.

'I suppose I trust you. Anyway, you're more likely to see someone you know than me. And this trip is supposed to be an adventure, after all.'

Churches and museums are usually way down on my list for sightseeing. I like hanging out in cafés, walking round city streets and watching the world go by in blossom-laden parks. For one day, though, I was happy to go along with Carlos's idea of a sightseeing tour. Despite my protestations at home that textile design was not going to be my life career, I also had to see the collection of pre-Inca weavings in the private collection at Miraflores, so had got Carlos to make an appointment for that late in the afternoon, which meant that I had effectively limited the time for gazing at altars and glass cases.

We started with the main museums, which were scattered all over the city. My perch on top of the precarious heels wasn't tested too much, just in and out of the car and around the exhibits. Not surprisingly Carlos lingered a little too long over the relics from the Spanish Inquisition, and he seemed to find the riches in the gold museum almost as interesting. In the centre of town we did the cathedral and nearby I caught my first glimpse of street sellers in traditional dress, which delighted me, though Carlos assured me I'd see plenty of that in Cuzco. I also caught my first glimpse of McDonald's, which was a bit disappointing.

'What do you expect?' Carlos asked, amused. 'This is civilisation too, you know. OK, it's not Europe, but it's not the third world either.'

'I suppose. It's just that wherever you go you see the same things. Before long you'll be walking down a street and you won't be able to work out whether you're in Bogota or Bognor.'

'You obviously haven't been to Bogota.'

'Yeah, and I'll put money on you not having been to Bognor either.'

Carlos decided we needed a light lunch as he was taking me to the best seafood restaurant in Lima that night. The little vegetarian café was half empty and he chose a corner table right at the back and tucked in next to me. We were half a dozen tables away from the cluster of customers who looked like lunching secretaries with the obligatory sprinkling of gringo backpackers. The darkly handsome waiter was obviously of Indian extraction and greeted Carlos with familiarity. Without even consulting me or the menu Carlos ordered.

'Don't I get to choose anything myself?' I complained.

He smiled his closed-mouth enigmatic smile. 'I enjoyed feeding you so much last night that I wanted to do it again.'

Before I could register what that statement might imply his left hand snaked round the back of my waist and grabbed my left hand while his right pulled my right to meet it. Without even having to look he fastened the gloves together.

'Carlos, this is public. You said no one would see,' I hissed. Still smiling but now with an edge of triumph to it he leaned over me, his left arm still around my waist and his right arm resting on the table top.

'They won't,' he murmured. 'As long as you stop trying to pull them apart.'

My vain efforts to loosen the seemingly simple fastenings meant that my tits were jiggling in the brief cups of the corset. His eyes were on them, and as I followed them I saw that my nipples had hardened in excitement.

Before I could tell myself to stop trying to get free and calm down, Carlos lifted his hand and rubbed my nearest nipple. My eyes closed with excitement and fear of being seen and I felt the colour rise in my cheeks. I sincerely hoped that the other customers were too far away and engrossed in their lunch or their conversation to take any notice, but part of me was melting with the embarrassment. Melting into a sticky pool in my knickers, that is.

He moved to the other nipple and teased it harder. My eyes were in constant movement, darting between the café customers, his face, the movements of the waiter and my now rapidly rising and falling breasts. Shamed and helpless I saw the waiter move towards us but Carlos's hand was back on the table before two glasses of yellow juice were set before us. Did the waiter's eyes linger on me with admiration or contempt? Or had I imagined his eyes registering anything other than just another punter?

The juice was delicious; papaya and mango, Carlos told me, as I sucked the nectar through the straw. His hand was, to my relief, around his glass and I relaxed, but not for long. The arm that was thrown caressingly around my waist was withdrawn to lie negligently in my lap and, as Carlos sucked nonchalantly on his juice, his hand snaked up between my silky body-lotioned thighs and rubbed at my knickers.

'I suppose it's all about power,' I said defiantly, almost condescendingly, as his hand slipped easily up and down the wet satin.

He laughed in genuine amusement. 'Sure it's about power. But more than that, Bliss. I take part of my pleasure from giving it to you, as well as from seeing you unable to help responding to me.'

'And why do you take pleasure from humiliating me in public?'

'No, Bliss. You're getting pleasure from that. Aren't you?'

Of course I was. Don't we all like that element of danger in misbehaving in public, even if it's only as a teenager, snogging in your bedroom when your mum might burst in at any minute, or being felt up in the back row of the cinema.

'If what I'm feeling now isn't a sign that you're getting pleasure, I can only assume you've wet yourself.'

'Most amusing,' I retorted, but I had to smile. 'The thing is, Carlos, where do you stop? I've always associated being tied up with being whipped or walloped, neither of which are my thing.'

'Nor mine,' he assured me. 'I don't need to hurt you. Anyway there's no point trying domination unless you want to submit: it's a two-way thing. But don't tell me you don't want to be bound. Your reactions so far have spoken for themselves.'

As if to emphasise it his fingers slid inside my knickers and encountered the full spate of my slickness. It was hard to stop myself from moaning as he poised his finger on the tip of my clit and stroked so delicately but rapidly that it was like the buzz of a mild electric shock. He withdrew his finger and put it to his lips, smiling quizzically.

'I think I'm right.'

The waiter appeared with a large plate of different vegetable dishes, which he placed between us, and two plates and knives and forks. I almost told him not to bother as I wasn't able to use the knife and fork and in moving the plate he'd put my juice, or rather my straw, out of reach of my mouth.

Once again I submitted to being fed and once again I

55

got a real charge from it. Why there should be a difference between picking up a fork and putting food into my own mouth and taking food from the end of Carlos's fork I couldn't say. Maybe it was because I was submitting to him obediently, but then again I didn't have much choice. Whatever, the food tasted good. There were potatoes in a delicious peanut sauce, a bit like a satay sauce, hard-boiled eggs, avocado, beetroot in a creamy mayonnaise and sweetcorn. He fed us alternate mouthfuls and as he lifted the fork to my lips I opened my mouth in readiness, turning myself on picturing the crimson lips parted ready to receive whatever he decided to put between them. God knows I can probably do without sex altogether and stick with my imagination. By the time we finished I'd stopped watching the waiter nervously and couldn't have cared less what he might have thought of the customer at table 15 being fed like a baby.

After lunch Carlos untied my hands and after sashaying through the Plaza de Armas again on my heels I was driven north, crossing the river, and he pulled over on to some waste ground and parked.

'Let me show you a part of Lima most tourists don't see,' he said as we walked up the busy road. I couldn't believe that there was going to be anything to see; the river looked brown and polluted and the road was full of traffic. Then we crossed the road and I saw what he meant. Stretching out along the river bank was a higgledy-piggledy row of makeshift wooden and cardboard shacks. They were roofed with dirty discarded carpet, which also did for a door, and though no bigger than beach huts some seemed to house a tangle of filthy children and their parents, or an old, hopeless-looking couple. We rounded a corner; the shacks seemed to go on for ever.

'Of course, it's better than a McDonalds on every street corner,' he said drily.

'Oh for God's sake, Carlos, the two are hardly the opposing choices,' I said, angered more by the squalor than his statement. 'Don't you think the two present an obscene contrast?'

He shrugged. 'You mean more obscene than people sleeping on the streets in London? It's a damn sight richer than Lima. What's worse, pushing aside a down and out on the way to a hamburger restaurant or on the way to the Ritz?'

'OK,' I said, slightly confused. 'I'll think about that one and we can argue later.'

He laughed almost tenderly. 'When I have your arms pulled back in the gloves, when your tits are pointing at the sky, when . . . I think maybe I should chain your choker to the wall tonight –'

His mouth stopped speaking and came down over mine. If his last words had turned him on they had done no less to me. We kissed properly for the first time, our tongues exploring each other's mouth. His arms were pulling me towards him and I could feel his cock hard and big against me. Totally oblivious to the surroundings I pressed back against his cock and his hands moved to my arse and circled my buttocks, then slipped under the skirt and under the leg of my knickers. My eyelids drooped, heavy with desire, and I suddenly focused on an old man watching us from the carpet door of one of the shacks. I pulled my mouth away.

'Carlos, we've got an audience.'

Seemingly ignoring me, his muscular arms propelled me round to face the wall and his hand resumed its quest in my knickers. As I started to protest he stopped me with his mouth and ran his finger along the over-heated moisture that had spread to my arse from my

57

weeping slit. His other hand was on my waist, where it was holding up my skirt. Putting myself in the old man's place I saw a girl dressed like a whore who allowed a man to pull her skirt up exposing her knickers while he caressed her cunt in full view of anyone who was passing by, and as Carlos stopped kissing me and spoke to the old man I hung my head in shame. More than shame; I was totally on the verge of coming as his fingers slid lightly over my clit and back to my glorious wet sex.

He didn't let me come, though. After the old man answered him, laughing, Carlos pulled his hand out and showed it to him. They both laughed and Carlos propelled me away, back in the direction of the car. My head lowered, unable to look the man in the face, I felt as though my cheeks were on fire.

'Nice, eh?' he asked teasingly.

'Christ almighty, Carlos, I can't believe you did that.'

His look feigned surprise. 'What, not let you come? I told you, I will but it'll be later –'

'Oh do shut up. You know exactly what I mean.'

'Oh, *that*.' Raising my head I saw him smiling. 'You mean you can't believe I combined giving you a major turn on with giving some poor old boy a treat? Seemed to make sense to me.'

As we got back into the car I calmed down. Put like that, what the hell. As long as I wasn't in the way of a BBC camera shooting a documentary about the slums of Lima, no one would know.

Apart from the fact that I was looking forward to finally getting my rocks off, I was glad to be back in the apartment. My concentration on the textiles – it was a terrific collection – was somewhat spoiled by self-consciousness about my appearance and the half-fear, half-desire that Carlos might at any moment decide to fondle me in public.

I was afraid that he was going to make me wait until after dinner before fucking me, as I'm not keen on sex on a full stomach, but although that didn't turn out to be the case he still made me wait. Achingly, tinglingly and desperately.

It was almost six when we got back and Carlos poured us both a beer and made a toast: 'To anticipation.'

'That sounds good.' I raised my glass in response. 'We won't have long for that though, will we?'

'Long enough,' he said cryptically, setting down his beer and diving into the wardrobe. 'Why don't you take off your skirt and top?'

The coldness of the beer sent a shiver through me, or was it desire? I stripped off quickly and efficiently, as he wasn't watching. Remembering what he had said about chaining my choker to the wall made my sex muscles leap and my nipples stand to attention.

Carlos looked up almost absently from his box. 'Panties.' He mimed for me to take them off, and I stood before him in corset, choker and boots. To my excitement he took off the velvet choker and replaced it with the wide one I had worn the night before. No gloves, though; instead he produced two black leather straps and fastened them around my body and arms; one over the corset, just under my breasts, and the other around my hips, just where the corset ended.

'I think it's time to take you to bed,' he said, his eyes narrowing. I almost expressed my disappointment – after all, where was the anticipation, and what about being chained to the wall? – but instead a moan escaped me as he fastened a short strip of plaited leather to one of the chains on the choker. It could only remind me of a dog lead and he almost dragged me like a wide-eyed puppy to the bedroom. Trembling with excitement I tottered on the high heels and as he pushed me down on to the bed and fastened a clip on the other end of the lead to the rail of the bedhead I could have fainted with pleasure.

'I have to go out for a bit and, as we've already established, you can't be trusted not to bring yourself off while I'm out, I'll have to leave you like this ... I hope you don't mind?'

'What do you think?' I asked him, my voice and my look charged with meaning. He smiled, his thin lips looking almost cruel.

'Good, because just one more thing.'

He pulled my legs apart and I thought he was going to give me another shot of anticipation. Instead he fastened a black cuff around each ankle and snapped the chains on them to the rail at the foot of the bed. Chained at neck and ankle, but with my arms tightly bound to my sides, my first thought was that if he was going out for too long I would die of desire.

'Oh, and another,' he added, lowering his face to mine. 'You are comfortable, Bliss?'

I nodded.

'Good. Can you lift your head a little?'

I thought he was checking to make sure I had enough freedom of movement on the chain. But no, he took the opportunity to slip a thick black band over my head and around my eyes.

'Carlos, it's a bit scary.'

Without being able to see his face, his laugh sounded satanic.

'I suppose it is. After all, when I get back you won't actually know it's me, will you?'

I whimpered.

'For all you know, I might have given the key to the old squatter we saw earlier.'

'Carlos, please!' My voice was anguished.

'I offered him a feel of you, but he said no. Don't be hurt, though. I think it was just that he was afraid that I was some kind of nut who'd slug him after he'd touched you.'

'You didn't!'

'I asked him if he wanted to put his finger up your cunt, and showed him how wet it was.'

My face flamed once more but Carlos found my real reaction to humiliation as he suddenly penetrated me with two fingers. Three, four times he thrust in and out as I arched my back to meet him, then he stopped as abruptly as he started.

'*Hasta la vista*,' he said mockingly as he left the room, and minutes later the apartment door slammed.

Time seemed to stand still. I could have sworn Carlos was gone for hours, but he had told me we had a dinner reservation for nine. Bitterly I regretted agreeing to anticipation. How did I know he hadn't decided to prolong my anticipation by going to dinner alone . . . or even worse with someone else? Or that he wouldn't come back with that someone else and let him or her loose on me as I lay bound and helpless?

Still, as long as it wasn't the old squatter; if it was a friend, or a girlfriend I might not mind. But then if he didn't take the blindfold off, how would I know? I tortured myself with the possibilities of what was to come, and tortured myself even more by imagining that after all he would do what he did last night and come back and put me to bed without allowing me release.

Finally the apartment door opened. I called out but got no answer. Minutes passed then he – or someone – came in the room.

'Carlos?' I began. A hand crushed my mouth and I froze. I thought it was his, but in any event took the hand as a warning not to speak. It moved away from my mouth when satisfied that I was silent and moved to my nipples. First one, then the other, were gently stroked then pulled harder until they must have been an inch long. Then the hand started stroking my mons, taking my hairs in between its fingers, and pressing down hard enough to start my clitoris fluttering. It moved again and caressed my clit, gently then harder, but it seemed to sense my nearness and stopped and instead the fingers slipped in and out of me again. Still I couldn't be sure it was Carlos. I couldn't smell his cologne but then, had he worn it this morning, or was that just put on for work the day before? I consoled myself that at least it didn't smell like a dirty old man.

Suddenly my ankles were unclipped from the bedpost and a body, warm, muscular and covered with fine hairs, pressed against me. Sure now it was him I raised my legs to wind them round his back, but he put them over his shoulders and clipped the ankle cuffs together. A cock pressed against my slit and entered me without difficulty and I pushed against it. It filled me wholly, satisfyingly, and having spent more than twenty-four hours waiting for it I knew that even if it wasn't him I didn't care. The choker tightened round my neck as I thrust up to meet him and he thrust even more violently inside me. I strained against my bonds, wanting my finger on my clit, but as we pushed even more furiously against each other I felt a finger on it, no, not a finger, because suddenly it was making a noise and my muscles heaved and crashed like the walls of Jericho tumbling down as the combination of the cock and the vibrator brought me to the best orgasm I had ever had in my life.

Of course I had to get away from Lima. Sitting in the guesthouse in Cuzco, I explained it in a postcard.

Kip, you bastard, you did it on purpose. You knew I'd get addicted to him, and I bet you've been rubbing your scarred lily-white little hands together in glee at the thought of me bound and gagged. Well I've escaped after a mere four days, and I don't mean the Houdini style of escape, out of the black bag and chains, I just got on a plane and left. Love, Bliss.

PS: Escaped, my arse, I'm meeting him in Chile in a few weeks' time.

I had to go. I'd only meant to stay in Lima for two nights and after the third I got Carlos to book me on to a plane out. After all, I'd come to South America to see the sights: what was the point of being blindfold? And instead of trekking bravely through the cloud forest I had been happily and helplessly tottering around Lima in four-inch heels. But as I explained to Kip, I only managed to tear myself away from him because we'd be meeting later. After a dose of sightseeing and intrepid adventuring I'd be more than ready to submit to Carlos's chains.

I'd arrived in Cuzco early the previous morning and had spent the day rambling around the pretty town, trying to get my breath. It was at a high altitude and the guidebooks advised a few days' acclimatisation was necessary before starting off on the Inca Trail. Carlos had been right: there were plenty of indigenous Indians in traditional dress here, though when I say that I mean the women. Traditional dress for the men seemed to consist of jeans and bomber jackets. All the women were selling something, and though I guessed that I'd end up with at least one alpaca sweater, so far I'd restricted myself to a woven braid for my wrist. When I pulled it tight it reminded me of Carlos.

I turned to the next postcard. The guesthouse had an

ideal set-up for chilling out, with its rooms arranged around a central hall with a glass roof, and furnished with sofas for lounging around on. Already I'd struck up conversations with a German couple and two English girls, though this afternoon everyone was obviously out sightseeing.

Dear Rachel, I bet you're kicking yourself . . .

'G'day! Do you mind if I join you?'

The accent was obviously Australian, which was fine by me. Even finer was the sight that met my eyes when I looked up.

Tall, probably six two, three? Broad and, while not rippling with muscle gym-style, a real sportsman's body. Combat shorts and T-shirt, both khaki. Skin tanned, face big and square. And short hair as blond as a peroxide bottle can get it. I found myself forgetting about Carlos, even about Gabriel Byrne, and denying that I'd ever had a thing for dark men.

'I've got a few to do too,' he said sympathetically, waving his own clutch of cards. 'Fantastic here, eh? We only got in this morning from Lima.'

'I only got here myself yesterday,' I confessed. 'Not that I've done much in the last two days, just a bit of walking around town, acclimatising.'

'You'll be doing the Inca Trail though, won't you?' he asked.

'Of course. I haven't booked up with anyone yet.'

'Oh, we're not going in a group, I can't stand being organised. This is the last chance to go alone, you know.'

'Do I know? Let me tell you . . .'

And I explained my solo predicament, looking into his quite stunningly blue eyes as I did so, thinking that once I had a tan and the sun had lightened my hair a

64

bit we could pass for brother and sister, but then did I want to think of him as a brother? What a lovely golden couple we would make.

While he was sympathising with my predicament another oversized crop-haired clone, though more mouse than blond, came out of one of the rooms and flopped down on the sofa next to him.

'Hey, Red, thought I heard your voice. Got the beers?' He smiled at me and held out his hand. He didn't compare with his friend as far as looks were concerned, but his attraction was in his deep, slightly rough, sexy voice. 'Robbie. How's it going?'

'Great, Robbie. I'm Bliss.' I looked at his friend and raised my eyebrows. 'And you're . . . Red?'

He laughed. 'No, not Red, Rad. I guess it's the accent.'

'Hmm. Not much of a difference the way you say them, but I think I prefer Red. If it's all the same to you.'

'No worries. My name's Magnus Radberg, but I'm not keen on Magnus.'

'Swedish?'

'Three generations back.'

'You know Magnus means big in Latin . . . yeah, of course you do, schoolteachers must have bored the pants off you with that one.'

'Too right.' He laughed. He turned to Robbie apologetically. 'You won't believe this, mate, but I started looking at postcards and forgot about the beer. This altitude must be affecting my brain. I'll go back.'

Robbie shook his head. 'Jeez, mate, this trip's not going to run on water. I'll go. I suppose if you're doing the dutiful postcard thing I'd better get some as well.'

He went out and Red and I went back to our cards, though my mind wasn't on them as attentively as it had been.

We stopped writing when Robbie returned with three big bottles of Cusquena, the local beer. Red told me I could get my round later on at the English pub, so after downing the beer I went to have a shower. As I'd already discovered the hot – sorry, make that warm – water only appeared at erratic intervals, and the German guy had said that five o'clock was a good time. I hoped so, as I'd already had two cold showers since I arrived in Peru, though God knows the way I kept bumping into stunning men it was probably just as well.

I have to admit that I got pissed in the English pub. Well, it was happy hour, and pisco sours are a lot more alcoholic than I had thought judging from the one I had as an aperitif in the posh seafood restaurant in Miraflores. The trouble is, once you launch into a series of five of anything made from a large measure of spirits, getting pissed is fairly inevitable.

But I'm not a quitter and managed a couple of beers with dinner, where we had a great time, getting mixed up in a multinational group of fellow backpackers. It set the tone for the next few days, though apart from the booze and the laughs we managed to do the local sightseeing and explored the valley, which was breathtaking. Finally when Robbie was on one of his daily trips to the internet café – he was a real line freak – Red and I spent the afternoon in my room.

The S&M crowd use the expression 'vanilla sex' to describe normal straight sex. I suddenly found out why. Fucking Red was really nice, or as he would say, rilly, rilly nice, but after Carlos it lacked a bit of edge, a bit of spice. I tried not to make comparisons, though, and did enjoy taking charge myself, which after being totally helpless and passive was great. I rode him every way I knew how, with the holdups having him almost creaming his combats before he even got inside me –

girlies in black stockings being, frankly, rare on the backpacker circuit.

And man, was he big. If ever a man was well named, etc. Everything else about him was, so I shouldn't have been surprised by the girth and length of his cock. The first time we fucked, after he'd calmed down at the sight of the stockings, I was happy purely to sit on him for a few minutes, moving minutely, just to feel the rock-solid hugeness of him inside me. He got off even more on my admiration – I suppose Australian girls are a bit tight with the compliments – and it was good. You could even say that after Carlos it was unrestrained, abandoned lust, but something was missing . . . such as the restraints.

It was inevitable that we would team up for the Inca Trail. The guys had a big tent – they had to, otherwise the two of them wouldn't fit in it – and said one more wouldn't make much difference. We queued up for our train tickets and set off before the crack of dawn one Monday morning.

The train journey was surreal. Women in traditional dress got on at every stop, selling all sorts of food. One sat almost opposite us carving slices off a lump of hot roast meat, just there on her lap, and you had to wonder what else had been on that skirt; the smell was not appetising. The train filled up and people sat on the floor, even one woman nursing a baby. Then we got to kilometre 88, the start of the trail, and shouldering our rucksacks we picked our way as delicately as we could through the mob, fearful the train would set off again with us still on it.

The first day's walking was fairly easy and we stopped at a campsite along with several others who had been on the train. You're not supposed to build fires on the trail but a group of crazy French guys did anyway – I guess that's why they're insisting on people

67

going in organised groups – and after we'd eaten our packet soup and pasta everyone gathered round it. One of the French guys had, believe it or not, a guitar and played old Simon and Garfunkel songs, in which thanks to my hippy mother I was word perfect.

Red kept plucking at my sleeve and suggesting we turn in, obviously wanting to screw before Robbie joined us, but I was having too much fun. By the time tiredness kicked in, and I always find that without drink it seems to do so earlier than usual, Robbie was already heading into the bushes with his torch for a last pee.

Modesty has to go out of the window when you're three in a tent, and I didn't think Robbie was looking, or even interested, as I stripped off my bra to put on the fine cotton Indian top I wore as a nightshirt. It was easy enough to wriggle out of my knickers while in the sleeping bag. But after turning over and back six times, Red reached over and pulled my hand on to his cock, which was doing a pretty good impersonation of Huayna Picchu, the phallus-shaped mountain behind Macchu Picchu itself.

'He's asleep,' he whispered. 'Bliss, I'm dying to get inside you. Look, he's got his back to us.'

OK, it was tacky. But he did have his back to us, and if you've ever camped you'll know that lying almost on the bare earth with just a canvas roof over you brings out the most elemental urges. As I had tried every position but the missionary with Red I lay on my back and submitted to him, raising my arms above my head and moaning with gratitude when he grasped them firmly in one hand.

'Hey, keep the noise down, guys,' said Robbie. I froze, but his voice was tolerant and almost amused. Red smiled down and winked at me as his cock nudged at me. I wasn't really ready for him and he realised and spat on his hand and rubbed the slippery wetness over my clit with feathery strokes.

There was movement from Robbie's direction and his torch clicked on. The next thing was the sound of his voice, reading from one of the guidebooks. I guessed he was just trying to forestall any embarrassment on either side by drowning us out but let me tell you when there's one hand holding your wrists together and one teasing your clit, the smell of a campfire outside and someone still strumming on the guitar, the addition of a deep, husky voice with an Australian accent talking about Incas only feet away is enough to get you there. I lifted my legs to pull Red inside me as I felt my muscles ready to pulse and as his cock rearranged the flesh of my now-wet pussy the muscles exploded around him.

Try as I might to keep quiet I couldn't stop a low moan escape from my throat as the orgasm tore through me. At the same time, feeling the strength of my contractions around his cock, Red let out a startled 'Jesus!' and Robbie turned up the volume and his voice washed over me with the helpless convulsions of my sex and I was in Inca heaven.

The next day's walk was hard. As we climbed higher we got slower and were easily overtaken by porters carrying around three packs each for the wimps in the tour groups. More than once I regretted hooking up with the guys as otherwise I'd be swinging along with nothing but a daypack, able to appreciate the flowers in the cloud forest rather than the load on my back.

Robbie acted as though nothing out of the ordinary had happened the night before and while Red was chatting with a couple of Uruguayan guys in Spanish I decided to bite the bullet.

'What you were reading last night, about the Incas,

that's so amazing. That they were so many and were just conquered so quickly by so few Spaniards; how on earth did it happen?'

'This book's got a theory about that. After you'd finished I carried on reading it.'

'Look, I hope you weren't embarrassed,' I interrupted. 'Just say, honestly.'

He turned to me, smiling conspiratorially. 'No worries, Bliss. I quite enjoyed it. How about you?'

'Shit. You know what, Robbie? Your voice gave it that little edge, you know?'

He gave a gravelly laugh. 'And do you know what, Bliss? You're starting to sound like an Aussie.'

'Yeah, well, I'm one of life's natural mimics,' I sighed, trying not to make it sound like a question.

'Sure. Well I'll read to you tonight too if you like.'

'So what is this theory about the Incas?'

'Well, there's two options. One is that they thought the Spanish were Gods and so they bowed before them. The other is that they read in the stars that their time had come to an end and so just gave up.'

'Wow. So what else have you got to read?'

He laughed again. 'Wait and see.'

It turned out nobody was in the mood for reading, or sex, that night. Despite coping reasonably well with climbing to over 14,000 feet, we were all knackered when we got to the campsite. After cooking the pasta we turned in and I don't think I was the only one to go straight to sleep.

The following night, however, we felt a bit better. For one thing we had been mainly descending, and for another we had reached the hotel where we got chicken and chips for dinner rather than pasta, washed down with cold, delicious beer. Whether it was due to a couple of days' abstinence or the altitude had made us lightheaded, after a couple of bottles we were all a bit giggly and ready to call it a day.

It was still early and not completely dark as we got into the sleeping bags. I wondered if Red was horny, because I certainly was. Without waiting to see if there was anything to drown out, Robbie began reading aloud. Seeing as Red didn't complain that he was trying to sleep, I guessed he was feeling the same way and reached out. Even through the sleeping bag I could feel his hardness and in the dim light he smiled and unzipped the bag.

He made to move towards me but I beat him to it and straddled him, bending to kiss him long and hard. His hands came up to my breasts and he rubbed my nipples through the thin cotton, then pinched them harder. I liked it but as he'd had a cold shower in the hostel I decided I wanted a taste of him and slid down and settled my mouth around his cock. Starting to suck him gently I was able to concentrate on what Robbie was saying just inches away from me.

'The Inca priests selected the prettiest young girls to train for priestesshood. The first of the initiation rites was conducted by the priestesses. The girls, all virgins, would be bound naked in the inner sanctum of the temple and anointed with precious oil on their breasts and vaginal area. Their clitorises would be stimulated so that they reached orgasm, and this went on day after day so that they became accustomed to climaxing quickly. In the second phase the oil was applied to the anus and the priestesses would gently insert a gold phallus into it in imitation of copulation, which would continue until the phalluses could be inserted easily.'

Never mind the trainee priestesses, my juices were flowing like a mountain stream. Robbie must have picked that passage of the book deliberately to get me going. I didn't know whether or not Red was listening or whether he was just enjoying my mouth action, but when he whispered, 'Turn round, Bliss,' I was more than happy to oblige and lowered myself happily over his mouth. It gave me a chance to notice that Robbie had abandoned his face to the tent wall position, however, and was interspersing his reading with looking unashamedly at us. As Red's tongue started to lap at my clit I decided I had no shame either and before getting down to his cock again I smiled at Robbie and moulded my hands round my tits like a page three girl. He smiled back and went on with his reading.

'The girls would then practise the masturbation and anal penetration with each other, as once they reached the priesthood they would be required to train the new initiates. Finally they were taught the arts of love by performing cunnilingus on the priestesses and each other, and then they were taught how to perform fellatio on the phalluses.'

Inspired by the Inca rites and Red's questing tongue my own performance of fellatio was practically deep throat, though with the size of Red's real live phallus there was only so far it could go. It was far enough for him, however, as he lifted me off his face and I knew he wanted me down on his cock, right now. He unwrapped the rubber and passed it to me and without losing any more time I put it on and sank down happily on to his magnitude. Sure, I could have turned and faced him, but that wasn't what I wanted. What I wanted was to half turn so I could watch Robbie watching us; I could hardly have turned away from Red if we were face to face.

'Once the initiates were deemed to be experts in the art of love, the priest would initiate them. Two at a time they would come to him and demonstrate to him their ability to please each other with hands and tongues. They then took turns to excite the priest with their mouths and once he was fully aroused they would be bent over the stone altar and he would penetrate one and then the other. However they were not worthy of receiving his seed and the priestess who had initiated them would receive that from the priest.'

Robbie had moved forwards in his sleeping bag and put the book down as, moving slowly up and down on Red's prick, I lifted my top over my head and held my arms up, my wrists tangled in the cotton, knotted at the nape of my neck. His eyes were on my tits. I dropped the top and massaged them as he picked up the book again, though he kept glancing up at me.

'The new priestesses would remain, technically, virgins unless one was chosen as the sacrifice, which was every new moon. Then before plunging the dagger in her breast the priest would penetrate her vagina. He would manually stimulate her to orgasm when he reached it himself and the death blow would come at the moment of their mutual climax.'

I had started my own manual stimulation before he'd even got to that point and moved faster and more urgently up and down on Red's cock. Not long after the priest and priestess reached their mutual climax so did Red and I.

Breathless, I peeled myself off Red and putting my top on got back in to my sleeping bag, suddenly feeling slightly embarrassed at my wanton exhibitionism.

'I never read that bit before,' said Red ingenuously as he tied the condom tight. 'What book's that in, mate?'

Robbie laughed his throaty, almost dirty, laugh. 'The one in my head, mate.'

Well, we had to laugh, though silently I blessed him for his shrewd instincts at what turned me on. I wondered if voyeurism was reward enough for him, or whether I should give him a special treat in thanks. But not yet.

Chapter Four

Dear Kip, Have managed to get over Carlos and
the thrills of bondeeism/bondageism – what the
hell – with a new hobby, exhibitionism. Really owe
you now, not only for introducing me to Carlos
and so the first, but also for putting Rachel out of
action so that I can indulge in the second.
PS Macchu Picchu is stunning.

I was in the restaurant of the Macchu Picchu hotel,
having lunched with the French Simon and Garfunkel
fans, and lingered over coffee with a couple of
postcards. Red and Robbie had deemed the set price
menu too expensive and had wandered back up to the
ruins with the remains of our trek food: stale rolls, a tin
of tuna and some disgusting local chocolate. I wasn't
going to let a few quid stand in the way of my awesome
Macchu Picchu experience so we'd gone our own way
for a bit.

I'm an artist, not a writer, and there was no way I
could put the day into words, hence the flippant card.
The walk to the sun gate, the first sight of the ruins and

the magical atmosphere had captivated me like nothing ever before, and I wasn't going to attempt to describe it. In part that was why I had decided to have lunch in the restaurant when the others ducked out; I wanted to be alone to savour the experience, though thanks to the *entente cordiale* that didn't last long. Solitary at last I went through the motions of writing cards though my mind was still in the ruins.

The noise in the café was starting to get to me, however, and I decided to make the most of the visit and wander round a bit more on my own. Following the crowd outside the café I realised that instead of going back to the ruins I was heading to the car park. Just as I made to turn back I saw a group of men in suits getting into a car. Nothing strange about that, except that the one who was doing the talking was Carlos.

Calling him, I ran towards the car but the doors had closed and it started off. The tinted windows meant that I couldn't see him and I assumed he hadn't seen me, unless he didn't want to introduce a girl he'd initiated into the rites of bondage to business colleagues.

But why was he there? I couldn't see how visiting Macchu Picchu was helping Peru with its development. The puzzle was still bugging me when I bumped into Red and Robbie a couple of minutes later.

'I don't understand why he didn't tell me he'd be here. After all, it wasn't that long ago I saw him, and he knew I was planning to do the Trail,' I said, having explained to them – without bringing in the sexual aspect of our acquaintance – that I'd seen my friend from Lima.

'I think I saw those guys before walking round the grounds of the hotel,' said Robbie. 'Four of them, two in white suits, two dark?'

'That's right. Carlos is the one in cream with a ponytail. I'm sure it was him because of his hair.'

'So how do you know this guy?' asked Red casually.

I told him about Kip and Carlos.

'And what does he do?'

'He works for some aid agency – no, not aid, development agency, helping the locals set up industry and so on. It's called ETP. I'm not really sure what they do.'

'Sounds very altruistic,' said Robbie a touch acerbically. I wasn't sure why; after all if anyone needed to be jealous of Carlos it was Red and not him. Still it was no skin off my nose.

'Not that it matters. I'm supposed to be seeing him in Chile, in a few weeks time.'

'Hey, don't say you're going to ditch me in Chile,' said Red in mock dismay.

'You should be so lucky to last that long. We'll have gone our separate ways by then, anyway.'

We had already vaguely discussed our future itineraries. I was definitely going to have a look at Bolivia, even if it was only for a couple of days, while they had said they might go and see Lake Titicaca but after that they would head straight for Chile. Still, that was further down the line. We got the bus down to the station and waited for the crowded, smelly, slow train back to Cuzco.

Just because you've spent a few days with a couple of guys, fucking one and putting on a live sex show for the other, it doesn't entitle you to any claim on their time, I know, but when I found them both out next morning and what's more not back by the next day I felt a bit peeved. Knocking round town on my own wasn't so much fun and, let's face it, after Macchu Picchu anything would be an anti-climax. Still on the second day I bumped into the Uruguayans and amused myself by practising my Spanish with them and flirting slightly. All right, flirting outrageously. I was almost minded to go back to their guesthouse with them for a pidgin Spanish threesome but I thought maybe my erotic life was running just a little wild and instead made do with lots of kisses on cheeks and went back to mine alone.

Red knocked on my door just as I was resigning myself to going out to dinner alone again and kicking myself for turning down the chance to be the filling in a Uruguayan tortilla.

'Thanks for inviting me,' I said drily before he launched into a sketchy apology for leaving me. Apparently they'd bumped into a couple of mates from home who persuaded them to go back up to Pisac, the mountain village we'd visited together a few days before. It sounded a bit of a coincidence to me, but it was none of my business. I suspected that Robbie was fed up with the rôle of voyeur and had persuaded Red to go off with a couple of girls, but hey, we were all free agents.

After a few pisco sours I got over it and we took the train together the next night to Puno and Lake Titicaca. Robbie was reading out loud from the guidebook about it being the largest freshwater lake in the world. I wondered if his reading was a hint that I should get fresh on the train but it was too full and I was tired and still slightly pissed off and, anyway, I hadn't turned into one of Pavlov's dogs. Puno was the nearest thing to a shit hole I'd seen since the Lima shanty town and I decided to head straight out for the island of Taquile. Maybe they'd gone back to close buddy mode because neither of them wanted to come with me, so I left most of my gear in the guesthouse strong room and wondered if they'd be there when I got back.

The boat was good fun, not least because there was

an English girl, Ros, who spoke fluent Spanish and interpreted the patter of the captain. He wore traditional dress: a rather dashing full-sleeved white shirt and an embroidered cummerbund, though to my mind a bit spoiled by a Wee Willie Winkie-type hat. He explained that because the end of his hat was plain rather than patterned it meant he was single, but if it was a hint it was lost on both of us. I mean, the islanders knit their own hats, and if there's one thing that's more of a turn off than a man in a nightcap, it's the fact that he knitted it all himself.

The fantastic thing about Taquile, apart from the knitting and the fact there are no cars, is that it's run as a co-operative, and the islanders refuse to have any hotels built. Instead you sign in and are allocated a place to stay. Ros and I were taken to a cabin built around a restaurant. It was fine though unlit, and the toilet could have been nearer, had a flush and not been at the top of a muddy sloping path, but I didn't expect luxury. We were told to present ourselves for dinner at seven and walked round absorbing the peace of the island until then.

Dinner was a bizarre affair. The food, which was quinoa soup (not bad) followed by a Spanish omelette (the local fish was off), was entertaining at least, but the turns the conversation took were even odder. The other guests were two couples, not together, one German-speaking Swiss and the other French. Ros turned out to speak French as well as she spoke Spanish but there was no means of communication with the Swiss couple, so they talked among themselves. Ros launched into a rapid-fire conversation with the French couple so all that was left for me to do was launch myself into the wine. Patrice, the French guy, was also knocking it back and I suppose that's why the conversation went the way it did.

First he was gesticulating and shrugging in that Gallic way and puffing out his cheeks, then he was leaning across saying something to Ros in a low undertone. Gabrielle, the woman, was smoking disdainfully and interjecting scornful remarks, while Ros was giggling coyly. I thought resignedly they were setting themselves up as a threesome and I'd be in the cabin alone, but then Gabrielle gave a final shake of her head and turned to me.

'Do you mind if I change with her? They want to have sex.'

'Doesn't matter to me. I only met her on the boat and I don't fancy her myself.'

She laughed. 'I don't know him very well either. We just met up yesterday and both wanted to come here.' She spoke to the others in French and they all stood, so I guessed we were going to play swapsies and sure enough Ros's stuff was removed from our hut and Gabrielle's installed.

'You want some more to drink?' I asked her, switching on my torch. Even with a bit of light it was pretty dark in there and it was still early.

'No, I'm tired. Patrice is such a bore. He hasn't stopped hitting on me since we set out this morning. I think he's creepy, don't you?'

'Not my type either,' I agreed. 'Well, I suppose we might as well turn in.'

'Look, you stay up if you like. To be honest with you I'm going to get in my sleeping bag and play with myself.'

Things were looking up, but as she was sick of Patrice coming on to her I decided against asking her if she wanted a hand.

'Well, I don't really want to stay up with nobody to talk to . . . do you mind wanking while I'm there?'

She laughed softly. 'No, as long as my vibrator won't disturb you.'

'Oh, wow, I wish I'd brought mine.'

'You can borrow mine if you like, after me.'

Decisions, decisions: shall I make do with my hands so we can masturbate together, or shall I take my turn with the vibrator, sticky with her juices? Either way I couldn't lose, and with her long black hair and sulky French girl mouth she was a million times more of a turn on than the rather plain Ros. I just smiled and started to undress. It was cold in the cabin so I kept my top half wrapped up in my sweater and fleece.

I had unrolled my sleeping bag earlier and now moved it sideways so I could sit with my back to the wall and my legs bent, facing in Gabrielle's direction. She was lying full length on her bed and had already switched on the vibrator. Her body was pretty near perfect; although my legs aren't fat they're a bit muscular, and I appreciated her white, slender thighs.

'God, this is so much better than having to put up with Patrice,' she murmured. 'This trip is just not a success as far as sex is concerned.'

'Mine's pretty good so far,' I admitted, giving my clit a little tease. 'First there was Peter on the plane . . .'

Five minutes later she passed the vibrator over with a satisfied sigh. I knew she had been inspired by my adventures, and hoped she'd reciprocate. While I'd been telling her about my trip I'd merely been toying with myself, having decided I'd hang on for the power pack.

'I decided on this trip because my sex life was crap,' she said dreamily, lighting up a post-orgasm cigarette. 'For six months I had an affair with a married man; you know, everybody does it in France. But he was – what's the word in English – decadent, perhaps? It doesn't matter, but he had done everything. He was forty, quite high-powered and successful, and apart from a stream of mistresses he'd had prostitutes from Biarritz to Bangkok. It was like everything had lost its interest for him: he'd seen it all before. I didn't think it would last, but he had taken me to nice restaurants and bought me some jewellery and shoes and so on; it was fine. Then one day we had a dinner date and I opened the door to let him in and he wasn't alone.

'There was a cameraman with him. He said he wanted to make a film of me, of us. First he got me to strip off, like for a porn film, OK, then play with myself. I didn't mind; the cameraman was all right; I didn't feel too bad doing it in front of him. Then, you can guess, I had to undress Michel and suck him and then we fucked for the camera, different ways, you know. It was a turn on, and he brought the film next time and we watched it; it was pretty good. Then he wanted another one, but this was a different cameraman, and after Michel and I had been fucking for a bit he got him to stop and then he took the camera and the cameraman fucked me. I wasn't very keen on it, but didn't want to make a scene, so I went along with it.

'After that Michel went crazy for filming me with other men. He got his own camera and started bringing other men round to film with me. He would even pay them sometimes, which was so degrading. Thank God they weren't too bad looking, and clean. I don't know why I went along with it . . . but I really liked him, you know? And he always fucked me afterwards so passionately. Then one day he brought a woman. I'd never done anything like it before; the thought had always turned me off, but he talked me into it and in fact I quite enjoyed it. I would have done it again, except that when we out to dinner a week later, before we went back to watch it, we bumped into a friend of his. "Oh,

Gabi, it's so nice to meet you. I've loved watching your films," he said.'

'Oh shit,' I muttered. With the aid of the vibrator I'd come as soon as she'd mentioned the other woman, maybe because I rather hoped for some of her myself, but the end of the story was a real downer. 'Hey, Gabi? You OK?'

She had gone awfully quiet.

'I'm fine,' she said at length. 'But I'd like to go to sleep now. Thanks for your stories; they helped me.'

'Yeah, well, I'd started to enjoy yours. I'm sorry it ended like that.'

'Me too. Still, I always wanted to be a film star. Goodnight.'

'Night.'

Back in Puno was a note from Red and Robbie. They would probably meet me in San Pedro de Atacama in a week or so, if not maybe Santiago where they'd be staying at the Hostal Australe – how apt. I wasn't going to hold my breath, and anyway Gabi and I were going to Bolivia together.

Quite why we ended up riding bikes down the precipitous road to Coroico, a jungle town twenty miles out of La Paz, I don't really know. She had met someone who had done it and I was ready for a bit of adventure. It was a different matter though when we were actually on the road contouring the hillside, with a vertiginous drop down into the forest below, the unwelcome squidge of mud under tyre, what seemed like a non-stop honking stream of cars, buses and trucks overtaking us and coming towards us, and the unnerving frequency of roadside shrines to drivers who'd gone over the edge.

Eventually we arrived, booked into the nearest cheap hotel with a pool and plunged into the freezing water, shrieking like a couple of teenagers. Back in the room we rubbed ourselves dry vigorously to warm up again and had one of those magical moments when two people suddenly look at each other and, click, they're in each other's arms, without any premeditation. We were both wired by the ride followed by the swim and maybe anybody would have done for either of us, but there was a definite spark that connected us and propelled us towards each other like a magnetic field. Our bodies were cold but our mouths and our cunts were warm and soft. I pulled Gabi's hair back from her pale fine-featured face while I explored the warmth of her mouth and then laid her on the bed and spread her legs to explore the other warmth. She wanted to reciprocate but first I wanted her to come and my tongue luxuriated in the wet pinkness of her and then teased her clit until I knew she needed my hand. Once I judged my fingers were doing a perfect job I put my mouth back on her and relished her jerk against my face.

'Oh, Bliss,' she breathed. 'What a good name for you – I have got that right, haven't I? Like really happy?'

'Yep, like blissed out,' I told her, stroking the soft gentle roundness of her belly. 'You know that expression?'

'Of course. Blissed out, that's how I feel. Come here and hold me.'

We snuggled together. She was a lot warmer than I was, thanks to my attentions.

'The only other woman I made love to was for Michel's benefit, and when I came with her it was as much because he was watching as because of her mouth and hands. But with you it's just so ... so normal, somehow. And exciting.'

'It is normal, Gabi,' I told her, looking into her still slightly defensive eyes. 'We can all be bisexual, if we

83

want to be. But only if we want to be, not for someone else's titillation.'

'You're right.' She smiled. 'Now let me do something just for you.'

Her mouth showered kisses all over my breasts and then circled one of my nipples. She started sucking, gently and hesitantly, and then more greedily, almost like a suckling baby. Her fingers echoed her actions on my other nipple and I closed my eyes and surrendered myself to the sensations, wanting to be completely passive so that she could choose for herself what she wanted to do to me. I knew she'd do it right.

Always sensitive, my nipples felt like they were on fire from her protracted sucking and nuzzling. Her other hand moved down past my belly and rubbed lightly over my fleece and then pressed firmly in a circular motion just above my clit. My whole sex was suffused with that velvety warm feeling, combined with the delicious certainty that I was going to come, and come hard. Then she turned around and I thought she was going to give me her sex to tongue again while she did the same to me, but instead she spread it over my tits and moved lightly from side to side. It was as though her cunt was sucking my nipples up inside it one by one as she swayed on top of me. Her hands meanwhile had found other work, with two of her fingers gently fucking me while her other hand played my clitoris like a violin, one finger fretting the hardness itself while the flat of her hand pressed down on my mons. I raised it up to meet her palm and she took the hint and pressed hard and fingered faster and I grabbed the trim pale globes of her arse as she slid crazily across my breasts and pulled them apart and mashed them together. She took up my rhythm with her hands and in my mind's eye I could see inside my cunt, see the walls swelling and reddening and throbbing and pulsating and then landsliding as the orgasm shook me.

We ate fondue and a massive salad in the hotel restaurant, spearing bread and dipping it in the molten cheese and scoffing the salad as though we'd spent the day labouring in the coca fields, then fell into bed and slept, satisfied in every respect.

There were two things they told us. First, the path down to the river was obvious, just start at the corner of the football field. Unfortunately after about an hour of walking in the intense heat we'd stopped exclaiming at the bananas and coffee growing at the side of the rapidly narrowing track and walked round a piece of old sheeting spread with leaves. Coca leaves.

I say unfortunately because the other thing they had said was, take care not to get off the right paths in the jungle areas and stray into the coca plantations. Whoops.

'Shall we go back?' asked Gabi nervously.

I looked around. There was no one in sight and I wondered how bad it would be if we were found in the plantation. Loads of tourists must make the same mistake and end up off the path, and it was hard to believe we would be harmed. The track was descending so I guessed it would still lead down to the river; maybe not at the point we'd expected, but we could always walk up or down stream. Retracing our steps and starting again would mean two hours lost, and it was too hot to walk uphill unnecessarily.

'Let's just carry on,' I decided. 'Just for another half an hour, and if we can't see the river by then we'll turn back.'

At that moment a couple passed us, going uphill; a man in jeans and a woman in the usual five skirts – how do they stand it in the heat? – both carrying bundles on their backs, which, no getting away from it, had to be coca leaves. They responded to my *buenas días* politely and I brushed off any fears and set off down the way they'd come up with an obviously reluctant Gabi in tow.

Life would be boring if all our decisions were right ones, but when three men appeared in front of us and stood stock still, waiting for us to walk towards them, I rather wished that I'd made the right decision and turned back earlier.

'Bliss, what do we do?' asked Gabi, agonised.

'Keep walking, smile and say hello and hope they get out of the way,' I said in an undertone. We had to brave it out, otherwise we'd clearly be running up the path away from them. I had no doubt that if they wanted to they'd be able to catch us.

Following my advice – another bad decision – we reached them but they didn't move. There was no way round them.

'*Buenas dias*,' I tried again with a smile. '*Podemos pasar?*' I knew *podemos* meant can we do something, and from the Spanish Civil War stuff I'd read I thought *pasar* must mean pass.

The one in the middle answered me in a torrent of Spanish of which I understood only the first word, which was 'No'. We seemed to be at an impasse, both literally and verbally.

'We're going down to the river,' I thought I said in Spanish. They laughed and spoke to each other, and the middle one stepped forward. He was small and dark-skinned with a moustache.

'You, no, be, here,' he said, jabbing a finger towards me. Gabi took a step back.

'I do be here,' I replied pleasantly, figuring that he wouldn't understand anyway. 'OK, if it means that much to you, we'll go back.'

One of the others who had a handsome Indian face said something in Spanish. Although my heart was thumping my fear was modified by the fact that neither of them sounded particularly threatening, and the average Bolivian is about three-quarters my size. Maybe they were just as frightened of me, though Gabi's back-up lacked a certain presence. Anyway, sometimes you have to live dangerously and the adrenalin rush was exhilarating.

'You, *Norteamericana*?' asked the handsome one.

'*Inglés*,' I answered with a smile, then pointed at Gabi. '*Frances*.' I almost felt I was getting the hang of this Spanish lark.

'*Inglés*?' he repeated, and put a hand on my arm. I decided not to assume they were going for a gang rape and smiled again and nodded. He was quite cute, and I was still charged up from the bike ride and sex with Gabi the day before. I couldn't resist making my smile a little bit pouty.

The moustached one slapped his hand away from mine and said something to him angrily then pushed me, quite hard, and then Gabi.

'You go,' he said fiercely. 'You no here.'

The handsome one intervened again with a bit of nudging and I started wondering if I shouldn't have smiled so suggestively, especially when he put his hand on my waist. Why do I always have to go too far?

'Oh shit, Bliss, what are we going to do?' wailed Gabi.

'Tell them we'd love to entertain them but we've left our condoms back at the hotel?' I suggested, but without much spirit left. The man with the moustache was looking as though he was considering a change of heart and my determined cheerfulness took a nosedive.

Suddenly they stepped backwards and started shuffling a bit, and then a voice came from behind us, rattling away in Spanish in what was most definitely a threatening tone. From our three chums' reaction I assumed, and hoped, that the menace was directed at them and relaxed.

Turning I saw the kind of guy I'd have been delighted to have been introduced to in any circumstances, but if he was going to save us from assault by three skinny farm workers I was prepared to blind him with my maximum charm. He was tall for a Bolivian, with an aristocratically pale face unusual for someone with such high Indian cheekbones and sculpted lips. His dark eyes flashed fire as he harangued the men and despite the heat he was dressed in smart khaki trousers and a white shirt.

After he'd finished they slunk past us up the path without looking back. I turned to our saviour.

'Thank you so much,' I gushed. *'Muy, muy gracias – habla Inglés?'*

He wasn't looking very happy. 'Yes, I speak English. But I would suggest that as you don't appear to be able to communicate with the field workers, your trespass is at best unwise, at worst completely irresponsible. It might be a good idea for you to bear in mind that English girls are seen as –' his lips took on a disdainful sneer '– asking for it.'

I was furious. 'Well that might be your take on it, *señor*, but I can assure you that to most people two women who have lost their way are not just easy game for any peasant who happens to be walking along the path. Anyway, she's French.'

He laughed tightly. 'In that case, don't be stupid. Your guidebooks tell you not to go near coca plantations. Don't they?'

'So how are we to know?' I asked innocently.

Not even bothering to answer me, and I don't blame him because it would have been obvious to anyone, his eyes hardened even more. 'When you're in a strange country you must respect the customs of that country as much as its laws. You cannot do just what you like, and go where you want to.'

It was all quite right, but he was really bugging me. In one way I was impressed by his authority but I wasn't too keen on being treated like a silly little girl.

'As I said, we simply lost our way. We had no intention of showing any disrespect for anybody. So, thank you for helping us. We'll be on our way now.'

Ironically he was blocking our path now but in the other direction, back the way we came.

'I will show you the right path to the river.'

'It's not necessary,' I said stiffly. 'I think we'll just go back to our hotel now – OK, Gabi?'

She nodded and he stood aside and let us walk on. However, I was aware that he was following behind us right up to a junction in the path, obviously where we had gone wrong. I swept past it and on to town without a backward glance, but I almost sensed him standing on the track, watching us to make sure we did indeed go back.

'Well done, Bliss,' said Gabi forlornly. 'I wasn't much use back there, was I?'

I put my arm round her. 'Doesn't matter. I suppose he was right, but he didn't have to be so bloody rude about it.'

'He was a bit frightening, I thought.'

'Yeah. But tasty!'

She laughed. 'You're terrible. Aren't I enough for you?'

I kissed her full on the lips. 'Of course. It's that bloody Carlos; he's given me a taste for powerful men.'

'You might have a taste for them, but I just can't raise any interest in men at all at the moment.'

I wasn't surprised, given the fact that her ex-boy-friend had made her into an unpaid and involuntary porn star. Poor Gabi; like too many women she'd been conned by a man playing the role of lover. We went back to the hotel and cooled off in the pool, and then I made her feel as special as I knew how.

Despite the delights of Gabi's slim body I couldn't get my mind off the man in the forest. Who was he, the plantation owner? He looked more like someone who would own a proper business, a legal one, rather than be involved in drugs. And what was he doing out there? Picking leaves surely wasn't something that needed much in the way of supervision.

I shrugged off my suspicions – after all, anything could have happened with the three peasants – and let the memory of his angular face and chiselled lips come between my hands and Gabi's body, which sent her whimpering over the edge, so he had done us a favour in more ways than one.

Back in La Paz we had a few days of half-hearted sightseeing and full-on fucking while we made our separate travel arrangements. Gabi was going south to reach Chile across the salt plains, while Carlos had recommended that I take the single-carriage train ride across the Andes.

'I wish you would come with me,' said Gabi on our last night together. 'It's the first time for months I've felt really happy.'

Bless. I was tempted to change my plans, but I was afraid she would get to depend on me. And realistically, while I love making love to women, after a while I really start to crave the attentions of men, especially tall blond ones and short dark ones. A pretty hopeless case, I'm afraid.

'You'll be right,' I said, copying one of Red's

expressions. 'I've got a feeling we'll meet up again, if not in San Pedro then further down the line, and in the meantime you're bound to hook up with someone else. Just try to stick up for yourself a bit more.'

My train left early in the morning, and Gabi came to see me off. We clung together and kissed passionately as the train pulled in to the platform, creating a bit of a stir among the couples who were to be my travelling companions. As luck would have it my seat was next to a middle-aged Englishman who kept trying to talk to me – oh of course, you want to know what women do to each other! – but I clamped my headphones on and stuck my nose in the George Orwell I'd picked up in the hotel's book-swap library and only removed it to look out of the window. He gave up and started a conversation with the people behind and I had a peaceful journey.

Unfortunately the other end of the line, Arica, was in close competition with Puno for the least prepossessing place I'd encountered so far in my travels. Food and accommodation were expensive compared with Peru and Bolivia, but I economised by eating hot dogs and booking the night bus south, which would save a night's lodging. There was little of interest in the town apart from a pretty little cathedral designed by Monsieur Eiffel – I wondered if it would have made Gabi homesick – so I beat a hasty retreat to San Pedro de Atacama.

It's one thing leaving a girl a note saying see you in San Pedro, but quite another actually meeting up with someone in a strange town, even a one-horse oasis like this. It was like being in a western, the waterhole in the middle of the desert. If Red and Robbie were around I guessed I'd meet them sooner or later. Meanwhile I booked into a guesthouse that had rooms arranged around a central courtyard and got talking to some of the other backpackers who were hanging around it, who included the French Simon and Garfunkel guys I'd met on the Inca Trail and the Swiss couple from Taquile. The great thing about backpacking is you're almost bound to meet everybody at least twice.

This point was proved when I got back to the guest-house later that day, having spent the afternoon at the thermal spring swimming pool with two American girls I'd met in the courtyard, to find Carlos sitting outside my door.

Chapter Five

'*H*ow on earth did you know I'd be here?'

I sipped my Tequila Healer. We were in San Pedro's ritziest cocktail bar, by which I don't mean anything resembling the Met Bar. It was a bit early for strong liquor but I needed some alcohol in my system to get over the shock of being tracked down when on an impulsive, where-shall-I-go-tomorrow type of trip. Not to mention to calm the seismic shifts my sex muscles were undergoing at the sight of the dark, delectable Carlos in jeans and T-shirt, the fluorescent whiteness of the latter being the only thing distinguishing him from your bog standard traveller. I'd forgotten how seductive that wide, thin-lipped smile was, with just a hint of tongue and tooth showing.

'You told me where you were planning to go, remember? It's not hard to work out how long you're likely to spend in each place. I bet there are people here you've met before.'

He had me there.

'So how did you know which guesthouse I'd be in?' I demanded suspiciously.

He shrugged. 'Deduction. Not rock-bottom cheap, but fairly basic, pleasant, courtyard ideal for a girl travelling on her own. Anyway it wouldn't have taken all day to go round every guesthouse in the town to find you.'

I sat back and shook my head. 'But you didn't know I was still on my own. What if I'd picked up some guy and was sharing with him?' Or a girl, I thought, but I decided to tell him about Gabi another time, probably when we both had most of our clothes off.

His look was opaque and for a second I wondered if he knew about Red, then realised there was no way . . . unless he'd seen me with him at Macchu Picchu.

'Of course, we almost met up before, but you got in your car and away without seeing me,' I teased.

'What are you talking about?' He stared at me, completely taken aback.

'At Macchu Picchu,' I said smugly. 'I saw you come out of the hotel with some other men in suits and get into a fancy car and drive off.'

He shook his head, smiling. 'Not me, Bliss. I haven't been there for . . . oh, months, when I first came down here.'

I didn't know what to say. Without doubt it had been him. Sure, he could have a double: dark handsome Latin types can be interchangeable, but a double with the same suit, even the same shirt?

'Carlos, are you sure?'

He laughed loudly and took my hand. 'Unless someone hit me over the head and I had a bout of temporary amnesia before being returned to normal, I am absolutely sure. Work's been taking up all my time. This is the first time I've left Lima, and I shouldn't really be here, but I've been working twenty-four seven and seeing you was a good excuse for a couple of days off.'

Puzzled? What do you think? It was him all right, so

why was he denying it? But as stubborn as I can be, there was no point sitting there all night pantomiming, oh yes you were, oh no I wasn't, so I dropped the subject and told him about my adventures though, as I'd decided, saving the Gabi detail for a later, private moment.

After dinner we wandered back to the guesthouse hand in hand and I was starting to wonder what restraints Carlos might have brought for me when he confessed he was going to exercise the ultimate restraint and go straight to his own room.

'I'm sorry, Bliss. After such a hard few weeks and the journey down here I'm completely done in. I don't want to disappoint you by giving you less than one hundred per cent. I'll make it up to you tomorrow, I promise.'

He pressed his lips to mine and then went into his room, leaving me feeling like I was in a reverse fairy tale where the handsome prince had vanished after a kiss. Sue and Donna, the Americans, were sitting with a group of Israeli guys in the courtyard and I joined them briefly but I couldn't get interested in the conversation. Feeling vaguely depressed I too went to bed.

Red and Robbie hadn't turned up; Gabi had gone south and Carlos had appeared almost miraculously only to disappear again. I almost wished I'd offered to buy Gabi's vibrator, but as I was on a promise from Carlos for the next day another night of abstinence would get me nicely ready for an explosive reunion – unless he had any more surprises up his sleeve.

There was no reply from his room when I banged on the door the next morning. Either Carlos was still in a really deep sleep or he'd got up early and gone out. Feeling more than a bit pissed off I went round the corner with Sue and Donna for an extravagant egg breakfast. We got back to the guesthouse having decided to rent bikes for the morning and explore – sod Carlos – only to find him sitting outside talking to Simon and Garfunkel.

'Oh, hi,' I said casually. 'Can't stop, we're off to rent bikes for the morning.'

'Great,' he said enthusiastically. 'Sorry I didn't get up when you knocked earlier. I was in such a deep sleep it took me ages to get my head together, and by the time I opened the door you'd gone.'

'How do you know it was me?' I challenged grumpily, wishing I hadn't made the bike arrangement.

He just laughed and put his arm round me. 'I've been talking to the tour guide. We can get on the trip to the Valle de la Luna this afternoon to see the sunset over the sands. How about it?'

'OK,' I said grudgingly. 'Sue and Donna are booked on to that trip as well.'

'Yeah, we're going too; it's supposed to be fantastic,' enthused Garfunkel, or should I say Marc.

'So, you go on your bike ride while I book the tour and get some breakfast,' said Carlos, kissing the tip of my nose.

I felt slightly aggrieved, as though he was calling all the shots, but then he had said he'd been tired so I could hardly blame him for sleeping in. It still seemed bizarre that he'd come all the way from Lima to spend some time with me and we had spent the previous night apart and now were going to have separate mornings too but, hey, I hadn't even expected to see him for a couple of weeks so I couldn't complain.

By the time we met up for a quick lunch I was in a better mood. We'd had a few laughs on the bike ride, even though the ancient ruins we'd planned to visit had somehow eluded us, but we weren't too worried.

The coach trip to the desert was a blast. Marc and

Christian took their guitar and turned out to know some other songs, mainly old Dylan stuff, which again thanks to Mum I knew better than most people, and the guide was happy to cut the commentary to the minimum so we could sing along. It was enjoyably naff, though I wasn't sure exactly what Carlos made of it; I think he was relieved when we got off the bus to tour the old mine workings.

The guide led us through one of the abandoned shafts. He distributed a couple of torches around but unless you were the one holding the torch it was a case of feeling your way along. At first we were able to stand up but soon got to a point where the guide told us we had to go on all fours. There was a delay as people got themselves crouched down to go through the narrow tunnel. Carlos, who was behind me, put his hand on my arse. I was only wearing thin cotton drawstrings and wriggled against him, enjoying the thrill of such intimate contact in a crowd who knew nothing about it.

He moved his hands round to the front and pulled me back against him. He was as hard as I could want and I rubbed against him as his fingers made their way purposefully down to my clit. Suddenly they moved to my tits and started squeezing and mashing ... until I realised they weren't the same hands. Carlos's hands – or so I assumed, though I started to wonder exactly whose hands were whose – were now snaking down inside the loose waist of my trousers and inside my knickers.

Was I going to shout for help? Like hell. Two people were fingering me and, frankly, I wasn't that fussed who they were. We had been in a fairly close group as we went into the tunnel, me and Carlos, Sue and Donna, Marc and Christian. I was happy to get some finger action from any one of them, especially in the weird darkness of the mine. I even started to wonder if the whole thing was a set-up. After all, someone must have been taking forever to get through the tunnel. As the hands on my tits started teasing and squeezing my nipples, which had quickly hardened, the hands down my knickers started to scoop up my wetness on to my clitoris. Just as I wondered if I could come without knowing who'd made me the person in front turned and got down on all fours to get through the tunnel and I got ready to follow.

Once through we found ourselves in a chamber where the torches cast a dim light and I looked at the people either side of me. Christian was on my left and Donna was on my right. I could have sworn the person behind me, who I thought was Carlos, had come out of the tunnel and moved to my right. It didn't take Sherlock Holmes to know that Donna was definitely not the one pressing a cock into my arse so I could draw no conclusions, which merely served to increase my excitement.

The guide moved off with the torch and gradually the other torchlight also started to disappear. I too moved towards the vanishing light only to bump straight into somebody who turned and kissed me hard on the mouth.

That was a man. But was it Carlos? His tongue was insistent and I responded but, even more eerily than before, there was no other contact; my body pressed forward but on to nothing. Abruptly he turned away from me and walked after the others. Following, once again I felt a hand grab my buttocks.

By the time we got out of the tunnel I was dizzy with excitement and desperate for some release. I searched the faces of my friends but no one gave anything away. Yet someone had touched me who wasn't Carlos. Someone who wasn't Carlos may have kissed me. But I hadn't cried out or complained, and couldn't ask all four of them which one had groped me in the dark. If it had been a set-up by Marc and Christian, Carlos would hardly have been over the moon himself. I kept quiet.

We arrived at the valley, where great sculpted hills of sand rose up from the desert floor. Wrapping up as instructed we climbed to the top of a massive sand dune and sat waiting for the sun to set on the desert. It cast a red glow over the landscape and everyone used up too much film, especially me. The best bit, though, was running and rolling down the dune like five-year-olds. I found myself lying at the bottom in helpless laughter watching Carlos trying to ski down the slope using feet only and slipping and getting sand all over his cashmere sweater.

We were all subdued on the way back. Maybe because it was getting dark; maybe because it had been so beautiful, or maybe because we had exhausted ourselves by running down the sand or even just by trying to keep warm.

Back at the guesthouse Carlos held my hand and took me along to the end of the courtyard where his room was. As soon as he closed the door I burst out, 'Who was it?'

He raised one eyebrow elegantly. 'Who was what?'

'You know. Groping me. Kissing me.'

He shook his head, an amused look on his face. 'Not me. Tell me what happened.'

It was impossible to believe that he hadn't been one of the perpetrators, or that he hadn't organised the other one, but I told him. At each stage of my story he moved his hands.

'Like that? Like that?'

'Yes,' I murmured, as his hand slipped down my trousers and into my knickers.

99

'Exactly like that?' he demanded. 'Someone else's hand felt exactly like mine?' He teased my clit with a feathery, barely-there touch.

'Yes – no, it wasn't the same – I don't know.'

'It excited you, though. Whoever it was.'

'Yes.'

'You don't care who it was.'

'No.'

'You preferred not knowing who it was.'

'Yes.'

He laughed softly as he pulled my trousers and knickers down to my thighs. I obligingly helped him by taking my shoes and socks off, then my sweater and vest.

'I've got sand in some odd places,' I breathed, hoping he'd get it out for me, but he was busy getting something out of his holdall. I had wondered if he'd brought any of his gear with him and I wasn't disappointed.

I thought it was a blindfold and when he moved it to my face felt a fraction cheated. It was good last time, but if he was going to dress me up at all I wanted to see it. But suddenly the black fabric was in my mouth, not over my eyes. I opened my mouth to protest but it was a proper gag, not just an improvisation with a piece of cloth. Not only did it cover my lips tightly, but there was something hard wedged between my teeth.

'I hope you don't mind, Bliss,' he said silkily. 'These rooms aren't soundproof, as I found out last night.'

It briefly flashed through my mind that he'd had someone else tied up in here last night and the neighbours had complained, but I dismissed it. Anyway I wasn't going to feel jealous if he had; I'd just like to know the details.

The black garment in his hand wasn't the corset. Instead he pulled round my waist what seemed to be an extraordinarily wide black leather belt, which came right up to my breasts. Turning me round he pulled both ends of the belt and fastened it together, with Velcro I guessed. I was turned once more and he arranged my tits over the black below them. I wondered if that was all I was getting to wear when the familiar black collar came out of his holdall, together with handcuffs. Two pairs.

First he cuffed my wrists behind my back and then got me to kneel on one of the beds with my back to the wall, knees wide. The other pair of cuffs then closed over my ankles, and then my head was jerked back. He was fastening the collar to the ankle cuffs. I was almost looking at the ceiling.

'I think it's unlikely you'll want to close your legs, Bliss,' he said drily. 'But just in case you do . . .'

He didn't need to say any more as he fastened a black leather tie around my leg just above one knee, then the other. Each one was yanked back, pulling my thighs even further apart, and secured, not to the cuffs, but to the wall. I couldn't see to what but deduced he must have pressed some sort of ring into the soft wood earlier.

Surveying what I could see of myself with satisfaction I thought I must be ready now for whatever he had in mind. As far as I was concerned I was definitely ready. The new ensemble was even more exciting than the last. I just wished there was a mirror so I could see myself properly. The caresses in the tunnel and the cave had already got me ready for anything.

Not, however, for a blindfold to go round my eyes followed by the sound of the door being opened.

'I won't be long. Think I'll just have a look at the menus on offer tonight . . . you won't be lonely?'

His voice was mocking and I tried to protest, but it

came out as the conventional 'mm-mm' of kidnap stories. The door closed.

The last time he'd pulled that one at least he'd left me lying on a bed and checked if I was comfortable. I wondered how long he was going to make me kneel, legs wide, my head pulled back, but at the same time I wasn't really complaining. If only he had the same predilections as Gabi's ex. I would have liked to see myself like this on celluloid, though strictly for my viewing, unlike hers.

Sensory deprivation is a strange thing. One sense compensates for another. I was suddenly sure that I heard someone move in the room.

Perhaps he hadn't gone out after all. He might just have closed the door and was waiting to see how I would react, whether I would try to move or talk, whether I would fidget or stay still. More likely, he just wanted to watch me, otherwise what was the point of tying me up at all?

If the gag hadn't been so tight I would have smiled. Good trick, Carlos. My ears strained to concentrate on the room rather than the sounds of talking outside, the clattering of pans where someone was cooking over a camp stove. I definitely heard him move towards me and almost shivered in anticipation of his touch.

Before he touched me, though, I had an auditory memory. After he closed the door I had heard him say hi to Donna. Unless it was someone else who sounded like him.

He touched me. He – not Carlos, I now thought, definitely not: it had been his voice talking to Donna – touched my nipples, lightly, exquisitely. He circled them with light fingers and then teased them in his fingers, gently then harder. Maybe a bit too hard; I made a noise in my throat. The touch stayed just as firm but I started to enjoy it as my nipples hardened and started to revel in it.

I tried to concentrate on the sense of touch now. Carlos had touched me, rolled my nipples in his fingers like this; surely I would recognise his touch? But no, I couldn't conclusively decide it was him.

Both hands mashed my breasts together now, squeezing them, scuffing over the hard points almost carelessly. I moaned, but not complainingly.

One hand ran over the back of my head, down to the collar, down the chain that held my head so high. It pulled it slightly and my head dipped further back. The other hand stroked up one leg from the cuffs to the bands above my knees and then, delicately, up the silky flesh of my inner thigh.

Suddenly it was as though he was desperate to make me come. The fingers of one hand were inside me, pumping in and out, while the other was on my clitoris, rubbing purposefully. If I had been in a position for being fucked rather than touched I felt he would have been pushing his cock in and out of me savagely; but, as he couldn't do that, he was doing the next best thing. Although I couldn't move much I could push hard against his hand and I did, furiously, determinedly. The tension had been building up in me all afternoon and it was finally, gloriously dispelled. I came uncontrollably and he must have felt it; my muscles must have been sucking his fingers in, and he slowed down gradually and stopped.

He moved his hands and his body moved away from me. The door closed.

This time I was sure I was alone. By the time my heartbeat and the stillness of my vaginal muscles had returned to normal, I couldn't detect any sound in the room at all.

A few minutes passed and then the door opened and

closed again. Surely this time it was Carlos. Surely last time too it was Carlos?

He sat on the bed, but didn't touch me. He got up – the bed creaked, and then creaked again – what was he doing?

The first thing I felt was his hair on the inside of my thighs and I knew without a doubt it was him; the abundant hair, black and coarse, was definitely Carlos. He must be lying on his back with his tongue just about to touch my clit.

But I've just come, I wanted to say. I don't want that now.

Although I'd come quickly the fingers had rubbed over me firmly and my clit was now too sensitive to appreciate the little licks he was giving me. Whether he sensed this I couldn't tell because he moved his tongue up to penetrate me. I could hear him lapping at my juices like a cat at a bowl of milk.

Did that give him the signal that I'd just come? If, that is, it wasn't him who made me?

His hands pressed against my pubic mound and for the first time I moved in response to him, knowing that I might get a little tingling aftershock to my orgasm. He seemed to understand and rubbed harder, deep, right at the root of my clit, and weakly but pleasurably I had a secondary tremor.

Suddenly my thighs were released from the wall and before I could register what was happening I was lifted up by two hands and a powerfully erect prick was thrusting inside me. My wrists and ankles were scraping the wall as he dragged me up and then let me go as he rammed in and out. This was definitely Carlos, but still he didn't say anything. His rhythm increased but I was helpless to encourage him in any way, though he didn't need or want any encouragement. I guessed that the fact that I was helpless was enough for him.

He came with a groan that comforted me that it was indeed Carlos.

'Blissful,' he said ironically as he pulled out of me. 'I hope it was good for you, too?'

I thought he was going to take the gag out, but he didn't.

'What about the first time?' he asked. 'What did he do to you? Oh, don't worry, I can imagine. I hope he was quiet, though. I told him you didn't want to know who it was. That was right, wasn't it? That's what you said about the tunnel: you preferred not to know?'

That was different, I had the choice of stopping that, I wanted to say. But he still didn't give me the opportunity.

'If it's any consolation to you, I don't know who it was either. He said they'd draw lots for you. So I'm saying he, but of course it might not have been.'

That I didn't believe. Whoever it was, he had let them in when he went out. The door had only opened and closed once. Still, I kept quiet. I had no choice.

'I'm having a shower, and then you'd better do the same; I just ate a grain of sand from you. We'll have to eat soon as we've got to be up early tomorrow. Oh, of course, I forgot to tell you, I've booked us on the tour of the geysers, which leaves at three thirty.'

The door closed again.

The bastard could have untied me, or at least taken off the gag and blindfold, before he went in the shower. The only consolation was that I was no longer bound to the wall, so with some effort I flopped down on to my side and indulged in the luxury of putting my thighs together. God, they ached.

'Bliss! I've missed you!'

I spun round. It was Red, with Robbie not far behind. Getting to my feet I hugged him. 'You too,' I said as

105

neutrally as I could. Carlos took another mouthful of his pizza.

Robbie hugged me. 'I've missed you too,' he said, his eyes narrowing appraisingly, like a true voyeur. 'If you know what I mean.'

Red had already pulled out one of the spare chairs at the table. 'You don't mind, mate?' he asked Carlos. I did the introductions.

'Oh, you're Bliss's friend from Lima?' Robbie said. 'Glad to know you, mate.'

They ordered a beer apiece. It turned out they had arrived in San Pedro a week earlier, done all the trips and sights and gone to Calama for a couple of days to visit the mine.

'We got back this arvo and got the tent set up and came to look for you, but you were nowhere,' Red explained.

I decided against telling him I'd been tied up and blindfolded in Carlos's room being fingered by a complete stranger. As far as I knew whoever it was might not keep it to himself and he'd know soon enough anyway.

The early start for the geyser tour was a blessing after all, because otherwise Red would certainly have asked me to spend the night in the tent, or at the very least he would have come back to the guesthouse with me. As it was we swapped experiences, though I kept my accounts brief as Carlos had already heard them. Red tried to ask him polite questions about his job, but he was monosyllabic. I guessed that he was irritated by the guys' appearance, but what could I do? Now Red and Robbie had to realise that Carlos also figured in my sex life, otherwise he wouldn't have come all the way down from Lima for a couple of days. I just hoped they wouldn't suggest he join in the exhibitionist/voyeur game, at least not to him.

106

We took off for an early night straight after eating. Red and Robbie both hugged me goodnight and made me promise to come and see them when I got back from the trip.

'You didn't tell me you'd planned to meet boyfriends here,' said Carlos tersely as we walked back.

'So what would you have done? Turned round and gone straight back to Lima?' I retorted. 'And I hadn't arranged to meet them; they left me a note in Puno saying they'd catch up with me here. I didn't know you were going to be here anyway.'

'So are you screwing both of them?'

'No. Just Red.'

'The other one thinks he's in with a chance as well. That's obvious.'

Just as I decided I wouldn't give him the satisfaction of telling him about what actually had gone on with Red and Robbie I was left without any choice. He pulled me into his room and pushed me down on to the bed, still littered with his paraphernalia. Quickly he cuffed my wrists behind my back and chained them to one of the rings my legs had been secured to.

'You can tell me all about what you've been up to with your Australians, and then get undressed and get some sleep, or not. I quite like the thought of you sitting there awake all night.'

'I thought you said you weren't a sadist,' I returned.

'No, I didn't, actually.' He laughed. 'I said I didn't like to inflict pain. A little psychological torture, though, that's different.'

'Sleep deprivation's not psychological: it's physical.'

'Semantics, Bliss. Either tell me and I'll untie you, otherwise I'll gag you as well so that I at least can get a good night's sleep.'

Bastard. I had to tell him.

'I didn't think we'd promised to be faithful to each

other,' I concluded sarcastically. 'Especially as you got some stranger to give me a working-over earlier. So can I go to sleep now?'

He untied me. 'Of course you don't have to be faithful. I'm just a bit disappointed you didn't tell me about your Australian *ménage à trois* earlier. Never mind, off you go.'

'What do you mean?'

'Off you go,' he repeated patiently. 'We've got to get up at three o'clock. It makes more sense to be in separate rooms. You've got an alarm on your watch, haven't you?'

'Yes, but –'

'But what? We've had sex; it's not even a double bed so we can't cuddle up together, and if you can't sleep I don't want you tossing and turning and disturbing me.' He opened the door. 'Goodnight kiss?'

Like hell.

To say the geysers left me cold would be trite because cold was the overriding problem. Not only was it still crack of dawn cold when we arrived but they were also at high altitude. Even the coffee they gave us for breakfast with the cheese rolls wasn't very hot. I wished more than once I'd let Carlos go alone, stayed in bed till a respectable hour and then gone over to Red and Robbie's tent in nice warm San Pedro and played look at me.

The day warmed up later, though, as we drove back towards town. The sun came out; we were at a lower altitude and we stopped at the promised thermal spring for a swim. I'd put my bikini on as underwear so I was among the first to get into the water, the other girls crouching behind nearby rocks to undress and put their costumes on. Carlos, Marc and Christian and a couple of Germans splashed in at the same time as me and we quickly found the deepest part of the pool – it was quite shallow – and sat down, warming ourselves all over. Carlos had intelligently brought his towel with him and put it on a rock just above our heads.

We luxuriated silently in the warm water, just waving our arms about negligently and sighing with pleasure. Carlos, Marc and Christian started talking about music while the Germans talked among themselves, and I was happy to close my eyes and warm up. Carlos's hands played over my thigh but not obviously so I didn't mind.

'Bliss, could you reach my towel? It's just above your head,' he asked. I stretched up but there was no way I could reach it. Why he wanted it I couldn't imagine but I stood to grab it.

At the same time as I stood he hooked his thumb in the top of my bikini bottoms and as I rose they fell. He had quickly taken his hand away so it must have looked as though I had wantonly decided to flash my bush at everybody.

'Oh, Bliss,' said Marc, with a look at once admiring and almost resigned, which made me suspect he had been the bringer of my first orgasm the day before. Christian just looked and nodded appreciatively. Neither of them was fazed at all – well, that's the French for you – but the Germans were open-mouthed. I sat down as quickly as I could, but not before Carlos had raised his hand to stroke my wet pubic hair.

'What did you do that for?' I whispered fiercely to him as I tugged the pants back up. I expected him to deny it, or pretend it was an accident, but instead he just grinned at me.

'Revenge,' he said simply. 'Next time you fuck the Australians you can remember it.'

Although my body had warmed up from the warmth of the water my attitude was still icy and that was the way I stayed until we got back to San Pedro. I disdained Carlos's offer of lunch and stomped off to the campsite to see Red and Robbie.

'Well, seeing as you're remembering it now, we might as well fuck.' Red grinned as I got to the end of the story. I was so pleased to find them sitting outside the tent and they cheered me up with tea, sympathy and bacon rolls.

'So you're not being faithful to us?' asked Robbie cheekily.

I hit him. 'To us! Get you! You're only the audience.' I laughed.

'And the narrator,' he protested. 'That's pretty important too, eh?'

'Yeah, of course it is. Well actually he did come first. But I wasn't expecting him to turn up here. He gave me the address of a friend's hotel in Santiago, and I assumed I'd see him there.'

'What did he say about being at Macchu Picchu?' asked Red curiously.

'He said it wasn't him, but it was! Honestly, I'm not imagining it. It was him all right, with his hair tied back, in the same cream suit and white collarless shirt I'd already seen him in. But why would he lie?'

They exchanged glances. I had that funny feeling there was something they weren't telling me.

'Come on, you know why! What the hell's going on? Are you involved in something with him?'

Red laughed but it was a short, tight laugh. 'We know him, Bliss. But we're not involved in anything *with* him; rather, against him.'

It sounded almost theatrically serious. I just sat there, had a gulp of tea and pinched the last bacon roll, watching their faces and waiting for an explanation.

'You know this agency he works for? ETP? Do you

know what it represents, not to mention what it stands for?'

I shook my head. 'I don't know what ETP means, but it's some sort of aid agency, though he said it wasn't funded by charity.'

Robbie cackled with laughter. 'You bet it's not! It stands for *en todas partes*, Bliss – even your Spanish can tackle that one.'

'Cheek. Everywhere, right?'

'Right. And if you were to take a guess at ETP's mission statement, it would read something like, we will infiltrate markets anywhere on behalf of our clients, no matter what the cost to the local community, any disruption it may cause, who else we have to put out of business or however much we have to manipulate, connive or bribe in order to achieve our aim.' Red sat back with a look of grim satisfaction on his face.

'You left out the use of force, too,' added Robbie.

'OK, manipulate, coerce or bribe. Pretty good from off the top of my head, eh?'

I had a feeling they could keep up the Bill and Ted all day if I let them. 'All right, if I can just have a bit more light shed on what you're talking about here?'

'Sorry,' said Robbie. 'In a nutshell, ETP is the South American arm of a US firm that represents big companies, massive companies. It gets them in to closed markets, usually by bribery but sometimes by force, manipulates local and national governments to give planning consents where they shouldn't be given, smooths it all over with a bit of PR, and even helps import cheap labour where necessary. Clear enough for you?'

'Christ. And Carlos works for them?'

'Carlos very big man for them,' said Robbie in a mock Latin American accent. 'If the agency specialises in troubleshooting, he shoot the troubleshooters – if that's the right expression.'

It might not be, but I was getting his drift. 'Is it legal?'

They both screwed up their faces. 'Part of it is, part isn't. More a bending than a breaking of rules . . . in the main.'

'So what was he doing at Macchu Picchu?'

'Failing, if my sources are to be believed.' Robbie grinned. 'You know they're going to expand the hotel, make a whole new tourist complex? Well, there are a couple of your mate's clients who are just dying to get their little hands on a contract for that. But I think he got in too late. He's only been down here for a few months, and the plans are already in progress. That's why the agency needs him. If he'd come down here sooner, he might have twisted a few arms. Metaphorically, of course.'

'Glad you added the last bit. But what do you mean, your sources? How do you know what he's up to, and how do they know he's failing? And where are they?'

'Questions, questions; you should join our little investigation,' teased Red. 'Now you know what the e-mail kid here gets up to. We're keeping in contact with our guys in the States and back home, as well as a couple of contacts down here. That's why we went off the day after we got back from the Trail, to meet up with our man in Lima. He reckons he's busted as far as Macchu Picchu's concerned. Though he's got another big project to go for next, and that's his own little pet scheme –'

'Hang on,' I interrupted. 'Who are you?'

'Good point, Red, who are you?' asked Robbie.

'Stop being such a tosser, Robbie. I've had enough of men for today, quite honestly, and if you're not going

112

to finish telling me when I didn't even ask you to start –'

'Sorry, Bliss,' he said contritely. 'ETP are in Australia, too, though called something different. We've been in this action group for a while now and came up against them there, so we linked up with a similar group in the States who tried to help us fight some of their plans. We've managed to put a spanner in a couple of their little projects, though the way they work, it's not easy. Anyway we were planning to travel in South America and when the guys in the States found out they told us about your mate getting things moving down here. The local support's a bit useless, so we said we'd see what we could do.'

'Hang on a minute. Your little action group, the one in the States ... what are you? Anarchists? Communists?'

Red laughed. 'Nothing so streamlined. We're just against multinational companies and the global economy and for local, sustainable, ecologically sound activity. Not too sinister for you?'

I was a bit taken aback. 'Of course not. I'm right with you in principle. I can't stand the way every city in the world is starting to look alike.' My memory stirred. 'Funnily enough, I said that to Carlos.'

'Oh man! I bet he was surprised.' Red was in fits. 'Don't tell me he agreed?'

'No way! We'd just been arguing about McDonalds.'

'Magic! But you don't have to get involved with us if you don't want to, Bliss. He's not going to harm you. If you want to just carry on seeing him like you are now, meeting up in Santiago, whatever, that's fine. On the other hand, you could help us just by asking him some innocent questions.'

I wasn't too sure I trusted them. 'Maybe. Let me ask you a couple first. Did you know that Carlos was having his meeting at Macchu Picchu that day? We were originally going to leave for the Inca Trail the day before, I seem to remember, then you suddenly changed it.'

'Well done, Bliss. You should be a detective.'

'Yeah, right. Then when you left me in the restaurant you were sniffing around?'

'Very good. Not that we found out anything.'

Now I had to ask the sixty-four-thousand-dollar question. 'And you didn't know at that stage that I was anything to do with Carlos?'

Blonds are so transparent. Under his tan Red's face turned the colour of his name, or rather my version of his name.

'Well . . . not exactly. I mean, we didn't know what your relationship was.'

'So how did you know I had any sort of relationship with him at all?'

Red looked shamefaced. 'This is the embarrassing bit, Bliss. We saw you with him, in Lima. We followed you into a restaurant, and then hung out around his flat and found out you were going to Cuzco. We were planning to go there anyway, honest.'

'You mean I've been followed by two secret agents?' I didn't know whether to be impressed or incensed. Mainly I was thinking that while I hadn't planned, or not yet, to share with them that my relationship with Carlos was conducted in cuffs and corsets, if they'd seen me in thigh-high boots and massive cleavage in Lima they must have some idea. Still, that could wait.

'Great! I won't even ask how you found out where I'd be in Cuzco, seeing as Carlos tracked me down to the right place here. So you decided to seduce me to try to find out more about him!'

'Hey, I'm not sure which one of us did the seducing.'

I guiltily remembered it might have been me who first suggested spending the afternoon in his room.

'OK, but –'

'Bliss, if you're pissed off and want to ditch us, no worries. If you're meeting him in Santiago, that's not really much help to us anyway. We're more interested in a project he's trying to get going in Chiloe, an island off the coast –'

'I know where it is,' I said impatiently. 'He mentioned he had some big thing lined up there.'

'What else did he say?' asked Robbie intently.

I scoured my memory. 'Not a lot ... that it's crying out for development.'

'Oh yeah, like a huge tourist complex with imported labour and materials, run by international corporations, food imported from global consortia; you see the problem?'

'Of course! Really, I'm right with you. But I didn't know that was what he did. He said that his agency helps to set up industry ... I took it like the Oxfam thing, you know, helping people to help themselves.'

Robbie ruffled my hair. 'Sweet. Look, Bliss, we're sorry we've got you into this. But if you get the chance, will you help us?'

It was a little on the unbelievable side. 'What, you mean see what information I can get out of him?'

They were both looking at me eagerly. It was hard to believe that these two endearing Aussies thought they could take on the forces of global capitalism, but if they thought I could help, I was in. After all I'd been brought up in a non-material household. Mum would be proud of me.

'Like a sort of double agent?'

'Not quite,' said Red drily. 'After all, we don't want you betraying us to him. Just the other way round.'

'Yes, of course.' I smiled at them both. 'All right,

you're on. You've recruited a new member to your cadre, or whatever they used to go on about in the seventies.'

'We're not going to be kidnapping anyone or bombing Wall Street,' said Robbie gently. 'Just a little information gathering.'

'OK.' I put my mug down and gave him a theatrical sideways look from under my eyelashes. 'The name's Bon. Van Bon.'

Red threw himself on me, laughing, and Robbie joined in and we tumbled around in the grass. There was nobody else on the campsite and Red's roughhousing turned into a kiss, then a caress. Robbie watched avidly. Although just a couple of hours earlier I had been furious at being exposed by Carlos, this was different, and when Red lifted off my T-shirt and started fondling my breasts in the bikini top, I gave a little moan of pleasure and turned to Robbie with pouty lips. He had a smile that began slowly but finished wide and I looked forward to the next story that would come out of that mouth. But in the meantime, Carlos was still here and presumably waiting for me, so I told the guys they'd have to hang on till he was gone or find themselves a couple of girlies to play with until I'd completed phase one of my investigation.

Carlos seemed completely unconcerned by my absence, sitting in the courtyard drinking beer with Sue and Donna. I joined them till the girls decided to shower before dinner and we were alone.

He looked at me sardonically. 'Got over it? It wasn't such a big deal, was it?'

'No, I suppose not. It's just . . . it's just that when it's people you know, it's not like strangers.'

'Oh? And when you let the Australian's friend watch you two fucking, that's like strangers?'

116

'No, but that's different. I choose that.'

'OK. I guess you've been having your own revenge with them?'

'No!' I said indignantly. 'I just stopped by and had a cup of tea with them to say hello.'

His smile returned. 'Good, because I'm leaving tomorrow, and I was looking forward to our last night for a while.'

So, he's not a very nice man as far as business is concerned, but I couldn't, and didn't want to, resist those brown eyes. He could – what had they said? – he could infiltrate and manipulate me as much as he wanted, though I was going to stipulate a strict two-some tonight.

Chapter Six

*F*or the first time since Lima he dressed me up for dinner. I wondered how many outfits Carlos had, and how many women he had to wear them, as he laced me into a white bustier, this one front-lacing and made of cotton lycra so I could wear it to the restaurant. I was glad that was all; this was a holiday town and I didn't want to look too over the top, although almost over the top of the boned cups was just where my tits were. I'd started to get a bit of a tan and they looked good against the white. The only other piece of his equipment was a solid white metal choker, which looked like any other item of jewellery, though when I teased him that I expected it would be chained to the wall later he grinned without denying it. A white thong and a short denim skirt were allowed while we were out.

Dinner was pleasant but I was disappointed when he told me he wouldn't be able to meet me in Santiago. I started to wonder if my chance to play superspy was over before it had begun until he said that instead he had to go to Chiloe a couple of weeks later, so we could meet up in Puerto Montt and go together.

'That'll be great,' I enthused, partly sincerely as Bliss the willing captive and partly warily as Bliss the spy. 'Did you say you had development plans there?'

'If it works out,' he said, shrugging. 'Sometimes the best-laid plans don't come to anything –'

I assumed he was thinking of Macchu Picchu.

'– but this is a big project. A major holiday complex, it could get tourists in from all over the world, never mind Chile.'

'I thought they had bad weather there?' I ventured, trying to remember the guidebook spiel.

'Only on the west coast. It's a pretty little place, Bliss. It'll be good to have you along because you can give me unbiased opinions.'

'Glad to be of service.' I was excited at the thought that I would actually be seeing him in action, though I didn't have the faintest idea exactly what sort of action to expect.

After dinner we went back to his room and he pushed me back against the door as soon as we got in and kissed me, standing up, his mouth hard and demanding. It was definitely the same kiss as the one I'd had in the tunnel and I responded just as positively.

'I really need you now,' he whispered, lifting my skirt and pulling down the thong; no finesse at all, but sometimes I do love the directness of real urgency. He thrust a finger inside me but it wasn't a caress; he was just making sure I was ready for him. After displaying my tits all over San Pedro and having my mouth penetrated by his tongue I was wet enough and he pushed me on to the wooden floor on my knees and got behind me. As he dropped his jeans and rubbered up I lowered my head submissively on to my arms because that's how I thought he'd like it, but frankly I don't think he even noticed. He pushed inside me and thrust eight, nine times, not many anyway, and came.

Of course, I expected him to get the condom off, maybe take his trousers off properly, not to mention his shoes, before giving me some well-deserved attention but, while I was waiting on the floor for some reciprocal action, he got up and stretched himself out on the bed.

'Hey! What about me?' I asked indignantly, kneeling up and looking at him.

'Oh, sorry, Bliss, I thought as you'd already had your Australians this afternoon you wouldn't be interested – and we did have an early start. I'm really knackered.'

'You're joking. And I told you, I just had tea with Red. What do you want me to do, beg for it?'

He sat up and laughed. 'Now, that would be something. But seeing as you're into exhibitionism, why don't you just masturbate for me?'

'Why don't you do it for *me*?'

He yawned exaggeratedly. 'I can't really be bothered, Bliss. But if you want to wank, I'll happily watch you.'

'Thanks a lot. Perhaps I'll just go back to my own room if I'm going to do it for myself.'

I pulled my thong up and my skirt down and stood up. I couldn't believe that was it. After all, why had he put the choker round my neck if he wasn't intending to tie it to something?

His eyes were laughing. 'Sit down, Bliss. Don't worry, you're going to get your share.'

Feeling resentful I sat on the bed with my back to the wall, ready for the chains but feeling more than a bit put out.

'If you really can't be bothered –'

'Well, to be honest, I don't have to.'

Before I could wonder what he meant he opened the door and looked up the courtyard. 'Oh, there they are.'

'Oh no!' I said firmly, standing up and walking

towards him. 'If you think you're going to have Marc or Christian fuck me again –'

He pushed me back on to the bed. 'Bliss, if you don't sit down nicely, I'm going to chain you to the wall. What on earth would they think then?'

'Probably just what they thought yesterday,' I said sulkily. But I sat down. What the hell. They were nice guys and they weren't into rape – I hoped.

They came in eagerly at Carlos's call and sat down: Christian next to Carlos on one bed and Marc next to me on the other. Carlos turned to Christian.

'Are you going to go first?'

'Christian, I'm sorry but –' I started.

'Just listen to what he's going to say, Bliss,' broke in Carlos, leaning over to detain me by the wrist. He held it firmly enough to make me think he meant business. What was Christian going to propose? Maybe not a two-pronged attack. Maybe he thought it was just his turn and he wanted me to go to their room while Marc stayed with Carlos.

Simultaneously my mind was running a mental porn video where Christian was fucking me and Marc had his prick in my mouth while Carlos watched, and my sex muscles contracted involuntary. I heard Carlos say, 'Bliss doesn't think she's going to be interested.'

'It's fascinating, Bliss.' Christian's eyes were shining. 'And it's set in Peru. This guy gets wind of a series of insights that, if everybody knew about them, would change the world as we know it. He goes off to Peru to find out more and they're gradually revealed to him one by one, though the authorities try to prevent him . . .'

The fucking Celestine Prophecy. Carlos, you bastard. His eyes were full of mischief and he couldn't control his smile. I bet he wet himself when he thought of that one.

I settled down to be bored as Christian rattled on enthusiastically. I'd heard it all before, but sod it. In my mind I replayed the foursome in various combinations, mostly involving me getting nonstop finger action on nipples and clit and three different cocks inside me, and hoped my resulting excitement was going to be satisfied by a hand other than my own.

'I thought you might have put up a bit more of a fight,' Carlos grinned when the guys eventually left. 'What if you'd been gang raped?'

'They're not the type. Well, that's just been demonstrated. I can't imagine a New Age rapist.' I gave him a sidelong smile. 'I hate all that stuff.'

'Me too. But of course you were relieved when that turned out to be what they'd come in here for, weren't you?'

'Of course.'

'And you weren't just in your mind, in your fantasy, imagining being held down and fucked by all three of us?'

'Well, I left out the holding down.'

His eyes swept over me and I knew that it was my turn now. Wordlessly he pulled me up and took off my skirt and thong, and after fastening the choker to the wall he gave me as much hand and cock action as if he were three men.

While I was sorry to say goodbye to Carlos next morning I was also looking forward to getting back to Red and Robbie to tell them of the trip we were going to make to Chiloe. He made sure I still had the address of his friend's hotel in Santiago.

'Hotel, sounds expensive. I might go somewhere cheaper, but I'll look him up,' I said distractedly. I didn't want my reunion with Red and Robbie interfered with by some hotelkeeper.

'Stay there, Bliss,' said Carlos quietly but firmly. 'He'll make sure you're all right.'

I looked up in surprise. 'What do you mean, all right? Why shouldn't I be?'

He shrugged. 'You should be careful. When you're in a strange country with different customs ... you should make sure you don't upset anyone.'

'Well, of course I won't!' I said impatiently. 'What on earth makes you think I might?'

'You never know. I'll just feel happier if you've got someone you know in the city. You'll like him; he's an artist. He only owns the hotel; he doesn't really work there.'

Something in Carlos's previous words had struck a chord in my memory. 'Carlos, do you think I might have upset anyone already?'

He was packing his bag and just shook his head without looking up. 'How would I know?' he said into his case.

How would he know? This man who had somehow tracked me down to San Pedro despite not having seen me since I left Lima, this man who had just echoed the words of the man in the jungle at Coroico, how would he know?

'You're having me followed.'

It was a statement, not an accusation, and he didn't refute it.

'Not exactly. I just asked someone to keep an eye out for you from time to time. No big deal.'

I sat on the bed, the wind taken out of my sails.

'But ... why?'

He finally looked up. 'Kip asked me to see you all right, so I am.'

'Carlos, that was in Lima! That was in the big bad

123

city! I don't need anyone looking out for me! Stop it! Please, stop it!'

'Hey.' He stroked my arm. 'If you want. He's fond of you, and I am too. It's just a little insurance, that's all. You take too many risks, Bliss. Javier told me he wouldn't have intervened if those guys hadn't pushed you around in Coroico. He didn't want to butt in, but he had to stop it before it went too far.'

'That's bullshit,' I blustered. He didn't have to know that at the time I really thought we were in trouble.

'And last night. You don't know me that well. For all you know I might have tied you up, let those two at you and then half of San Pedro.'

I suppressed a smile. 'You already did.'

'Not precisely.'

We were getting off the point. 'But Carlos, how can you do this? Is it just that you want some power over me?'

He grinned and fingered the handcuffs he was just packing. 'Don't tell me you don't know I like having power over you.'

'Sure, but . . . where does it end?'

'When you say,' he said simply, zipping up his bag. 'If you don't want to see me again, OK. Tell Jorge and he'll pass on the message. Otherwise I'll meet you in Puerto Montt at the end of the month and we'll soak up the sun in Chiloe.'

He kissed me a little regretfully, as if he believed it could be for the last time. 'Take care, Bliss. I hope I see you then.'

Then he was gone, leaving me wondering what on earth I'd got into. He had had me spied on. For my own good, he said. Not only did he like having power over me sexually, but he had exercised a more threatening power. He knew how to buy it too, he knew how to hire muscle like Javier. And he had lied to me about

124

being at Macchu Picchu. If I had doubted Red and Robbie at all, his own actions told me that he wasn't just an ordinary businessman.

I couldn't trust him, and part of me was tempted to go to Santiago, book in to the youth hostel and call Jorge and tell him I wouldn't be staying with him or meeting Carlos in Chiloe. But the other part of me, the stupid, risk-taking part of me, was excited and seduced by my role as spy. Unless Red and Robbie decided it was too dangerous I was off to stay with Jorge.

'Imagine waking up to this every morning,' said Jorge, gesturing to the crashing waves of the Pacific Ocean through the wall of window. 'It would be impossible not to be an artist with this feeding your spirit.'

We were in one of the homes of Pablo Neruda, Chile's greatest poet. Not being an avid fan of poetry I had had only a cursory interest in him until Jorge had taken me to his house in Santiago. I was enchanted by it and clamoured to visit his oceanside home.

Had I walked away from San Pedro determined never to see Carlos again and told Red and Robbie I was quitting as a secret agent I would have turned down a fistful of experiences. First of all an idyllic two days in the tent with the guys in San Pedro, followed by the trip to the capital via a visit to Antofagusta and a couple of days' sunbathing on the beach at La Serena. Then I would have missed out on Jorge and the Hostal de Arte.

Arriving in Santiago Red and Robbie had decided they would first head south of the city to do some walking in the mountains, so we arranged to meet a few days later and I got a taxi to the most unconventional place I had ever stayed in.

On the ground floor of the Hostal de Arte was an art

gallery, then on the first floor Jorge's own exhibition area and the hotel reception. As Carlos had told me, Jorge didn't work in the hotel himself, but the staff who did wouldn't have got jobs in The Ritz, I can assure you.

Ulla was from Norway, and a severe-looking blonde who normally wore a pristine white overall. With her hair scraped back from her face and her flat lace-ups she looked more like a nurse than a receptionist. Isabella on the other hand had cascading black curls and dressed exotically, always with stiletto heels and extravagant makeup. And Manuel, with his long dark hair, suspiciously smooth cheeks and impeccable clothes, looked as though he really wished he were Manuela.

I didn't think too much of it at first. When I checked in they called Jorge from his studio and he greeted me with a bear hug. I liked him immediately. He was short and stocky, around forty, and wore his curly hair shoulder length, a bit like Che Guevara. In fact, with his wide-mouthed, amiable smile and his hands constantly gesturing complete with habitual cigarette, he looked like one of Mum's old hippy friends I remembered from my childhood, though with a Latin exuberance rather than a laid-back London passivity. Maybe that was why, despite the fact that he was a friend of Carlos, I immediately felt safe with him.

After he took me personally to my room he walked me round the gallery, and then took me into his studio. In the centre of the room was his work in progress, a half-finished installation he called *Casa de poeta* – the poet's house – a tangle of objects centring around a ship's figurehead, including seashells, beermats and brilliantly coloured glass, with photos of the exterior of three houses. The objects were similar to those in

Neruda's houses, which he enthused about at length and promised to take me to see.

Lining the walls were some paintings and many photographs. Nearly everything was almost garishly colourful, apart from a series of photographs of a woman. Bound. By corsets, cuffs, chains and cords.

'I see what you have in common with Carlos,' I said tartly, inspecting the pictures. They all portrayed the same woman. She had pale skin, her face almost ghostly, set off by dark eyes, red lips and flaming red hair. Her body was matt, chalky white against the glossy black satin and leather of her bonds, corsets and belts.

'Susie, yes,' said Jorge, amused. 'I didn't think you would have met her.'

I spun round. 'What? I meant bondage.'

His face was in an oh-silly-me expression but I think he took a sly delight in my shock.

'Sorry. That too.'

I studied the woman more closely. So they shared her? I knew Carlos would have at least one woman, and now I'd found half of one. The black corset was certainly familiar, as was the wide black leather belt. We were obviously the same size, although her feet were bigger than mine.

'She works here sometimes, and sometimes in Lima. She uses the office there,' he said indicating a door marked 'Private'.

'Is she South American?'

He laughed. 'No, she's from New Orleans. Do you like her?'

'Who wouldn't? I wonder if Carlos might bring her to Chiloe with us.' My mind was already going over the possibilities and running completely out of control.

Jorge was talented, no doubt about it. As I was considering taking up photography seriously we had plenty to talk about, and he was keen to show me the galleries of Santiago. Meeting him was a terrific plus as he took me to studios I would never have found without local knowledge, while he didn't neglect to show me the sights of the city and, though the memory was hazy in my mind thanks to over-zealous tasting, a trip to a vineyard.

I'd been in the hotel a couple of days when it occurred to me that although there were always plenty of people about, there was usually only me and maybe one other couple at breakfast, which was served by the polite but unsmiling Ulla. Jorge wasn't an early riser but sometimes Manuel would join me for a chat in Spanish, which still being rudimentary meant we weren't really communicating. Then on Saturday morning, before we set off for Valparaiso, there were loads of people sitting in the breakfast room as though they were waiting for something.

'What was the crush at the hotel this morning?' I asked Jorge curiously as we wandered out of the house at Isla Negra on to the beach.

He winked, rather absurdly. 'Saturday morning, no work. Courting couples, of course.'

'What?' I started to catch on. 'You mean coming for sex?'

'Sure. Great money spinner. They usually only take an hour each, sometimes less. You know, Chile is a Catholic country, and one where most people live at home till they marry, apart from screwing in the car – where else?'

'I thought they'd want to stay virgins until they marry.'

'Most do. These are just the fast ones.' He raised an eyebrow satirically. 'Unless they take it up the arse, of course, which a lot of them do.'

'I never realised that was a method of contraception.'

He smiled widely. 'Very practical. Sometimes makes a mess of the sheets, mind you – but then so does Manuel.'

I had an inkling then of exactly what sort of establishment he was running.

'So most girls want to stay virgins ... so the men hanging around during the week are ... clients?'

He nodded. 'I wondered when you'd put two and two together. Good operation, don't you think? Minimal effort, maximum income, I can get on with my art.'

'So Manuel is a male prostitute?'

'Almost male. Some men want to be faithful to their fiancées. Or they just like him.'

I felt I'd been a bit naïve to not fall in before, but what the hell. It was rather amusing to be staying in a brothel.

'So what about the other guests? The Austrians who are there now?'

'What about them? They come in off the street by accident. We don't turn them away.'

I wondered whether Ulla specialised in correction – she certainly looked the type – but in view of Carlos and Jorge sharing Susie I didn't want to question him too closely in case he took it for an invitation.

He didn't need encouraging. In the car on the way back to Santiago he stopped abruptly in the middle of a conversation about Man Ray and Herb Ritts and said, 'I want to use you in my work, Bliss. The gallery will be open tomorrow afternoon. Will you be an exhibit?'

'An exhibit?' I asked cautiously. 'How?'

'Bound. Sometimes Susie has done it; you remember the clown photo?'

I did. Susie's natural pallor had been completely whitened and she had clown-like red spots on her cheeks and black clown eyes, with the regulation teardrop. Her hair had been pulled back and waxed into three points. Her big clown's ruff was made of black leather and chained to the wall, as was her black leather-belted waist and her black-booted legs, but her hands were free, juggling with three red balls. Apart from that she was naked, her body as pale as her face apart from rouge-reddened nipples and her brilliant red pubic hair.

'That was taken from an ... exhibit?'

He nodded vigorously. 'Performance art is always part of my work, and if it can be a woman in chains – will you?'

Was this taking exhibitionism too far, I asked myself? It was one thing fucking Red while Robbie looked on. To be naked and chained as an art exhibit before a crowd of strangers was something else.

Jorge shook his head impatiently as I voiced my thoughts. 'It's an invited crowd, not a free for all. Come on, Bliss, you're an artist. The boundaries have to be constantly pushed back, you know that.'

One thing I do know: I love it when someone calls me an artist.

'I'm in.'

In chains wasn't to be taken literally, I found out next morning when I reported to the studio at ten o'clock.

'Everything off,' Jorge instructed. 'No make-up – good. Ulla will do your hair after.'

'After what?'

He produced a huge catering pack of clingfilm and a reel of transparent twine. 'After I've wrapped you up.'

I was dreading a skinflick oven-ready-chicken-type scenario but it wasn't that demeaning, though it was more bizarre.

My arms were pulled back and bound in place, the transparent twine going carefully around my arms and body at elbow and wrist level. Nothing else needed to be bound. That was just to get them in the right position.

The plastic wrap was next. Starting with my feet, Jorge meticulously wrapped me, tightly, making sure it overlapped by exactly the right width. He placed the clingfilm on the floor and rolled me over and over as he wrapped. All the time he kept up a stream of chatter about art, the difference between the erotic and the pornographic, and the necessity to shock.

As his hands brushed against my pubic mound I quivered, just a tiny, involuntary movement, but he felt it. His hand lingered.

'It would be even better if you were shaved. Do you ever?'

'Yeah, but only for work. I always let my beard grow on holiday.'

He grinned and encouraged by my eyes his finger pushed gently along my cleft and brought out my moisture. 'Carlos said you love to be restrained.'

'This isn't exactly the same, is it.'

'No. I'd like to fuck you, Bliss.'

'Not as an exhibit.'

He laughed, moved his hand and carried on wrapping me. 'No. Later.'

I kept my options open.

By the time my whole body was encased in the clingfilm I was feeling hot. Maybe it was just being wrapped in plastic or maybe it was because Jorge's hands on my sex and breasts had put me into horny mode. He had certainly spent a long time on my tits, squashing them with the clingfilm, pulling it even tighter than on the rest of my body as though he was trying to flatten them. He had left me on the floor and was beating something in a bowl.

'You're a slug, Bliss. You're going to crawl across the

floor and leave a trail just like a real slug. What do you think?'

Sweating, I looked up. The bowl contained something white and translucent.

'That looks like come.'

He laughed softly. 'Egg white. But in an ideal world it would be semen.'

Kneeling down beside me, he put his face close to mine. 'In an ideal world I'd have ten men masturbating over you, so that you could leave a trail of come as you crawl along the floor. What do you think about that?'

As there weren't ten men in the room and this was purely fantasy, I liked it. Like any girl I have the orgy fantasy, not to mention the degradation fantasy, and ten men wanking all over me simultaneously was just fine as long as it wasn't real.

'I would like to wank on you, Bliss. In fact – you look so naked like that, so soft – will you suck me?'

He undid his trousers. He wore nothing underneath and his cock sprang free. It looked curiously boyish and eager to please. I raised myself into a sitting position and manoeuvred on to my knees. Wrapped, I was rapt, as with my hands helpless behind me I sucked.

He came on to my subdued breasts and it trickled down my front. I knew what he wanted and lay face down on the floor and tried to wriggle forward. Progress was difficult; my body isn't quite as flexible as my mind.

Jorge turned me on to my side and kissed my mouth, but there was no time for tenderness. Ulla came in to pull my hair back and wax it to lie close to my head, and it was covered in a transparent cap that came down over my eyes. The plastic wrap, which Jorge had stopped at my throat, was extended to cover my mouth, leaving my nose free to breathe through. Finally, feeling rather like a Spam fritter, I was coated in beaten egg white along one side and instructed to lie on it. It worked; I could easily wriggle along in what seemed to me quite a slug-like manner. Jorge was pleased.

So were the guests. A bohemian crowd, they treated Jorge with great respect. As instructed I slid around the room; not too easy when you're trying to avoid a couple of dozen people, and I was a bit concerned when passing under anyone holding a cigarette. I tried to avoid the chain-smoking Jorge like the plague.

I wondered if anyone would touch me: the imagination worked overtime again, with the poor slug being groped with fascinated horror by the assembled company. However they were a sophisticated crowd and I escaped physical contact apart from the toe of one woman's shoe. Bitch. I wished my mouth were unconfined so I could bite her leg. I resolved to have more sympathy with dogs in future.

While I enjoyed the wrapping-up process and the initial attention, being a slug soon got a trifle boring, especially as the guests were launching into the wine. I'd just started to wonder how long the show was going on for when Jorge signalled me to make for the gallery door and I wriggled as fast as I could towards him. He was in the lobby with the door marked 'Private' open and I slid in there with relief.

'Photocall, Bliss. You've been wonderful. Won't be long now, then just one more thing . . .'

The flash blinded me. Like Susie I was going to be immortalised on his gallery wall; would Carlos see me? He took several shots from different angles and then took off the cap and removed the clingfilm from my mouth.

'Wine!' I said urgently, and he laughed.

'Wine, sure. But first you need to get that plastic stuff off your body, and I thought after you've showered

Ulla could massage you with some essential oils. OK?'
He started to unwind me.

'Fine, as long as I can have a drink at the same time.'
I would have agreed to anything for a large glass of
wine.

'The other thing is, I'm getting into audio as well.
What I'd like to do is tape you talking while Ulla
massages you: first describing being tied and wrapped
up, what it was like being a slug, what you were
thinking, and what you're thinking about Ulla's massage as well, describing where she's working and so
on; and try to put the tape and photographs together.
What do you think?'

'It sounds like a candidate for the next Turner prize.
I'll do it.'

He smiled. 'Good. We'll see if it works. Being in
English will be great. You get your shower and I'll get
you a drink and fetch Ulla.'

'And now I'm having a massage from Ulla, the one I
mentioned in the nurse's uniform, to get some essential
oils into my skin after the plastic wrap – can I have
some more wine? Oh, sorry, but I expect you'll be
editing this, won't you?'

'Yes to both,' said Jorge, grinning and getting up for
the bottle. The microphone, which he had been holding
to my mouth, was propped on the pillow. 'Don't stop,
though. What exactly is Ulla doing now?'

Before he poured the wine he took another photo.

'Massaging me, I said,' I repeated, getting slightly
exasperated, though frankly I think it had more to do
with two large glasses of wine on an empty stomach
than any real disgruntlement. After all I was quite
appreciating Ulla's hands on my back, especially now
as she rotated them firmly over my buttocks.

'Detail, Bliss,' said Jorge as he handed me another

glass of Cab Sav. 'Actually turn over, it'll be more interesting.'

I assumed he meant for the photo he took as I turned and settled lazily on my back, though I realised what he really meant when Ulla's capable hands moved on to my breasts. I giggled.

'Right, I know what you mean. Her hands are on my tits – breasts – edit out what you want. It's nice.'

'Exciting? As exciting as being the slug?' He zoomed in to my tits.

'Different. I told you, I liked the crowd watching me, legitimately, as an artist, even though it was a bit like being a stripper. But contact is ... well, more immediately pleasurable.'

Her hands moved to my stomach, which was a bit disappointing. I was starting to hope for some nipple teasing at least.

'How exciting, Ulla?'

Why was he asking her? I didn't have to wonder for long as she pushed two fingers inside me. Well, I said she was like a nurse, but I must admit it wasn't much like a medical.

'About as good as it gets,' she said quietly, moving her hands back to my stomach. I started to wonder if I'd imagined it but, no, she'd definitely penetrated me. This wasn't going to be an ordinary massage.

'Bliss?'

I was neglecting my commentary duties.

'Ulla just penetrated me with two fingers, obviously on instruction to see if my excitement had produced lubrication,' I enunciated pedantically. 'And it had.'

'Does that mean you're hoping for sex, Bliss? And with who?'

'Whom,' I corrected, a touch acidly.

Jorge laughed and took the wine out of my hand. 'Enough of that. I've got a better idea.'

Before I could say sorry, yes I am hoping for sex, you'll do nicely, he pulled my arms above my head and fastened each wrist to a corner of the massage table with leather straps. Massage table, that's what they'd called it. I started to wonder if I'd been right about Ulla being more into flagellation than Swedish massage. She was busy fastening my ankles to the bottom of the table, of course.

After the inevitable photo I dutifully told the tape machine what was happening and admitted that I was not displeased. I had to confess as well that when the oily hands pulled my labia apart and smeared my wetness over my clit and started to massage me with feathery strokes rather than the firmer ones I'd been enjoying on my body I was equally happy. Describing Ulla's every stroke, probe, rub and caress into the microphone turned me on almost as much as the fingers themselves and Jorge's eyes flickering from Ulla's attention to my face didn't make it worse. I was slightly tipsy and it made me loud and maybe slurry and slightly theatrical as my voice rose to tell the tape how she had two fingers pressing inside me and her little finger ringing my arse but most of all her other hand was on my clit. My orgasm must have been about two seconds away as Jorge raised his hand and she stopped abruptly.

'Hey! I was just about to come!' I tried to sit up but only managed to lift my body, which had anyway been straining upwards towards Ulla's practised hand.

'Not yet,' said Jorge. 'I want more words. Tell me about the sex you've had in South America.'

'Oh shit,' I muttered. Not that there was anything to hide – he was Carlos's friend and they shared Susie so I knew there would be no secrets there, and I wouldn't have been surprised if Carlos hadn't already told him about Red and Robbie – but because I was loving the manual attention. 'Only if I can have some more fingering.'

'Of course. Just more slowly, Ulla. A slow build up. Go on, Bliss.'

With my arms and legs tied and almost farcically desperate to come I didn't feel I had much choice. Ulla moved her hands over my breasts, ignoring my over-heated sex for the time being, and talking about my introduction to bondage while having my nipples teased was just fine.

I'd moved on to exhibitionism and the size of Red's prick by the time she'd moved her hands back down. She was bloody good at this.

'And who are these men? Australians, did you say?'

'Yeah, mature students, from Perth, into the environ-ment and, what do you call it, ethical consumerism and stuff.'

Ulla's fingers were playing me like a harp and the melody was sweet. I just hoped he'd let her pluck me to a climax this time.

'Interesting. So are they studying here?'

'No, just backpacking, though they're doing some work while they're here. They went to visit the big copper mine up north. I forget why, something about one they had on some island near Australia that was polluting everything, stuff like that.'

Her little finger was in my arse while the other fingers brushed lightly over my cunt. The other hand was the one with the finger that was made to massage a clitoris and that's just what it was doing. Unwillingly I dragged my attention back to Jorge who was asking about activism.

What?

OK, let's not be paranoid about this. A close friend of a powerful and possibly unscrupulous businessman who is being spied on by two activists has you tied up and has rendered you desperate for an orgasm. As you're on the verge of one he's asking you leading questions.

Just because he's out to trap you doesn't mean you're not paranoid.

Luckily I have this knack of putting sex first. While my mouth formed words that appeared to be the beginning of an answer to Jorge's question, my body tensed and pushed against Ulla's hands. Despite her light strokes my muscles were strong enough – practice, practice – to go over the top into a tumbling, spiralling spasm and my words trailed off and my eyes closed. Apart from the climax itself I was damn pleased with myself for pulling it off. I reckoned I could make a pretty good spy after all.

'Sorry, Jorge, that orgasm took my breath away – do you want me to describe it for the tape?' I asked innocently. 'Where were we, anyway?'

'The Australians,' he said. I don't think I was imagining the slightly defeated look in his eyes.

'Oh, yes. Activists?' I laughed dismissively. 'You know, they might be called mature students, but I don't think they're either mature enough or bright enough for that. But then I don't really care about their brains; it's their brawn I'm interested in.'

I yawned theatrically. 'God, I'm tired. What with the wriggling, the wine, the massage and, oh, thanks Ulla, the sex, I'm really beat. Do you think you've got enough on the tape now?'

Five minutes later I was in my room smirking at my brilliance, though underneath the bravado I felt a bit wobbly about Jorge's questions. It proved that Carlos suspected that Red and Robbie were up to something. The question was, did he think I was in with them, or did he assume I was an innocent caught up with these fearsome radicals?

As far as Jorge was concerned it didn't matter; it was my last night in the hotel. The next day was Monday, when I was due to meet the boys. We were heading south for a town called Pucon, where they planned to walk up to the crater of a volcano. I thought I'd probably had enough personal eruptions for the time being, but you never know.

I slept the sleep of the just, the stupid and the satisfied, feeling slightly like I had elements of all three.

Chapter Seven

*R*ed and Robbie were unsurprised by Jorge's attempt at espionage but impressed with my avoidance of his trap, though I expected more lavish praise. I think they were still distracted by the thought of me slithering around the floor in nothing but clingfilm, my debut as a performance artist being the first thing I had told them.

They had news, too. Their contact on Chiloe had told them that Carlos was renting one of the most prestigious houses on the island. He hadn't moved in yet but had set up meetings with important local government officers and wealthy businessmen.

'How does your contact know all this? And how did you get a contact there anyway?'

Robbie shook his head. 'You don't need to know that. The safe way for us to work is with minimum information, Bliss. We don't know much more ourselves.'

I was impressed. They clearly knew how to do this properly. I'd read the same thing in Mum's favourite novel about a revolutionary in the US back in the good old days before I was born. But in the book they were blowing up banks and oil companies. This seemed trite in comparison.

'Are you sure you're not being a little bit theatrical about this? We're talking about a holiday complex, right? A sort of Club Med, Center Parc effort? Is that such a big deal?'

Robbie nodded. 'A very big deal, Bliss. We're talking about a massive development here. One that could spread over the whole island and turn it into a theme park rather than a real place. A theme park with only one employer dictating wages and conditions. Buying up land thanks to bribing government officials and kicking off the indigenous people. Reproducing the local handicrafts in sweatshops, probably in China. Taking over the local hotels and restaurants, disenfranchising and disempowering the local people, and sending all the profits to the States; doesn't that sound like a big deal?'

'OK. So from the sound of it he's going there to start the bribery and so on. But he told me we were taking a bit of a holiday, and he wanted me to give him my opinion of the place. What am I going to be doing while he has his meetings?'

Dim, Bliss. As the words came out of my mouth a picture came into my mind of Carlos and Señor X sitting by the pool while a bikini-clad waitress brought them a tray of drinks. I just hoped that waitress was the extent of the job description.

'I assume you two would tell me if your "contact" implied that the local bigwigs were being offered any sexual favours in return for their co-operation?'

Red looked genuinely indignant. 'Shit, Bliss, what do you take us for? Can you believe that we'd really let you go into this if we thought he was going to try to use you as a bribe?'

Robbie too seemed horrified. Bless. Given the nature

of my relationship with Carlos, not just the bondage but the participation of unknown others, it hadn't been too great a leap to imagine myself bound and blindfolded while Señor X got his reward for pushing through planning permission or selling his land. Equally, given the boys' ignorance of that relationship their shock at my suspicion was normal. I realised how far I'd come since I arrived in South America; maybe too far. It was time to tell Red and Robbie about Carlos's tastes and my own happy accommodation of them, but I would save it for when we were alone.

Uncannily, my thought appeared to prompt Red to tell me something; not that I believe in telepathy, or any of that psychic stuff, but it was strange.

'Robbie's got some adventures to tell you about later.' So, we could take turns.

Robbie raised a sardonic eyebrow. 'Yeah, but as we'll be on the bus all night I reckon it'll have to wait.'

'Oh I don't know. I haven't managed to get to sleep on a bus yet. You know how to whisper, don't you, Robbie?'

In view of our saving on another night's lodging by taking the night bus we were splashing out on a terrific lunch in Santiago's fish market, which was brilliant, full of restaurants that were all packed and noisy, though according to Red the one in Sydney was just as good. We'd met up in the office of the shipping line to book our passage on the boat down to Patagonia. Luckily we all agreed we didn't fancy being in a 20-bed dormitory-type-cabin but the smaller ones only came in even-numbered berths. Robbie quickly invented a friend, whom I christened Miss Bertha Vida, to share our four-berth cabin but without Bertha's presence or passport they would only book her in provisionally. As it was unlikely that Bertha would turn up in their office to claim her place it looked like we would have a stranger to share with. You win some, you lose some. It might spoil our games, but on the other hand the right person might provide us with a new source of mutual pleasure . . . I put that thought out of my mind. Three in a sex game was, frankly, more than enough.

We wandered around the city, watching the chess games in the central square, strolling up the hills of Cerro Santa Lucia, where I tried unsuccessfully to get the guys to split up and pretend to be on the pull, it being a big gay area. But I guess that men just don't feel the same way about bisexuality as women, or at least if they're macho Australians they daren't admit it. It would have been a bit of a blast to hear about their adventures; I felt sluttish and demanding and wanted Red to give me lots of hands-on attention while Robbie supplied the eyes-on variety. My performance the previous day had left me with an erotic charge that was still smouldering enough to communicate itself to the boys, though the only place I could think of to satisfy the edgy hunger we were all infected with was Jorge's hotel, which in the circumstances was not one of my better ideas.

The bus wasn't full and we had arrived early so we spread ourselves over the back seat, talking loudly so as to put others off sitting near us. Red propped himself up in the corner and pulled me close but facing away from him towards Robbie. As we draped our fleeces and sweaters over us as blankets and the video started its Spanish dubbing of *Clear and Present Danger*, Robbie's deep, rough voice started telling me about the girl he'd met in the mountains.

She was with a friend – Red had been unfaithful! Though Red pointed out that he'd only gone along with the foursome because Robbie hadn't been getting any for a while – and the two guys thought they'd done pretty well for themselves when they got talking over the camp stoves on the first night.

The girls were Becky and Tasha from New York State. The guys had taken a couple of cartons of wine with them and they shared one and Tasha started flirting with Robbie. The logical conclusion to the evening was that Red moved in to the girls' tent and Tasha took her sleeping bag and bedroll in to Robbie's.

'Up till then it was fine,' he said gloomily. 'But, Jesus Christ, Bliss, though she'd been all over me and stripped off and cried out when I played with her breasts, when it came to touching her down below she was as dry as – as –'

'A kookaburra's khyber?' I supplied from my Barry Mackenzie guide to Australian slang.

'A nun's nasty?' offered Red slyly, giving me an alternative and somewhat unpleasant addition to my slang vocabulary. It confirmed my growing suspicion that Australians may be great at sport, terrific at fighting globalism and superb sexual partners but when it comes to the finer cultural points they belong firmly in the bottom division.

I shrugged. 'So, you know what to do with a girl, don't you?'

'Sure. I moved my mouth down there and she was gasping and *oh my God*-ing, as American women do, as though she was on the verge of coming, but I just knew she wasn't getting anywhere near ready. I tried a little more and then fingered her and fucked her and fingered her some more but I knew she was just putting on the verbals.'

'Shit. I'm sorry, Robbie. After you've been so good with me you deserved it.'

'Yeah, that's what I thought. But to be fair she was sucking me and rubbing her tits over me and saying fuck me and so on, so I guess she was trying, but

144

without her getting something out of it I wasn't interested. So I started talking to her like I do to you and she seemed to breathe a bit quicker, so my hands were working overtime and when she said fuck me now, I'm ready, I did and I came, but she didn't.

'"Tell me what you want me to do," I said to her. And she burst into tears. I just held her, wishing to God you hadn't gone to Santiago and then she started going on about being worthless, how she was just a tramp for the way she came on to me, what was I doing with a slut like her and so on. Really over the top, you know? So I cuddled her and told her that was bullshit and she wasn't at all worthless and she kept insisting she was, and how I must think her such an easy lay but then she wasn't any good for anything else, and suddenly I got the message.'

I did too. I've been there – haven't we all? Insult me, degrade me, abuse me – it's a great turn on. As long as it's not for real. I let Robbie carry on.

'So I stopped the cuddling and the caring and lay back and yawned and said I wished I'd gone for her friend: she looked like she'd be a better lay. She stopped sobbing and started listening and I carried on wondering if Becky would be just as much of a pushover. I said I'd really fancied Becky more, with that long curly hair, but seeing as Tasha was obviously a goer it would have been stupid to turn her down.

'Anyway I could see she was breathing harder; her tits were rising and falling, so I sat up and beckoned her towards me. "Open your legs; that's what you're used to, isn't it?" She stood over me and did what I said and I heard a little noise in her throat. "Show me your cunt, slut." She put her fingers in and pulled it apart and I could see it was creaming nicely. So to cut a long story short I got her to take me in her mouth to make me hard again and we fucked long and slow with me talking all the time and when I felt like I was going to come again I put my fingers on her and she just took off.'

His eyes had been lowered while he'd told his story but he raised them to mine. 'Don't think I'm proud of that, Bliss. No way would I talk like that to a woman unless she wanted it. To tell you the truth it made me feel pretty worthless myself.'

Men can be so sweet, and so naïve. I put my hand on his arm.

'It was brilliant of you to pick up on the hint. I reckon you *ought* to be proud of yourself, not ashamed.' I winked, just imperceptibly. 'And to be frank I quite like that sort of thing myself from time to time.'

In fact I'd quite liked that sort of thing in the telling and wanted to hear more later. We would be in Pucon around nine and I decided that as we'd do no more than catnap on the bus, the best move would be to pitch the tent, have a bedtime story and a fuck and then catch up on our beauty sleep and be ready to face the afternoon.

Relationships between two people change so minutely it's sometimes hard to grasp until it's too late that there's been a subtle shift in balance. Between three it was easier. I hadn't noticed at first, though as we put the tent up in Pucon I sensed something had altered. Red and Robbie kept up their usual banter but somehow I was excluded; I was the outsider. It was understandable; I'd not been there for a few days and they'd gone round in a foursome with two girls. Not that I thought they'd rather be with Becky and poor old Tasha, but I felt they'd bonded again without me and they weren't as prepared to open up to let me in as when we first met. That had to change.

'Seems a bit of a waste of time sleeping. Think I'll

leave you two to it and take a look round town,' said Robbie casually.

'Hang on, mate, I'll come with you. Bliss is the tired one,' said Red.

They were practically out of the tent door. The choice was simple: I could go with them and feel like I was tagging along, or make sure they stayed and got back in the old routine.

'If you guys want to explore, fine, but having got me going telling me about Tasha I want a fuck now.' I pulled down my drawstrings and knickers together and stepped out of them. 'Just a quickie, Red. And if you don't mind, Robbie, would you do me a favour and hold my wrists tight? I don't think I mentioned I'd got into bondage with Carlos, and Jorge tied me to a table while the Norwegian woman fingered me ... I just don't know if I'll really enjoy it without being restrained now.'

That did the trick. The tent door was zipped firmly from the inside as I kneeled with my back to Red.

'Robbie, if you could just come round here and hold my arms down, really tight?' I turned my head over my shoulder towards Red, businesslike. 'I think I'm ready – are you?'

As Robbie moved round as though hypnotised and crouched down in front of me I held his eyes with mine and pushed my hand down to my sex. 'Yeah, I'm wet. Thought so, after your story.'

I showed him my hand, glistening with peachy juices. 'Looks like I'm the slut round here,' I said softly. 'Now, where were we? You were getting Tasha to wank for you while you told her what a whore she was –'

'I thought we were talking about you liking to be restrained,' said Robbie, his voice even more throaty than usual. It was tempting to place my wet hand on what I'm sure would have been a completely rigid

147

cock, but *that* subtle shift in the relationship was a long way off . . . not that I'd ruled it out.

'Right now you're supposed to be restraining me,' I ordered. He grabbed my wrists and held them, a little too tight. But I liked it. 'And you're going to continue with the Tasha story. Please.'

The slightly satirical note in my 'please' wasn't lost on him. He smiled and sank on to his knees as well and as I felt Red's prick nudge at me I leaned forwards and let Robbie take my weight. Slowly the huge heft of my Australian Swede pushed inside me and with my arms braced against Robbie I pushed back against Red, luxuriating in being filled up by him again. I saw Robbie read the satisfaction in my eyes and raised an eyebrow as a starting signal.

'She was shocked at my suggestion that she masturbated in front of me, or she pretended to be. I laughed disbelievingly and told her that a horny bitch like her probably wanked all the time so there was no need to pretend she didn't know how to do it. She was lying on the sleeping bag and I moved my head to watch her close up for a bit, telling her I'd never seen such a slippery cunt and that her fingers moved to her clit so fast they must have plenty of practice. She was saying, oh my God, over and over, and stuff like, I can't believe I'm doing this, and I told her to shut up because she knew she wanted it any way she could get it and she was going to have to wait for me. Then I had a flash of inspiration – pun coming up, Bliss – and gave her the torch and told her to fuck herself with it. It's not a huge torch, but big enough, and it filled her up.

'I kneeled over her and started moving my hands up and down my cock and wondered out loud whether I wouldn't rather just wank over her than put my dick in her big wet cunt and debated whether to spunk all over her tits or her face, or just to get her to blow me and swallow it. Then, sounding a bit reluctant, I said after all I thought I would fuck her.

'I took the torch off her and rubbered up and lay down and pulled her on top of me, facing away from me as though I didn't want to see her face, and jiggled her up and down and told her to get on with it. She started moving up and down on me like she meant it, not like the theatrics she'd put on before, and I put my finger on her clit. After a few strokes she started the verbal and I just stuck that torch in her mouth, covered in her love juices, and said that while I didn't mind fucking her there was no way I was going to listen to her whingeing. What with that and my fingerwork I felt her tense up and she came, so hard I didn't have to move at all, my cock just responded to her going haywire all round it and I shot my load as well.'

'I'm going to do the same in a minute,' I said. 'Give me some finger.'

My eyes were on Robbie but I meant Red. He didn't know that, though.

'Which one of us?' he asked. I wondered if he cared. I wondered if I did but as I said it would be a while before we got to that point, etc.

Robbie, who had just demonstrated his intuition as far as what women want sexually is concerned, picked up the cue I'd given him earlier.

'She doesn't give a toss, mate. You do it; I can't reach that well holding her hands.' He smiled at me crookedly. 'You're right, Bliss. You are the slut round here. I would have thought that screwing one bloke while his mate watches would be enough for you, and it turns out you're doing a whips and chains number with your smooth little Carlos guy as well.'

I laughed but it came out all breathy and uneven thanks to Red's gentle fingering distracting me. Bracing my arms harder against Robbie I pushed back to encourage Red to touch me harder. I wanted more verbal as well.

'No whips, just the chains and corsets and so on – like the sound of it?'

'Haven't you ever had enough?' countered Robbie. 'Can't you even go a few days without sex?'

I shook my head wordlessly. Though I wanted to say no my body was crying out yes and one more scornful remark would do it.

'You're all cunt, Bliss,' he said witheringly and that was it, for a moment or three I was indeed all cunt as my muscles heaved so hard my mind suspended itself.

My arms were suddenly freed and I almost overbalanced, I had got so used to leaning against Robbie. I realised that Red, whom I had practically forgotten about except as the mechanical means to my orgasm, had obviously come as well and had just withdrawn.

'Don't think for a moment that I meant that,' said Robbie, with just a trace of anxiety in his voice.

'I've got too much brain to think you did. And I reckon you've got too much brain to say it if you did. If you see what I mean.'

We were a threesome again.

My plan for the next couple of days was to relax by the lake with a book and let the boys get on with the volcano stuff but it was no good; I felt I had to consolidate our reunion rather than let them drift away into Bill and Ted again. So after we explored the town, which didn't take long, and went into one of the many agencies offering trips up Villarica, I had to say I'd go too. The only respite I got was that, as it was a crack of dawn start and we were still tired despite a post-coital nap, it was put off till Wednesday and we had one great day off with nothing to do but throw stones in the lake and read and talk about sex and world capitalism. I was being allowed to finish my novel before starting *No Logo*, which Red had promised me wouldn't be a boring read at all, though frankly I feel that travelling is the time for feeding the mind with the ideas of the great fiction writers rather than feeding it with facts. However as the best I'd been able to find at the last book swap café was a Joanna Trollope I couldn't demur.

'So, this was your first time?' asked Robbie after I'd been persuaded to describe my introduction to bondage. 'You know when we saw you with him in Lima you were dressed in black with high boots and gloves; we thought you were just into the Goth look. I wondered what had happened to it but decided you probably dressed different for the city.'

'Women, eh,' said Red but I knew he was trying to wind me up and ignored him.

'Yep, absolutely the first. And it was on that tour round the city he gave me a taste for exhibitionism as well.'

I told them about the old man and then thought what the hell, let's have everything out in the open and confessed to the unknown others in San Pedro.

They were quiet when I'd finished and I thought, big mistake, I should have left that bit out.

'So really it's thanks to Carlos that we're in our little *ménage à trois*,' I pointed out. 'Quite frankly a few weeks ago I'd have said it was really tacky having sex in a tent with an audience, but after he had put me in touch with my latent talent for exhibitionism I went for it.'

Robbie smiled and put his arm round me. 'Good thing you did, don't you think?'

'Oh yes.' We were smiling at each other and though Red was my fucking partner and sitting on the other side of me my sex muscles skipped a beat as our eyes met. I knew he wanted me, and badly. Maybe at first the voyeurism had been enough or maybe a proper threesome had always been on his agenda; I didn't know, but right now his eyes were cloudy with desire. And, let's be honest, I expect mine were too.

The ludicrous thing was it seemed a bit late in the day to ask Robbie how he managed to get his own release. Did he masturbate in his sleeping bag after supplying the commentary to our sexual athletics? I didn't think so. Not usually being a fan of bedtime sex, just thrown into it by circumstance, it was rare for me to go straight off afterwards. I usually just tucked up in my sleeping bag, listened to Red start snoring and thought about the day's events. Presumably Robbie was excited by his own words and our actions, so what did he do with his hard-on? I wished I'd asked before, but tore my eyes away and changed the subject.

'Now we've had my little true confessions I reckon it's time you shared your Becky experience with us,' I said, turning to Red.

He shrugged. 'Not much to tell.'

'Don't you want it later, back in the tent?' asked Robbie.

We were definitely moving on to dangerous ground there. I don't know how that came across to Red but it seemed to me that if he were the chorus then Robbie would be the one involved in the action, and at this stage in the game that really did have the potential to end in tragedy. Robbie's eyes had just told me that that was what he wanted, but not yet.

'No, now.'

Robbie got up. 'OK, I'll leave you to it.'

'Don't say you've heard it before?' I grinned. So it was true about men being worse than women when it came to discussing their sex lives.

He laughed. 'No way! I'd just rather forget about

those two and move on. Anyway I want to get down to the internet café and see if there's anything for us.'

'You sure, mate? Don't you want me to come with you later?'

'No worries. You two stay here and I'll bring back some sambos for lunch, OK?'

It still took me by surprise how many words in Australian English were, first of all, abbreviated and then embellished with a final vowel. I'd got used to brekkie and the constant lament that dinner wasn't cooked on the barbie, but this was a new one on me.

Becky started out to be as dull as Tasha was exciting. Red's storytelling skills were far short of his friend's and rather than a full-on fantasy fulfilment like Robbie and Tasha it was just a boring vanilla sex story.

'Then on the second night she said, "You can fuck me up the arse if you want. I've got some lube."'

'Christ, talk about be prepared. I bet you did.'

'Yeah, you bet. Do you –'

'Not any more,' I said firmly. 'And it's not negotiable. So, how was it? Was it your first time?'

He nodded, looking slightly embarrassed. I wondered if men were ever likely to be mature enough to admit that there are aspects of sex they hadn't explored.

'So tell me about it!'

He opened his mouth and closed it again. Had something awful happened? Had he not been able to get it up once faced with his first experience of anal sex? Surely – a worrying thought came to me – he hadn't neglected to use a condom?

The answer was none of the above. He'd loved the preparatory lubing and fingering, though not as much as the actual penetration. I'll gloss over the usual how tight it was, the undercurrent of the transgressive, etc. He told her it was his first time – I almost applauded –

153

and she got off on that and kept asking him what it felt like, how different it was to a vagina and so on.

'So I asked her what it was like for her, and didn't her cunt feel empty? And she said, "Oh yeah, why don't you go and get your friend and I'll take you both at once."'

'Jesus! Why didn't Robbie tell me this before?'

'Because I didn't get him.'

'Oh.'

Just when I was thinking how predictable men were, he dropped this bombshell. Can you believe it? How many men do you know who would turn down a chance like that? Maybe Red was more of a puritan than he appeared from his willing participation in sex as performance art. Must be that Scandinavian blood.

'Sorry to disappoint you.'

There was an edge to his voice. I shrugged. 'It doesn't matter to me. The main thing is, you enjoyed it?'

'That put me off a bit. I felt like I wasn't enough. Anyway I pushed three fingers up inside her, thumbed her button and she came and so did I. The next night I told her she was an insatiable little slut who wanted it both ways, and gave her my torch.'

He was avoiding my eyes. No wonder.

'So Robbie had been telling you about what he did with Tasha and you copied it?'

'Too right. It did the trick.' He looked up at me, slightly defensive. 'We don't have to share everything, OK? Just because we share you doesn't mean to say I want to give him a go at every other girl I screw.'

'You don't *share* me, Red. We have a relationship where we all play our part. I'm not a toy you pass around.'

'Sorry, wrong choice of words. I just get a bit pissed off sometimes. My part in our relationship is just to provide the cock and the finger. The rest of me might as well not exist.'

What could I say? Only the day before I'd felt the same thing. Red had noticed that Robbie and I were connecting mentally and he was jealous. I felt a pang of guilt, not only towards Red but also on the part of poor old Becky, who'd made a generous offer only to be punished on my behalf, not that she would have noticed.

No wonder I had felt left out; Red had feared he was being excluded and so he had pulled Robbie in closer to leave me in the cold.

I hugged him. 'I don't want you to feel like that. But if you and Robbie changed over – well, that doesn't seem right, does it? Him fucking me and you watching?'

'No,' he admitted. 'I guess I've been a bit stupid.'

'Not really. I don't want to come between you and Robbie, though. There's no reason why I shouldn't book into a hostel and we can just meet up during the day if you like.'

He moulded his hands round the cheeks of my arse and pulled me towards him. I felt him hard against me.

'I don't want to stop having sex with you. Unless you do.'

I looked up at his blue eyes. They were happy again though just a bit anxious that I'd turn him down. I shook my head.

'You're kidding. Why don't we go back to the tent right now for a quickie? We'll probably beat Robbie back here anyway, and if not he'll hang on for us.'

The campsite was deserted, which was just as well as it would have been obvious what we were going back in the tent for. As soon as he had finished zipping up the tent door I unzipped him, pulling his jeans and shorts down just far enough. After some preliminary tongue play I stripped down to my bra and mounted him.

Sometimes an efficient, functional quickie is even more satisfying than a long session of hazy eroticism. I rode him hard, with concentration, and when his stomach muscles started to quiver I started to finger myself and, taking a leaf out of Tasha's book, added a few verbal encouragements, though in a more succinct Anglo-Saxon vein. Well, if he could copy Robbie's technique, I saw no reason why I shouldn't copy hers. Frankly, as far as sex is concerned, as long as all participants are happy with it, the end justifies the means.

Red's orgasm followed mine by a split second and I relaxed my full weight on top of him. It was only the second time we'd fucked without Robbie there, and it was quite nice for a change, though like any performer I guess I missed the appreciation of the audience.

I *know* I'd seen the pictures of the snow-capped volcano. I *know* some sort of equipment was mentioned when we booked the trip. But for God's sake, this was summer. I was astounded to be climbing up a long, steep, snow-covered mountain, the sort of slope that should only be ascended by chairlift and only ever skied down. But not as astounded as when I lost my footing on the way down, felt my ice axe fly out of my hand and found myself rolling over and over in the snow towards what would appear to be certain death.

My life just isn't full of drama, though, and I don't expect my death to be either. I slithered to a halt, unharmed, and sat there watching Red and Robbie running down the snow towards me.

'You looked comical doing that,' I told them as they lifted me up.

'Not as comical as you did,' said Robbie. He tried to

make his voice normal but it was shaky and his face had gone pale under his tan. Red held me and brushed the snow from my back without a word. They'd both been worried, and they both clearly cared about me. Although we hadn't seen any flames and the crater had smelled of rotten eggs, it had been worth the trip.

We had a great week wandering around the Chilean Lake District, camping by the shores of azure lakes, walking through meadows full of spring flowers and exciting each other verbally as well as manually. I made sure Red didn't feel excluded and we grew closer than ever.

Finally I got round to asking Robbie how he managed without sex, apart from what he'd got from Tasha. He laughed.

'You obviously haven't noticed how long I take going off for a pee before turning in,' he said mockingly. 'After that first night in the tent I knew I'd be busting my balls if I didn't get some relief, so I jerked off before bed. It doesn't mean to say that I don't get hard again once I start watching you, but it means at least it can subside reasonably easily.'

'So how do you make sure you're ready for a wank?' I asked.

He gave me a sideways look. 'I'm usually sitting next to you or opposite you all evening. All I have to do is start thinking about watching you later and I'm ready for anything.'

A thrill went through me. But Robbie was going to have to stay in his current rôle until Red decided he wanted to hand over to the understudy.

It was nearly time to travel to Puerto Montt to meet up with Carlos. We spent the last day together in a pretty little German-style town, where we gorged on terrific cakes and tarts in a teashop playing Christmas carols before going back to our guesthouse, a treat for the last night. Our room was up in the attic, dominated by a huge brass bed bang in the middle, which straightaway sold it to me. A small single bed was tucked under the sloping roof and every inch of the old-fashioned dressing table and tallboy was covered by flowery china ornaments.

At first the landlady had looked slightly suspiciously at a mixed-sex threesome so Red told her we were brothers and sister, and I guess with our communal blondness and height we looked the part.

We flopped on to the beds, our bodies heavy and lazy with cake. The brass glinted in the sun flooding through the dormer window and lying on my back I reached my hands up to grasp the rail. From the other bed Robbie smiled.

'I think I should tie your hands there. I don't see why Señor Garcia should be the only one to have the pleasure of restraining you.'

I shivered. There wasn't any logical reason, of course not, but I didn't want it. My relationship with the guys was different and I wanted it to stay that way.

'You can't tie your sister down and have your brother fuck her, mate. It's not legal.'

Robbie and I laughed at Red's get-out.

'Imagine if she came up with a cup of tea for us and found us screwing while Robbie watched. Jesus, she'd probably have a heart attack.' Red grinned mischievously. 'Talking of brothers and sister, did you ever play doctors and nurses?'

'Did I? How do you think I got launched in my brilliant career as a sex kitten?'

'So lie still, Miss van Bon, while Doctor Sullivan and I prepare you for examination.'

At the same time as I realised that Red had practically invited Robbie to put his hands all over me, it occurred to me that as we were outside the normal routine Robbie hadn't had his night-time pee. Or wank.

Red started with my socks and worked up to my trousers and pulled them off me, while Robbie started with my sweatshirt and then removed my T-shirt. His hands grazed my breasts as he pulled it over my head. I was only wearing a thin crop top and my nipples responded straight away.

'I think our patient's got a slight swelling here,' he said, fondling one erect nipple. 'And on the other side too. You investigate, doctor.'

I watched their two hands, both large, both tanned, as they teased my nipples into tingling points of longing.

'It's actually further down I have the problem,' I put in. 'I think it must be some sort of inflammation.'

'Let's have a look.'

Red pulled off my knickers slowly and then parted my thighs. 'It's a shame we haven't got stirrups for your legs; we'll just have to hold them up.'

Robbie took his cue and they each held one of my thighs up and wide apart and took turns gazing intently at my slit.

'That's a decidedly abnormal quantity of secretion, I agree,' said Red. 'What does it feel like?'

His question was addressed to Robbie; he wanted him to touch me. I almost fainted when for the first time his hand reached out and stroked me. Despite the fact that Robbie's voice had been such a key factor in my excitement in our previous encounters I didn't even hear what he said as he probed me and fleetingly touched my clit before ceding to Red. We'd moved on another stage but it was Red who had instigated it and I wanted to stop playing games and get seriously raunchy.

'Let's stop the doctor crap. Where are we going from

here?' I said, my voice as husky and dangerously seductive as I could wish. And that wasn't even intentional, just a by-product of my excitement.

Red smiled at Robbie and then at me. 'No map. No plan. No limits. Yes or no?'

Oh, man, yes.

The sun on our bodies, the soft bed with the brass rails, the first time Robbie and I had exchanged more than words or touched with more than hands, whatever happened it was going to be the best. Although we were committing no crime the mention of incest hung in the air, making me feel opulently sinful. An atmosphere of decadence and debauchery had pervaded the chintzy room and I revelled in it.

Robbie wanted to taste me but while I held my breath waiting for his tongue he picked up a spoon that nestled in a pretty china cup and saucer on the dressing table. Carefully he mined my cunt for the abundant juices, bringing out a spoonful and looking at me while he slowly sipped from it, then rubbed the cold hard metal over my clit. I thought my head would explode but there was more to come.

The idea of tying me down had taken hold of him. When Red turned me over on my knees facing the bed head, Robbie moved and crouched down on the other side of the bars, facing me. I took my bra top off before Red entered me, hoping Robbie would touch my breasts while I was being fucked.

'You look like animals in the zoo,' he observed, almost insolently. 'I suppose that's just what you are.'

'Just as primitive,' I agreed.

'But probably more promiscuous and less discriminating than most. Hold on to the bars.'

I grasped the brass rails and his hands immediately closed over mine. I made as if to pull them away and he tightened his grip.

'You can't escape,' he said teasingly. With Red push-ing slowly and satisfyingly into me, I didn't want to and I don't think Robbie thought I did for a minute. The image of being a shameless animal copulating publicly, combined with the big hands holding mine firmly was electrifying, but not as much as Robbie's mouth suddenly reaching forward and touching mine.

Kissing's never been my thing particularly. It was down to those early experimental days with boys, when you seemed to spend endless hours with a flabby wet tongue in your mouth before he plucked up the courage to feel you up. Not that I dislike it, and lately I'd especially enjoyed both Gabi's and Carlos's kisses, but if someone asked me to rank kissing in a league table of turn-ons I'd put it at the absolute bottom. Until Robbie kissed me through the bars of the bed.

It started off gentle and tender, but not sloppy. Our lips were like positive and negative connecting and setting off a long, slow charge. His tongue explored my mouth firmly though gently but I was hungry for him and responded urgently. His mouth hardened against mine and the probing of his tongue was as thrilling as Red's penis inside me.

I knew I was moaning deep in my throat as the kiss went on and when finally he started to withdraw I felt I'd been thoroughly fucked. One touch and I would come but I didn't want to yet. Was Robbie going to take Red's place? I wasn't going to risk losing out on anything by bossily demanding an orgasm, however much I wanted one.

'Your mouth is as beautiful as your cunt,' said Rob-bie, his voice rougher than ever. I think he had been shaken by the intensity of the kiss as much as I had. 'Can I feel it here?'

He moved his hands from mine and unzipped and lowered his jeans and shorts. I hesitated briefly, wondering if I should do a Tasha and admire its size and heft vociferously before taking it in my mouth but decided against it. He wanted to feel my mouth around his shaft, not hear it pronounce the results of its inspection. The praise could come later.

His hands closed over mine again as I ran my mouth teasingly over his hardness. No, he wasn't as big as Red but he was plenty big enough and more than hard enough. I guessed he wasn't going to take long.

'Having fun, mate?' asked Red, breaking my dreamy mood. I had slipped from my mood of illicit lust into a romantic, dewy-eyed, first time scenario with a new lover, which was frankly rather absurd. I put the sloppy stuff on hold; with one man in my mouth and one in my pussy it wasn't hard to recapture that feeling of depravity and dissipation, especially when they started comparing notes.

'You didn't tell me how good she is at this,' Robbie answered, his voice jagged. 'If you'd rather fuck her than have her suck you then she's got to be bloody wonderful.'

'She is, mate. Tight but soft, magic muscles. Don't you want to swap?'

I lapped up the way they talked as though I had no say in the matter as eagerly as I lapped at Robbie's prick.

'No, I think I'll come in her mouth. I suppose she swallows?'

'What doesn't she do?'

Red's comment came with an increase in the intensity of his thrusting. He pulled me hard back on to him as Robbie's hands gripped mine harder. They were both nearly there.

'Tell you what, mate, leave her for me to finish, if you don't mind?' That was Robbie.

'No worries,' said Red breathlessly and groaned as he came. 'Jesus.'

Robbie's arms were trembling as his hands slackened and tightened rhythmically over mine and I knew he was nearly there. I took him as deep as I dared and in less than a minute he spurted into me. Red had lied, of course – I never swallow – but instead I dribbled it slowly out of my mouth so that it spilled down to my breasts. As Robbie unclasped his hands from mine and sank to his knees I rubbed his warm cream into my tits. His last remark would have sent me completely over the brink if only hands-free orgasms existed.

I expected him to get up and come round to the bed but he stayed where he was.

'Sit down, Bliss.'

I sat back, still facing him, wondering how long he was going to make me wait till he let me come. Suddenly his arms came through two of the bars, grabbed my legs purposefully and pulled them through. They were uncomfortably far apart and my sex gaped, framed by the brass rails.

I had fallen on to my back, my head against Red's knee, reminding me of his presence. Robbie hadn't forgotten him, though.

'Hold her down, Red, with her arms above her head. Close your eyes, Bliss. I want you to concentrate. Red, keep your mouth shut.'

The sudden silence in the room, my anticipation and the fact that Robbie didn't touch me for a full half minute reminded me of waiting, bound and gagged, for Carlos. Of course I'd told Robbie about how agonisingly exciting that had been and he was trying to recreate it for me. I concentrated on what I must look like to him, my pink lips plump with desire, my slit creamily expectant, flaunting itself through the bars like a monkey pressing her arse to the cage.

His tongue caressed me with a delicacy that sent shivers through me. As gently as he had kissed my mouth he kissed my pussy, licking and probing slowly. It seemed forever before it touched my clitoris, but when it did I felt overwhelmed with the need for release. Winding my legs behind him I tensed my muscles ready to come but he replaced my legs in front of the bed, leaving his hands on my thighs. His tongue continued to lick my swollen bud slowly, too slowly for me to come, a delicious torture. Once again he moved to my molten slit, where his tongue replayed its action in my mouth, thrusting harder inside me. My breathing was getting more and more shallow and then his warm mouth moved down, lapping away from my overheated sex, and then started softly rimming my anus.

I don't know if he heard the sound that escaped my throat but Red took Robbie's earlier instruction for silence to mean me as well. Without a word he placed his free hand over my mouth.

Robbie's tongue moved back up to my pussy and then to my clit and I knew this time he would let me come. As he started to increase the pressure his hands moved from my legs and one finger of each hand pressed gently in a circular motion just above and each side of my clitoris. His tongue needled my inflamed clit with rapid but firm strokes and then he swept it broadly up and down and increased the pressure with his fingers. It was totally out of my control and my own enforced passivity and blatant exposure jarred my body into the violent reaction I'd been waiting for.

'Nice one, Rob,' commented Red as my orgasm subsided, bringing us back down to earth. My hands and my mouth were my own again.

'How do you know?' I asked, though my voice was weak. 'How do you know I came?'

They both snorted with laughter. 'The bloody bed vibrated with it, for one thing,' said Red. 'Even your face tensed up. Your legs twitched. Your fanny bucked.'

'You can't see my legs or my fanny. I hate that word. Don't use it again.'

'Yes miss. I've seen them loads of times.'

I pulled my legs through the rails and grinned at Robbie. 'Anyway he was right, it was a nice one. I was a bit put out when you turned down the offer to swap places, but you more than made up for it.'

We had a group hug on the bed. Just the sort of thing Mum used to go in for when I was a kid – though not post-coitally, you understand, but fully dressed and with her consciousness-raising group. OK, I was disappointed that Robbie hadn't technically fucked me, but figured that we still had something to look forward to.

Chapter Eight

*A*fter two days on Chiloe I stopped waiting for Carlos to tie me up and threaten me if I didn't tell him what Red and Robbie were up to. Maybe he wasn't as unscrupulous as I'd allowed him to become in my imagination. Yes, he'd had me followed but for my own protection, as he said. The boys' warnings, not to mention the Bond-type drill I'd been put through before leaving them, seemed preposterous.

I'd been made to learn two e-mail addresses, though my request to eat the paper they were written on afterwards met with slight exasperation. One address was theirs and one belonged to the anonymous contact on Chiloe, who I teasingly christened Moneypenny. After checking that Carlos wouldn't know whether I'd had one before they gave me a mobile and made me learn its number as though I'd had it for years. They programmed in Moneypenny's phone number, though that was only for emergencies. If I needed urgent help and couldn't talk I was to phone him, call him Steve, an old friend, and ask him if he could get Mum to put some money into my bank account. Moneypenny would try to make himself known to me by introducing himself as 'Franco, as in General'. So already he had three names; serious espionage or what?

But in two days of sightseeing on the delightful island nothing more sinister had occurred than listening to Jorge's edit of my tape while looking at my slug photos. He had sent me a note via Carlos to say he was going to exhibit the pictures at the end of the month with the tape on continuous loop; would we be able to go? Sadly I would be in Patagonia but Carlos said he would try to get there.

The slug pictures were good. Mid-slither I looked pretty impressive, wrapped up in my transparent mummy outfit and a quite amusing look of determination on my face. I have to say though that the ones on the massage table were more sleazy porn than erotic art. Not that I minded much.

Carlos played the tape at full volume on the first night we spent together in the rather nice house he was renting. I couldn't relax and appreciate it because the maid was bustling in clearing the remains of dinner and fetching the coffee. At least I managed to get the photos out of the way.

'Can't you wait till she's gone?' I hissed, embarrassed. Exhibitionism has its place and frankly before a middle-aged female servant just wasn't it in my book.

'She doesn't understand English,' he assured me, though as she had returned with the coffee just at the moment where I was describing rather loudly and thickly that Ulla was fondling my arse, cunt and clit I felt myself blush. Even I knew the Spanish for the first two. Apart from anything, my voice sounded exactly like the voice of someone on the verge of an orgasm. However she seemed completely oblivious to the sound effects, her lined face bent in concentration over the tray.

My embarrassment deepened for different reasons when I heard myself describing sex with Carlos and even worse with Red and Robbie. He was obviously taken aback by my enthusiastic description of the size of Red's cock. Jorge had left out his questions about the guys and ended the tape with me coming. You know I would have sworn I either shut up or shouted but I was groaning and moaning just like, well, like the American girlies. I wondered if I was always like that or whether I'd put it on a bit to avoid Jorge's spytrap, but I could hardly ask Carlos.

I liked it better when he replayed it later after he'd dismissed Maria. He took the part of Ulla, touching me when she did, and as you can imagine also tying me to the table. As he brought me to orgasm in sync with the voiceover I self-consciously gritted my teeth and came in silence. But though listening had turned me on it didn't seem to affect Carlos; after he had made me come he untied me and said he wanted to wait for me. It wasn't the first time, so I shrugged and went to bed.

We had our own rooms, which was fine by me. Bed was usually the only place that lent itself to sex when you're camping, but in a big house with a secluded garden and swimming pool, the next week was going to present plenty of opportunities

So I thought on night one. However the ensuing two-day tour of the island gave us little time to ourselves at all, never mind time to indulge in a relaxed screw. Carlos drove all over the island; he genuinely seemed interested in my reaction to the place as a potential holiday destination. He explained that parts of the island had been spoiled by logging operations, so it could only be improved. Some of the beaches on the populated east coast were good; the towns were attractive and the people were friendly. We ate superb seafood in quaint wooden restaurants set on stilts over the sea and picnicked in the national park on the west coast, on the longest, whitest, sandiest beach I've seen in my life.

Red and Robbie often went on about deforestation and for the life of me I couldn't see why a holiday park would be worse than a neglected forest. I had to point out to Carlos, however, that I myself hate formula holiday resorts and wouldn't have visited the island if there was any danger of being forced to go on tours with jolly bus drivers handing out bingo cards.

'This isn't going to be that tacky, Bliss. But you know millions of people do want organised tours and on-site entertainment. Look at the Caribbean. Most people who go there are in tourist complexes. That's what people like.'

Well, I couldn't argue. Even friends of mine who used to rough it in India and Morocco had taken up packages to new resorts in Salvador or the Dominican Republic. It was so nice, they said, to have everything laid on and not have to spend all your time with your nose in guidebooks deciding which were the best places to go and the cheapest hotels to stay in. But it made me realise that Red and Robbie were right; those Caribbean compounds surely weren't owned by local businesses, but by multinational corporations. I even wondered if maybe the dangers of travelling freely in the Caribbean islands hadn't been exaggerated by those same corporations to frighten people into staying in the compounds, buying their food and drink and souvenirs there. And what had the boys said about importing the food and drink as well?

I decided not to run that one by Carlos. After all I was supposed to be gathering information, not trying to dissuade him from getting on with the job.

He promised we would spend the next day relaxing by the pool, though my first encounter made me anything but relaxed. The gardener was trimming a hedge – not too surprising, as I didn't see Carlos brandishing a pair of shears, though I bet he'd pounce on a roll of garden twine – and greeted me with a *'Buenas días, señora'*. Then he added in English, 'My name is Franco, as in General.'

'Oh, good. I mean, hello, Franco.' Was I supposed to say anything else?

He smiled and moved to the other side of the hedge. I quickly figured that there was no point having a code unless you suspected someone might overhear or maybe even that the garden would be bugged – can you bug a garden? Well, I suppose if you can bug the president of the United States, there's no limit. I feared I was being a hopeless spy and stopped peering at the hedge for a hidden microphone and sat by the pool.

I guess I was supposed to be comforted by the presence of Franco/Moneypenny/Steve but, although I had dismissed the idea of Carlos doing me any harm during the last two days, I was uneasily aware that unless both the guys and F/M/S were nuts, there was obviously some danger involved here. But as Carlos joined me dressed in nothing but blue swimming shorts I rationalised my reawakened fear. F/M/S was also intelligence gathering, just like me. Just because I had his number in case of emergency didn't mean that they thought Carlos was out to harm me, but that they were taking unnecessary if rather sweet precautions. It was a bit like my dad's insurance policy, a well-meaning but extravagant safety net put in place just to show they cared.

Carlos and I had fun racing each other – his crawl was better but my breaststroke is quite honestly superb – and rubbing each other with suntan lotion while we talked non-stop. Maria appeared with a salad lunch and a couple of beers and then Carlos said he had to work but he could do it at the poolside. It was fine by me because I had neglected my postcard duties for weeks so I settled down to the ones I'd bought in Castro the previous day.

G'day Kippo!
  Carlos – sorry, Charlie – and I are having a week's holiday on lovely Chiloe. Weather is great, no restraints so far – geddit??! – but after two days touring the island and today relaxing by the pool I have great hopes that we'll be tied up later, if you get my drift. You'll see from the greeting I'm also still getting into my Australians, or rather vice versa ... hope your end holding up too. Blisso.

Carlos looked up from his laptop as Maria came out to ask if we wanted coffee. We didn't, but I seized the interruption to ask him what seemed to me to be a key question.

'I thought we were going to be relaxing in other ways here,' I said with a raised eyebrow to illustrate the sort of ways I meant. 'There's this terrific garden, the pool, a great big house; but there's also Maria and the gardener.'

'Franco,' said Carlos automatically. I nodded. I hadn't known whether he would know that I knew his name. 'So? You want to involve them?'

'Very funny. Just the opposite. What I mean is, as long as they're around, we're hardly free to take advantage of this nice private garden, are we?'

'Oh, I see. Well, Franco's only here twice a week for a few hours; I think you'll find he's gone now. As for Maria, I've got quite a bit of entertaining to do while I'm here and it seemed a bit presumptuous to expect you to do the cooking and cleaning.'

'Sure. But couldn't she just come in the evening to do the cooking? She's in and out all day.'

The chair scraped harshly on the concrete as he pushed it back and came round to stand behind me. He pulled my bikini top down and fondled my breasts with both hands. I closed my eyes and luxuriated in his attention, fantasising about where it was leading.

'Maria!' he shouted.

Oh, shit. He laughed and I realised I'd spoken out loud. Maria bustled out through the French doors and stood in front of the table. I saw her eyes flicker over my breasts, where Carlos was busy teasing the nipples into hard points, her coarse face impassive.

'*Si, señor?*'

He spoke to her quickly in Spanish while I lowered my eyes. It was far too quick and informal for me to pick up on. She answered him, her voice giving no clue as to what she might be saying or thinking, but I could guess. What a shameless tart, so far sunk in depravity she didn't think anything of being groped semi-naked in front of the staff.

I could hardly tell her how wrong that was. For a start, my Spanish wasn't good enough to explain that although I may be a tart, I was an unpaid one. And it would have been difficult to convey that I did indeed feel shame, and in fact I was feeling it keenly right now. But what I would have had most trouble communicating was the fact that it was precisely because of the shame that I had a pulse throbbing hard between my legs.

Carlos said something else and she turned and went back into the house. He raised me out of the chair and undid my bikini top.

'I explained your "fear" of exhibitionism,' he said almost contemptuously, still idly toying with my breasts, 'and that I hadn't got round to telling you that

172

the terms of her contract are that she may see many things of a sexual nature while she works for me. She's indifferent and unshockable and she won't talk.' He smiled cynically. 'Not as long as I keep paying her twice the going rate.'

'So what did she say?'

'That it's none of her business and it doesn't offend her in the slightest. You know, Bliss –' he sounded thoughtful '– I think she rather enjoyed that little display, don't you? I bet you did.'

His hand darted down my bikini bottoms before I had a chance to guess what he was going to do and he laughed as my wetness proved he had won his bet. His dark eyes mocked me, glinting with mischief. Then he lifted his face from mine.

'*Gracias, Maria. Momento, por favor.*'

She was back. Holding a coil of rope, the kind we used to hang washing on when I was a kid. Standing patiently with it in one hand, a knife and bottle in the other, her narrow, glittering eyes watching Carlos's hand moving in my pants. Watching Carlos pull them down to my knees and watching his hand move back to my blatant, wanton sex.

Her eyes didn't move from that spot. As he rubbed my clitoris she stood there as though she was studying it until she raised her eyes to mine. Something glinted in there – insolence? jealousy? excitement? – and I think she almost smiled. I came without remembering not to make a noise, my legs buckling slightly.

'Then I asked her to fetch the rope and knife and sunblock,' he continued, as though there had been no gap in his explanation of their earlier conversation. He took the sunblock from her hand and rubbed it over my breasts and back, then pulled my bikini pants right off and rubbed it over my buttocks and bikini area. 'I don't want you to get burned.'

He sat me down on the chair and took the rope and knife. Maria went back inside and he turned back to me.

'She was so impassive at the interview I knew she'd be perfect,' he said conversationally as he wrapped the rope around me twice, just above my breasts, knotting it firmly at the back. My arms and body were tied tight together round the chair. Then he crossed the rope diagonally down and in between my breasts in both directions like a crossover bra, and pulled it around again underneath, winding it right down to my waist. Picking up the knife he cut the rope and knotted it once more. Then he pulled my legs slightly apart so he could lash each ankle to the chair leg.

This was different from corsets and chains and smooth black leather restraints. I'd thought he'd taught me everything I would need to know about bondage, but I realised that so far I'd only dabbled in the softcore stuff. This was the hardcore.

In black leather I'd felt sexy and desirable, which had been emphasised by the tightness of the belt or lacings. Naked and bound with washing line didn't make me feel an object of lust, though as long as Carlos thought it did it was fine by me. At least the rope didn't feel as rough as it looked, but he'd tied it tight enough to bite into my skin. I wondered if it would leave red marks and if that was what he wanted.

'I hope you enjoy this as much as our previous little games,' he said equably, sitting down at the table again and adjusting his chair for a better view of me. 'It's not quite as soft focus, but it's to my taste. What do you think?'

'I think I should have waited before I wrote my postcard to Kip,' I said faintly. 'Apart from that, I'll let you know later. I'm used to thinking on my feet, not tied to a garden chair.'

He chuckled. 'Lovely, Bliss. I've been dreaming about this, sitting here working with you at my side, beautifully bound. The rope is so much more real, isn't it? Not so elegant, of course. But we'll save elegance for the evening.'

'Great,' I said. 'As long as this is only my daywear and I'm still to be dressed for dinner, I'll survive.'

'Talking of which, we're entertaining some important contacts tonight,' he added casually. 'So you'll definitely be dressed to impress.'

'Let's just get one thing straight here,' I said warily. Being tied naked to a chair meant I didn't have much bargaining power but I had to make sure from the start there were no misunderstandings. I wasn't going to be gangbanged by half of Chiloe just because Carlos assumed I'd like it. 'I didn't come here to screw your contacts, or whatever you call them, either willingly or unwillingly. If you thought I'd be up for it you're wrong and I'll go now. And if you don't give a toss and you're going to have me raped, I'll scream. Until I'm sick.'

He laughed. 'I sincerely hope you don't seriously think I'm a rapist, either in person or by proxy. And no, I'm not expecting you to screw my contacts. What I would like, if it doesn't outrage your sense of propriety too much, is for you to be well dressed, flash a tantalising glimpse of cleavage and stocking, be as charming to my guests as your appalling Spanish will allow and generally just let them see what lovely companions can be bought if they'll only hitch their wagon to my star. *Capisce?*'

'That's Italian,' I said sulkily. 'OK, I didn't really see you as a rapist, but a girl has to make sure we're all in the same ballpark. How many men have I got to flash my tits at?'

'Only three,' he replied. 'Three very important men,

however, as far as my project's concerned. Two are government officials and one's a landowner. But don't worry, you won't be the only girl. A friend of mine from Lima is coming as well. *She* can speak Spanish, so she'll be more use than you.' He looked at his watch. 'She'll be here pretty soon, actually.'

I had a glimmer of an idea as to who that was. 'Susie, I presume.'

'Jorge told me you'd seen the pictures,' he teased. 'Attractive, isn't she?'

'Stunning,' I admitted. 'So does that mean she'll be the recipient of your attentions tonight?'

'Maybe,' he said consideringly. 'Maybe you will. Or neither of you. Or both. Although –' he leaned towards me '– if I spend the afternoon watching you motionless and helpless, that delicious juice trickling out between your parted thighs, then I don't think I'll be able to resist you.'

His eyes were on my pussy, displayed for him. He got off on watching me, helpless. I had an inkling of why this turned him on, and shivered myself.

Carlos came towards me again and softly fingered my wetness. I sighed. Helpless and displayed. Motionless, defenceless. I could buy into this.

'Then again, sometimes after dinner I don't feel very . . . active. Sometimes I like to watch. Maybe you and Susie? I know she'd like to – if you wanted?'

Not only was I *not* required to sell myself in the cause of mass tourism, not only was I being instructed in the finer, or rather rougher, points of bondage, but also I was being promised a luscious redhead *and* an audience. Didn't I do well?

It seemed forever since I'd left Gabi and while I tried to picture myself turning down the chance of a scene with Susie I had to admit that I'd have more chance of having a shit in the Queen's handbag, as Kip would so succinctly put it.

Six sophisticated adults sat round an elegant dinner table, laughing, eating and drinking. The women were glamorously attired and the men wore smart dark suits; the conversation was in two languages. The food was good and the wine the best Chile had to offer. On the surface it was a civilised evening.

But the guests were strangers, invited in order to assess how easily they could be bribed. The women were there to inspire lust in the guests, if only for the money that could buy them. And, as far as I was concerned, it was a prelude to lazy and luscious, or fast and furious, sex with Susie. I didn't care which way she wanted to play it. The various undercurrents lent the evening a surreal air.

It amused me to flirt with the 'contacts'. When Carlos had mentioned local politicians I instantly thought they'd be like some of the borough councillors I'd met through Vicki – the loud-mouthed, thick as two short planks, only elected because no one else wanted to stand variety. Mind you, if you knew the borough she works in . . .

These men were charming. I found myself thinking that I'd really been too precipitate with Carlos and I wouldn't have minded flashing more than cleavage at Señor Riviera, or was it Ribera? I ought to find out for Red and Robbie. But I immediately erased that thought from my mind; I was turning into a really *bad* girl.

Señor R, or Miguel, as we were on first name terms, was the junior of the local government guys, slim and dark – well of course they were all dark, being Chilean – with thick eyebrows, an elegant nose and sensuous lips. Maybe I liked him best because he could manage a few words of English and seemed to understand my

Spanish better than the others. His boss, Fernando, was the only tall man at the table, cadaverously thin with a wolfish face. I reckoned Carlos would be all right there; he would definitely be the type to take backhanders.

The other guest had been introduced as Raoul Delgado, but everyone called him Señor Delgado. He was obviously Mr Big, and actually he was big in the chubby sense as well. Bliss the spy deduced that he must be the landowner, and the way the others deferred to him he must own a hell of a big parcel of land. Carlos was equally affable to all three men but even he treated Raoul with special attention, discussing wine and cigars with him as a fellow man of the world. The big man was jovial and charming to me and even more so to Susie. I wondered if she'd laid down her ground rules as well?

She had arrived early and to my dismay while I was still tied to the chair, although she greeted me with a kiss on both cheeks as though she was accustomed to greeting new acquaintances roped and naked. She and Carlos talked business and I listened hard but not much came out that I didn't know already.

I would have recognised her flaming red hair anywhere, though her face wasn't as pale as in the clown photos. Her southern drawl was intimate and caressing. Briefly I considered whether I should be jealous of her relationship with Carlos but, hey, he was just a holiday romance.

Carlos had explained that she would be bringing clothes for me. As I knew, we were a similar size. After I was untied and showered she knocked on my door and came in with a huge suitcase.

'Not exactly cutting-edge fashion, hon, but the standard hostess-type thing,' she explained, pulling out half a dozen cocktail dresses, mostly low-necked and with either short or split skirts. 'If you're a fashion designer I guess you'll be appalled by this.'

'Fabric,' I corrected. 'It's OK, I don't mind dressing like a tart from time to time.'

She laughed. 'Yeah, it's kinda fun, isn't it? The first time I entertained somebody for Carlos –' she pronounced it Car-lowss '– I thought I looked like my mother, for heaven's sake. But I guess it's kinda like corsets.' She shot a glance at me. 'That seemed so tacky at first, but now I can't go out in the evening without one on; I just don't feel sexy.'

I nodded non-committally, wondering if I too were to be corseted this evening, and whether for what she would assume to be my own benefit, for Carlos's titillation or maybe for hers later on.

I didn't have to wonder for long. After she'd suggested which dresses we both would wear – mine was white, with long sleeves but bare shoulders, straight and calf-length but with a crotch-high split on one side, while hers was black, short and sleeveless but deeply plunging – she brought out the appropriate underwear. I wondered if Carlos had been leading me on about her fancying me as she had me lean forward so my breasts fell into the tiny satin cups and started pulling the back together to fasten the hooks. Her eyes were as clinical as if she were a nurse bandaging a patient.

'This is tight, hon,' she said as she squeezed my ribs with the stiff satin. 'He said we were identical but you're a bit bigger than me. Never mind, it'll be more fun.'

'Fun for who?' I asked, bewildered and breathless.

She didn't answer while I felt her pushing me into the corset but finally as she stood back and inspected me I saw an expression I recognised in her eyes. It was desire but it was mixed with power and satisfaction.

'I get it,' I said quietly. 'You don't just like being bound, do you?'

She smiled. 'You catch on fast, honey. No, I love to play both parts. Not that I get the chance with Carlos. He'd rather have his ass roped to a bucking bronco than be tied up by a woman.'

An interesting thought went through my mind. If Carlos was telling the truth about not wanting me to prostitute myself for him with his 'contacts', had he brought me here to be Susie's plaything? Did he need to keep her sweet from time to time? What about her relationship with Jorge – did he get to be the one in chains from time to time?

I decided it didn't matter much as Susie placed a tight gold choker on me. It was made up of a dozen thin chains and I wondered if later one of those would be clipped to a wall or even a lead. How far did she go?

Right then she went far enough for the time being as she stroked my pubes below the corset.

'I guess you'll have to do without panties, hon, with that high split. Stockings would be a little too vulgar. But a garter would be nice. Just something those boys can see through that split.'

So, that's how I came to be sitting with Miguel on one side looking down my cleavage and Mr Big on my garter side. I should explain that it was less a garter than a bracelet, expandable like those slave bracelets, thin white metal in a wave-like pattern. Susie had made sure it gripped tight, and had spent some time adjusting it around my leg, her fingers grazing the soft flesh of my inner thigh, close enough to my sex to make me shudder with delight. My only disappointment was that she hadn't let me dress her. I supposed Carlos had that pleasure.

While I would have been happy lingering over coffee

180

and brandy, though frankly cigar smoke has never rung my bell, Susie suggested we leave the men to it and repair to the sitting room. Although I had to smile and agree politely I cursed her; whatever they were going to discuss now was just what Red and Robbie might be interested in.

'How long will they be?' I asked as we settled ourselves on the sofa. I wondered whether I dared make a quick move on Susie while the machinery of bribery and corruption was set in motion, though I guessed she wouldn't want to risk jeopardising the deal by having three shocked Catholic men finding their two hostesses *in flagrante delicto*.

'I don't suppose they'll be too long, hon,' she said. 'Knowing Carlos, he's researched this thoroughly enough so that all he needs to do is give them sufficient inducements and they'll be only too happy to help things move along.'

'What sort of inducements?' I asked innocently.

Susie touched my bare shoulder. 'Don't worry, sweetie. Carlos told me you'd made it clear you weren't going to be one of them.' She laughed softly and moved her hand down my throat and on to my breasts. Reaching in gently she scooped one, then the other, out of the small cups of the corset and toyed with my rapidly stiffening nipples.

'I did just wonder if you'd be averse to putting on a little show with me for our guests, however.'

'Hang on a minute.' The mixture of vodka, wine and brandy has never been one of the better cocktails for keeping a clear head. 'You mean Carlos wants me and you to – Jesus, what? A bloody table-dancing act?'

She giggled. 'Oh my gosh no. That would be totally tasteless. No, I mean more of a cabaret act, if you see what I mean.'

The penny dropped. 'Of course I see what you mean,'

I said grimly. 'Carlos suggested it to me himself. The only thing is, he didn't tell me there would be more than one in the audience.'

You know what? I was suddenly turned right off. Despite the fact that my body was betraying me, my nipples hard as bullets and my sex heating up and liquefying, my mind said no. It detached itself and suddenly felt crystal clear and sober, considering my plight as though it was someone else's. It wondered with cool interest whether my body would continue to respond to the mere mechanics of the situation, were I to be persuaded or forced into it somehow, if only to try to get some more information for Red and Robbie.

'He told me you liked an audience,' said Susie, moving one hand to the split in my skirt. 'It wouldn't be the same for them as it would with just the three of us, of course. Just a little sexy stripping and kissing and fondling, like a soft porn film. Lots of gasps and loud orgasms, you know the kind of thing. Later on we could get into the real thing.'

'You don't sound too fazed by this. Is it normally part of your job?'

She let me go and lit a cigarette. 'Sometimes. Things have to get done and if money's not enough it doesn't hurt to smooth the way with a little game. It can be quite enjoyable. I think it will be tonight.'

'I'm afraid you might be wrong there.'

We looked up at Carlos who was standing in the doorway, smiling faintly at the scene before him. 'He wants you, Susie,' he said, nodding in the direction of Mr Big. 'He's not interested in watching, and the other guys are definitely not interested in anything but dollars and cents.'

Could be my first instinct about the good Catholic boys was right. I looked at Susie, who didn't seem too put out.

'Some you win, some you lose.' She shrugged. 'I don't suppose he'll be too painful. Apart from his weight.' Stubbing out her cigarette, she smiled at me. 'Maybe later?'

Carlos held the door for her. Before following her he looked back at me. 'Put your clothes in order, Bliss, the other guys are coming in to say goodbye.'

I suddenly felt very small, a little girl playing at spies who'd got out of her depth, an adolescent caught up in a sex game that had turned nasty. Cursing Kip for introducing me to Carlos and cursing Red and Robbie for introducing me to espionage I pushed my tits back in my corset. I felt lost and lonely and I wanted my mum.

With an effort I put on a glitzy smile to air kiss Francisco and Miguel goodnight then sank on to the sofa as Carlos brought in his brandy. I'd gone right off the idea of booze.

He sat opposite me and looked at me coolly. 'Susie said you weren't keen on playing ball, Bliss. I thought when I suggested you and she got together with an audience you seemed very enthusiastic. Maria's still trying to get the stain out of the cushion.'

It stung like a slap in the face, but before I could recover enough to come back at him he carried on.

'I'm sorry if I don't know exactly where I stand with you, but you seem to have suddenly moved the goalposts. In view of your delight at being groped and fingerfucked by someone unknown in San Pedro, your obvious relish at exhibitionism with your fellow back-packers and your willingness to be photographed as another woman masturbates you while describing it on tape, it didn't occur to me that you might object to making out with Susie before a small, exclusive audience.'

His voice hardened. 'If I had made an offer of that

little tableau and you had then refused to go through with it I would have been very embarrassed. I think I've given you a fair idea of the importance of this project and even you must realise that it's not something that's going to happen without very delicate negotiation.'

Anger seeped out of every pore of him and I felt abject. He was right; I'd almost salivated at the prospect of sex with Susie, especially before an audience. I couldn't blame him at all for assuming that the bigger the audience, the bigger the thrill. And let's face it, if I'd not met Red and Robbie and consequently cast him in the role of baddie, I would probably have strutted my stuff with Susie glorying in the appreciation of four men.

Mind you through my contrition I did feel a flash of pride that I'd almost played a more active part in foiling his plans than mere information gathering. However, I felt it would smooth things over if I made an apology.

'I'm sorry, Carlos. I guess you're right and I was stupid. I don't know why I got so uptight about it. Maybe if you'd prepared me earlier. I had just a bit of a shock when Susie said we were expected to put on a show.'

He sighed. 'Well, no harm done. But I don't think I'll be introducing you to any more of my business connections.'

Well done, Bliss, I thought sourly. Mission aborted.

'Carlos?' I asked tentatively. 'How did it come about, him wanting Susie? I mean, you said you didn't expect me to screw them, so how come she has to?'

He raised an eyebrow. 'It's part of her job; I sometimes think it's the part she enjoys most. And it's very useful. Powerful men often like to be tied up by whores.'

'But she's not a whore, is she? I thought she worked for you.'

'Oh, Bliss. She does work for me, and in different capacities. Tonight she's playing the role of whore. So are you, in fact, except that I told them you were a lesbian I'd hired because I enjoyed watching you and Susie screw. If they'd showed any interest in that, I would have offered to let them watch too. Fortunately Raoul just wanted to get his rocks off with a redhead, as he's never had one before, and Francisco looked horrified by the very idea of women making out together.'

'What about Miguel? I thought he rather liked me.'

Carlos's smile was patronising. 'Oh yes, he did. But he's married to Raoul's niece. He would have been allowed to watch if the others wanted to, but of course not to touch. Raoul has a lot of influence. One does not upset him.'

I got the subtext; i.e. I had come close to doing just that. No wonder he was angry.

The clock ticked loudly in the silence.

'I really am sorry,' I repeated. 'Can I make it up to you?'

'No.' Carlos got to his feet and held his hand out for me. 'I mean, there's no need. As I said, no harm done. Just go to bed, Bliss. I'll see you in the morning.'

I surprised myself by sleeping well but woke feeling stupid. In one fell swoop I'd blown my chance with Susie, made Carlos angry with me and, what was probably in the great scheme of things most important of all, put him off introducing me to any more of his business connections. Without that I didn't see that I'd be able to help Red and Robbie much, and wondered whether it would be better if I just packed my bag and headed back to the mainland.

I dreaded getting up, not knowing what reaction I'd get from Carlos and Susie. But when I finally summoned the courage to dress and go out to the pool, where I could hear their voices, I was greeted like their best mate and offered Bucks' Fizz and croissants.

'Looks like you're dressed for going into town already, Bliss,' said Susie, who wasn't. Her pale body was still gleaming with water after a swim. To anyone else's eye she was wearing a perfectly innocent one-piece black swimsuit, with cutouts banded with gold around the high neckline and a chain belt wrapped twice round her slim waist. I knew that innocuous-looking chain could be tightened around her arms and body, or slipped through one of those cutouts to keep her fastened tight to a wall or a post, or led around like a dog. Had I been forgiven enough to join in a game like that, or did she mean they were sending me off to town while they played without me?

'I didn't know what the plans were,' I admitted. 'Are we all going to town?'

'Sure thing, hon. Maria's having a night off and I thought I'd like to make some gumbo for us all so I'm going shopping. Carlos has got a meeting to go, to so if you want to come along with me we'll all meet up for lunch after. How's that sound?'

'Fine.' I felt better already. It was obviously just going to be the three of us tonight and everyone was being nice to me. The silly child had indeed been forgiven.

Susie's shopping didn't take long. The fish market provided nearly all the ingredients for her Louisiana gumbo – 'Grammy's recipe' – and after we'd bought some bread and fruit and cheese we went to a café to while away the time until we were to meet Carlos for lunch.

As much as I was desperate to find out what had happened with Raoul, whether Carlos had discussed

186

me with her, and if they had finished off the night after Raoul had gone, I was chastened enough to wait for her to raise the subject. Not surprisingly, she read my mind.

'Go ahead, hon, I know you're just dying to ask me what happened last night.' She was smiling with barely suppressed amusement.

'Yeah, well, quite honestly I feel a bit of a fool,' I explained. 'I almost expected Carlos to have my bags packed this morning. The best thing I can do is speak when I'm spoken to, I reckon.'

She squeezed my hand. 'Don't worry your head about it, darlin'. He was mad last night but mainly because he thought he'd come close to upsetting Señor Delgado. Once it was all just fine he calmed down.'

'What happened then?' I shot her a sideways glance but she shook her head.

'I think he is planning to tell you about that later. And since you're afraid to ask, the big guy wasn't too bad.'

'Did you know I was supposed to be your lesbian hooker plaything?'

Susie laughed delightedly. 'Do I know? It was my idea. Carlos told me before I came down here that he was going to introduce you as his English cousin, so they wouldn't get any ideas that you could be part of any deal. But then when he said you wanted a scene with me and you liked an audience but didn't want anything to do with the guys I came up with the lesbian whore idea. It quite amused me, though I'll keep my mouth shut in future as it could have got us into trouble.'

'Oh Christ. So all along Carlos was going to protect me?'

'Sure, hon.' Her eyes watched me shrewdly. 'What kind of guy do you think he is?'

I declined to answer that one directly. 'But, Susie, you had to put out for Mr Big. What kind of guy expects his assistant to do that?'

She raised her eyebrows. 'The kind who gets his assistant a profit-sharing deal, and listens to her when she suggests that if money and freebies won't do the trick, something else might, I guess.'

So she wasn't forced into whoring, but had volunteered for it. I could understand it if you fancied one of the guys you needed to bribe – after all I'd had a few thoughts myself about Miguel – but not with someone like Raoul.

'But why can't you just get a girl in? I mean, someone presumably cleans your office but you get a cleaner, right? You don't say, OK this is a job I can do myself so I will.'

She laughed appreciatively at the analogy. 'That's true. Look at it this way. Say you owned an old and expensive car, like a vintage Rolls Royce, and you were an expert mechanic. Would you take your precious car to an unknown garage for a service just so you didn't get your hands dirty?'

'Well –'

'No, you wouldn't. And when we're dealing in big bikkies like here, there's no way I'm prepared to risk some whore upsetting anyone when I can do her job better myself.'

Fair enough. She explained that without Raoul's land and his influence on other landowners the whole deal would come to nothing. It was obviously in his interests to help the project, as he was getting a good price for acres of land he wasn't getting anything out of, but he had been reluctant to help with their negotiations with the others – until last night.

'So is that it? You won't have to do a replay?'

She grinned. 'He said he'd be interested in seeing me with my lesbian whore next time he was in Santiago.'

'Oh God,' I groaned. 'You'll have to get another girl in.'

'No problem.'

I realised what she'd said. 'Santiago? That's in the Hostal de Arte, right? You've got an office there.'

'That's it. Having an office in a hotel makes my little incentive schemes quite easy to put into practice, of course.'

'Sure.' My sluggish brain seemed to be functioning better. 'So is Jorge involved in your company, then? I've forgotten what it's called; ETA?'

'ETP. Yes, he does some jobs for us, and we use the studio for meetings sometimes.' She looked at her watch. 'Time we went to the restaurant.'

Everything was going so well again. Susie and I seemed to be back on track; I'd got some more little snippets out of her about the development project and ETP, and she had implied that Carlos was going to give me a little description of last night's action, presumably as background to something steamy. But things didn't go well for long. As the three of us sat down at the restaurant table Red and Robbie appeared in the doorway and ambled over, calling my name. Carlos's face showed he was not at all pleased.

Just as he'd come round after my stupidity last night they'd gone and spoiled it. I tried to make faces to tell them to back off but Robbie was bending over Susie in full-on smarmy mode and Red was exclaiming over the coincidence of bumping into me so hammily that I shrank with embarrassment.

'Sorry I can't ask you to join us,' said Carlos pointedly. 'We were just about to order. But it was nice to see you again.'

They finally got the hint and went. I kept my eyes on the menu.

'I didn't realise you'd arranged to meet your fan club here, Bliss,' said Carlos in a tight voice.

'I didn't,' I said honestly. 'I left them in the Lake District and wasn't expecting to see them until the day before we get on the boat to Patagonia. How could I arrange to meet them when I didn't even know which town we'd be staying in? It's a coincidence, but not a very odd one.'

He couldn't argue with that, but neither did it convince him. Susie tried to mollify him and he smiled at her little stories about the making of gumbo, but I could tell he was not a happy bunny. At least, I consoled myself, he thought that the guys had come to the island to see me and didn't suspect they were here to pry into his business. That was the best scenario, so I stopped protesting my innocence and tried to join in the conversation.

'I'm really cross with you for spoiling our lunch, Bliss,' said Susie as we got out of the car back at the house. 'If you hadn't told those boys where you were going, we'd have had a really nice time. I think you ought to get some practice in keeping your mouth shut. Don't you agree, Carlos?'

The bastard, he answered her in Spanish. He was shaking his head and wrinkling his nose distastefully. She too switched languages and they threw the conversation backwards and forwards vigorously for a few minutes while I stood not knowing what to do except, of course, keep my mouth shut.

Maria ended their argument by coming out and telling Carlos he was wanted on the phone. With a final word he walked inside. Susie immediately grabbed my arm and frog marched me into the house.

'You're coming to my room, hon, and shutting up before you spoil anything else.'

She pulled her big suitcase out from under the bed and beckoned me over. Meekly I stood before her. I had guessed what was coming.

The gag wasn't too bad. She put it on carefully, with that little gleam of lust coming back to her eyes.

'Strip for me, please,' she said imperiously. There was no question of not obeying. After all, I'd been waiting twenty-four hours for her already.

She dressed me, if that was the word, in the black choker and gloves I'd worn for the first time for Carlos, fastening the gloves behind me, though not attaching them to the choker. Next came the black leather boots, except this time they too had chains around each ankle, which she clipped together, just as Carlos had hobbled my shoes in his apartment. She looked me up and down without a word, then suddenly jerked down one of the chains of the choker so that I was facing the ceiling.

'Don't upset him any more,' she whispered almost menacingly. 'I'm going to try to bring him round. Don't spoil it.'

With that she hooked a lead on to one of the chains and pulled me through the door. Instead of going straight to Carlos's room she led me into the kitchen, where Maria was stowing our shopping in the fridge. She turned towards us, a tiny smile on her face. I cringed at her look and cursed Susie for deciding I needed degrading as well as gagging.

Susie spoke to Maria in Spanish and I silently – not that I had any choice – thanked God that I couldn't understand. However, just as she finished she continued in English, obviously translating what she'd just said for my benefit. Or rather, for the benefit of my humiliation.

'Thanks for doing that, Maria. What do you think about our little puppy here? Isn't she the cutest thing you ever saw?'

Maria, who had smiled and been about to reply before Susie had spoken in English, answered. At least she couldn't translate for me. But Susie could.

'You think she looks ridiculous, but as you know that's what the señor likes. Now be honest, Maria, don't you like to look at her?'

The Spanish followed and Maria laughed her answer. Her little eyes were fixed on me as they had been the day before, and I realised she relished the English girl being humiliated like this.

'You think she's got a good body? Do you want to touch it?'

The maid's smile disappeared when that was repeated. She shrugged, and Susie carried on in Spanish, tweaking one of my nipples with one hand as she did so. Whether it was her action or what she said I couldn't tell but it made Maria laugh coarsely. She came close to me and I shivered. She smelled of tomatoes and onions and clothes worn once too often and stood so close I could count the lines on her face. I couldn't believe she would really touch me.

'I just told her that it didn't mean she was gay, any more than me, but she should see how shamelessly you enjoy anyone touching you.'

I felt Maria's hands brush my pubes and hoped she didn't feel the corresponding leap in my sex muscles. My eyes closed as Susie continued, 'I told her to stick her fingers up your vagina to see how wet it was.'

The rough, calloused fingers thrust inside me. I imagined they had just finished chopping garlic and unwrapping the fish we were to eat that night. It was awful, so awful that I couldn't help it: I groaned. Susie laughed at Maria's comments and answered her. The fingers pushed inside me again, once, twice, three times.

'Yes, she's got to be some slut to get that wet when an old woman touches her. Go on, do it again. Give the whore a treat.'

'Susie, you've gone quite far enough. Let her go.'

I raised my eyes to Carlos, totally shamed and humiliated. I expected his face to register either disgust or excitement, but instead he was looking at me with an expression of patience and regret. His face changed however when he barked something rapidly at Maria, which made her scuttle from the room. When he looked at Susie his face was dark with anger.

'I suppose I guessed it wouldn't be long before the bitch in you came out,' he said furiously. 'You choose to play the whore, Susie: no one makes you. You've got no right to take it out on Bliss. I told you to leave her be.'

He crossed the room and pulled me into his arms, hiding my scarlet face in his neck. 'I wish to God I'd never told you that story,' he continued to Susie. 'Anyway, you've done your job here, so just get back to the office. I don't really want you around for the next few days.' He turned back to me. 'I just want to be alone with Bliss.'

Chapter Nine

*I*t was a hard call deciding whether I should tell Red
and Robbie about the Susie and Maria incident. Every
time I recalled it colour flooded my face and I closed
my eyes in shame and disgust. To be fair to Carlos,
however, I wanted them to understand that however
much bribery and corruption he might be happy to
perpetrate, he hadn't tried to exploit me at all and in
fact had been my knight in shining armour as far as
that bitch Susie was concerned. I wouldn't have to tell
them how tenderly he had untied me and led me to the
shower so I could wash away all traces of Maria's
hands, and how sweetly he had made love to me to
wash away my humiliation, or how he had blamed
himself for telling Susie about the old man in the shanty
town. Or, of course, go into details about the rather
more hard-edged scenes we had over the next couple
of days while Maria took a little holiday.

I decided it was more scrupulous to tell them. I did
it quickly and with lowered eyes, adding, 'I'm hating
every minute telling you about this, but I just want you
to realise that Carlos isn't a complete sleazebag where

women are concerned. But it's over, end of story; don't mention it again.' And I burst into tears.

Red hugged me fiercely and Robbie slid off the other top bunk to put his arm over both of us. They were so sweet, and I felt such a girlie. I can't even remember the last time I cried; I think it was when the games teacher I had a desperate crush on left my school, about eighteen years ago. Mind you, as they both stroked me protectively I thought that after having been an object of degradation the prospect of playing the weak girlie was quite pleasant, and I made a mental note to consider changing my style when I got back to England.

We were on the boat to Patagonia. The previous afternoon we'd met in Puerto Montt and I'd been congratulated on the amount of information I had for them. Quite frankly I'd felt that apart from a couple of steamy encounters at the end of the week the whole thing had been a bit of a waste of time, but Red and Robbie seemed to think I'd done a good job. They were pleased with their own investigations, though kicked themselves for coming in to the restaurant. They had tailed Carlos from his meeting but not being experts at it feared he might have seen them, in which case it would have been more suspicious if they hadn't come in.

'Thanks to Franco and his pals we've got a pretty good file of sleaze, bribery and corruption stacked up against him,' Robbie had said excitedly. 'We've got plenty of photos of the site and tapes of interviews with people who've already been intimidated by Delgado and his cronies. Wheels are being set in motion already.'

Which is why I came clean the next day. We appeared to have struck lucky with the cabin. Of course, we weren't alone, but Michael, our fellow traveller, was a taciturn German who said how much he enjoyed sea travel and after putting his rucksack away went up on deck. Now three hours later we were still alone.

I cut the crying act and explained that I wanted to be fair to Carlos. 'I mean, what's going to happen to him when all his dealings are exposed? Don't tell me he deserves all he gets; he didn't do me any harm, and came to my rescue.'

Robbie laughed cynically. 'Please don't worry about him, Bliss. Look, we've done our job. But nothing at all may come of it. Even if we can get a public outcry about the project itself, there's never any mileage in naming individuals. It's the agency and the multinationals that employ them that we're after, not their employees. Let's face it, if he went someone else would take his place.'

I understood and was relieved by that part, but his first comment took me aback a bit.

'How can you think nothing might come of it? Surely once this is leaked there'll be questions asked all over the place?'

Red stroked my hair and looked up at Robbie. I could see they were thinking, oh bless.

'This sort of thing happens all the time,' said Robbie gently. 'If the public gave a toss about what corrupting influence companies like this have, don't you think we would have a few more reforms? But people are kicked off their land on the instructions of oil companies, virtually enslaved by sportswear manufacturers and have nuclear reprocessing plants planned for their back gardens. What's changed?'

Christ, I was depressed.

'But sometimes,' Red added, 'people do take notice. Very occasionally. And this might be one of them.'

'We have to try,' Robbie put in. 'Don't you agree?'

I nodded, but it was hard to understand how they could carry on such frustrating work.

'Anyway, we'll have a bit of a nose around Puerto Natales. There's a rumour going round that Patagonia could be phase two of Chile, the holiday resort,' said Red brightly. 'Never give up, Bliss.'

I was buggered if I could understand how they could be looking forward to another investigation that could be a total waste of time, but was impressed by their dedication.

Thanks to Michael the German's fascination with the ship's engine room we had a brilliant couple of days on the top bunk of the cabin. He only came back to sleep, by which time we too were snoring; at least the boys were. It hadn't been too bad in the tent where I could reach out and turn them over, which usually shut them up, but in the cabin I just had to put up with it. Luckily I was usually sated enough to ignore the symphony of snores and sink into oblivion myself. The exception was the third night where thanks to rough seas we all queued outside the toilet for our turn to be sick. So much for my confident assertion that I was a good sailor.

We hit Puerto Natales a few days before Christmas, which to my relief meant that phase two of foiling Carlos's plans were put on hold so we could spend the holiday in the national park. Pasta and instant soup wasn't the ideal Christmas dinner, so we bought a couple of cartons of wine and some fruit cake as a festive addition to normal rations. We were leaving a lot of our stuff in the guesthouse, so we had room in the rucksacks for a few luxuries. We spent two nights stoking up on steak and fish dinners, beer and pisco sours before we set off.

The Torres del Paine are three granite rocks sculpted by nature into massive, perfect phalluses – I kid you not. As we got off the bus and walked towards them they sparkled in the afternoon sun. We were going to spend the night at a campsite as near as possible to the towers and walk up to the best viewpoint before dawn to see them blushing pink in the sunrise.

For the first time for ages I felt completely happy. I might have glossed over it but there's no doubt that being a spy is a touch stressful, especially when you're also dealing in unusual sexual practices. Now that Red and Robbie were happy with the Chiloe investigation and we were just going to be walking and sharing the tent together for a few days, not to mention celebrating Christmas, I felt like the old carefree Bliss. I almost skipped up to the campsite. Well, that's not quite true because the path was a bit steep and although I may have given the impression that I hotfooted my way effortlessly through the Inca Trail I'm not really that sporty.

A few tents were dotted around the campsite, which was in an idyllic position, sheltered by trees. We walked around the site to assess the best spot but were stopped in our tracks by the sight of a fox sidling around between the tents.

Silently we watched it circling each tent, none of us daring to move in case we scared it away. I was surprised when, turning, it seemed to know we were there. I don't know what a fox's eyesight is like, but I suspect it could smell us. Rather than fleeing, which I would have expected, it stood looking at us.

'Don't worry, you won't frighten it off. It's used to being fed by tourists,' said a voice behind us. The guys turned with animated faces to talk to the stranger, but I didn't have to. Carlos's voice was easily recognisable.

The change in expression on Red and Robbie's faces was quite comical, but I had other things on my mind; like, what was he doing here?

He kissed me on both cheeks after shaking hands with the guys.

'I couldn't decide how I wanted to spend Christmas. Seeing you has made me homesick for England, and as I couldn't get over there I thought the next best thing would be to come down here and spend it with my favourite English person.'

He was looking sincere and I wanted to believe him, especially after the last three days we'd spent together. But I knew Red and Robbie would pour scorn on any suggestion that he really did just come to be with me, and I could hardly blame them.

Robbie's eyes had moved back to the fox, which was trotting over to a man squatting by a tent, holding a morsel of food in his hand.

'Isn't it amazing how his natural instinct to avoid human beings goes on hold when someone offers him a piece of bread or cheese.'

Carlos shrugged. 'That's what happens when you're hungry. And not just to animals.'

Robbie nodded slowly. 'Hungry – or greedy. I guess you're right, humans or animals, we're all quick to overcome our fears, or even morals, if the price is right.'

It was as if he'd said, we know what you're about, but Carlos was completely unfazed. I told myself he may not have caught Robbie's drift.

Carlos smiled faintly. 'Anyway, I hope you don't mind me being here. I've got a proposition to put to you.'

He indicated a large tent near the back of the campsite, on the edge of the wood. I'd noticed it before, because it must have been big enough to stand up in. Trust Carlos to have the best tent on the site.

'Shall we dine together?' he suggested formally, as though we had all met up by chance outside the Ritz. 'I saved a space next to my tent for you, so after you've pitched yours let's share resources. I'm only going to be around for a couple of days so I had room to pack some wine in my sack.'

He looked at his watch. 'I'm going for a stroll now. I'm afraid the weather's going to break, so just in case I don't get up to the viewpoint in the morning I'll at least have seen something of the towers. Why don't you bring your food over in a couple of hours' time? If it should rain, there's plenty of room in my tent for all of us.'

'Great,' I said briskly. Red looked as though he was about to prevaricate and it seemed best to get rid of Carlos so we could at least discuss him alone. 'See you later.'

I pecked him on the cheek, suspecting he was the only man in the whole of the national park who smelled faintly of expensive cologne.

We put up the tent without a word and laid out our bedrolls and sleeping bags. I put the plastic sheet down in the doorway and Red and Robbie sat on it, looking up at me.

'So? You think I shouldn't have said, OK, we'll come to dinner at yours?' I asked, slightly exasperated by their look.

'Bliss, you didn't – you didn't invite him, did you?' asked Red quietly.

'Oh for fuck's sake.' I was really quite cross. 'You think I wouldn't have told you? No, scrap that remark. You really think that I would have invited him in the first place? Surely that's ridiculous enough, never mind doing it and not telling you.'

I plonked myself down on the sheeting and gave them an evil look. 'You turn up in Chiloe and he thinks it's my doing, now he turns up here and you suspect I invited him. Doesn't anyone trust me?'

'OK, calm down,' said Robbie. 'Of course we trust

you. But it's a bit surprising that he's arrived here on the same day as us.'

'I was thinking about that as we put up the tent,' I admitted. 'But let's face it he knew which day we were sailing on, and if he doesn't suspect you're out to do a little undercover work in Puerto Natales he could easily have worked out that we'd be here today at the latest. After all, it's not the most exciting town in the world, is it?'

'He can't spend all his time deducing where you'll be and when. Don't forget that's how he said he found you in San Pedro,' said Robbie thoughtfully. 'He admitted he had you followed in Bolivia. What's to say that ever stopped?'

A shiver went through me at the thought that I'd been stalked for weeks, but I dismissed it. 'No, he did that for my protection. Honestly, I believe him. And I think you should give yourselves credit for noticing if we'd been tailed all along.'

Carlos wasn't out to harm me, I was sure of that. We sat in gloomy silence for a moment, then I had a brainwave.

'Got it!' I said triumphantly. 'We booked the bus tickets the day before we came. He wouldn't need to have us followed if he had a contact working for the bus company.'

The guys agreed that was quite inspired. We certainly knew that Carlos had plenty of contacts in various places.

'So, not necessarily sinister. He really might have just wanted to join us and phoned a friend.'

Red and Robbie didn't look relieved in the slightest, however. I started to lose patience with them.

'Look, you don't really believe he's followed us to do us some harm for trying to expose him, do you?'

201

They didn't answer.

'Well, do you?' I repeated.

'I guess I do,' admitted Red. 'He's turned up here to have a nice family Christmas. Can you buy that? And I think we're all forgetting he said he's got a proposition for us.'

Robbie smiled crookedly. 'Let's cool it and assume for now that he's going to propose that Bliss sleeps with him rather than us. The little shit – I hope you say no. But apart from that, look at all this.'

He gestured at the tents dotting the campsite. Even as we'd been putting up our tent and talking more people had turned up, obviously with the same plan as us. Others had come down the path from the viewpoint, exclaiming how beautiful it was, and were diving into the tents that had been unoccupied when we arrived.

'It's going to be a pretty full house here. He might have expected to be able to threaten us in some way, but with all these people around he's got no chance of getting away with it.'

Stubbornly, I couldn't believe that Carlos was out to harm us. 'He is *not* going to threaten us,' I said fiercely. 'I'm telling you he won't hurt me, I know it. He – he's fond of me.'

God, that was hard to say to the guys, because I knew how fond of me they were too. I just wanted to get them to relax rather than waiting for Carlos to pounce on me at any minute. If he was up to something we'd find out sooner or later, and not only were we three against one but frankly we were all somewhat bigger than him.

Dinner was most pleasant. As Carlos was only spending four days in the park as opposed to our eight I had no compunction in rifling through his food. He was obviously not an experienced tramper, having brought impractically heavy things such as cans of corned beef and soft things such as a hunk of truffled pate. Seeing as that was already squashed into a formless lump I decided we might as well have it as an hors d'oeuvre before the pasta with instant sauces. After one of his litre cartons of wine the sporadic conversation livened up a bit and once we started on the second carton – the guys were all for saving it for the next day but I overruled them – I found myself explaining how lucky we were at getting Michael the German as our cabin mate.

'Obviously we wanted a bit of privacy.' I looked Carlos straight in the eyes and, OK, I was flirting. As I said, I'm turning into a bad girl; having all three of my lovers round the metaphorical dinner table had rather turned me on.

My hint hadn't gone unnoticed.

'It seems a good time to discuss my proposition,' said Carlos softly. 'I guess you guys are a bit pissed off that I've turned up just as you're going to share a few nights with Bliss. Or share Bliss for a few nights.'

'Or share a few nights of bliss,' I added childishly.

'I'm sure they will be. Especially as she has been staying with me for a week, although we encountered a couple of little problems. Which she may have told you about.'

'That's right, mate,' said Red aggressively. 'She tells us everything – make no mistake about it.'

'Yes, including how you got rid of Susie-cow,' I said, touching Carlos's arm. 'Not to mention that I was a complete tosser, thinking you were going to use me as a prostitute. And that I led you on about wanting an audience.'

'Not so loud, Bliss,' grinned Robbie. 'Are you pissed?'

203

'Just relaxed,' I said defensively. 'Anyway, proposition away, Carlos.'

His eyes were on mine. 'You told them about Susie. So they know that the only time I've been the spectator was unwillingly.' His eyes moved to Robbie. 'I want to play your part. But I want to watch both of you with Bliss. And I want her tied up.'

'Jeez.' Red sounded as though he was about to burst out with outraged refusals but Robbie waved his hand for silence.

'You only want to watch? Bliss will be tied up but we'll be free? Is that why you've got such a big tent?'

Carlos had nodded to the first two and laughed his assent to the last. Of course in his job he's used to planning in advance, I thought, half amused.

'I've never fucked Bliss,' Robbie stated baldly. 'If that's what you want, she's got to agree.'

'It's about time you did,' I said, putting as little inflection in my voice as I could. God knows how long I'd been wanting him to! Even when we played the no limits game he'd hung back from it, and on the boat Robbie had watched from his top bunk as Red and I screwed in the other. In fairness to Red, however, I didn't want to sound too desperate.

'Red?'

He stirred uneasily. 'I'm not keen. It's one thing having your mate there, but I'm not used to performing in front of strangers. Not to mention having her tied up.'

'That's essential, and I don't mean just from a selfish viewpoint,' said Carlos. 'I know Bliss will like it. Won't you?'

His face was close to mine and his dark eyes hypnotised me, but not as much as his words. 'Tied up, being screwed by your two lovers, one for the first time, with someone watching. Someone who also wants you.

Watching and wanting, but not having. Don't disappoint me by saying you're not interested.'

Fat chance of that. 'Maybe I'm disappointed that you're not going to join in,' I said archly.

'Insatiable slut,' said Robbie with a smile on his face, and I knew we were on. He'd started already.

'That sounds good,' said Carlos, his eyes narrowing. 'I've heard you provide the commentary too.'

'Why won't you join in, Carlos?' I asked. OK, I am an insatiable slut.

He looked thoughtfully at Red. 'I will if you want me to – after,' he said obliquely.

'After what?'

'Well, I would like a little rôle play. You're going to be tied up. All that's missing is an element of coercion.'

'Oh, fuck off. I'm not going to bloody well rape her,' said Red.

'No,' said Carlos quickly. 'Just ... let's say she's willing, but not enthusiastic? Let's say the scenario is that she's agreed to be tied up by her boyfriend but didn't know his friend was coming round. And that ... somehow –' he looked at Robbie '– she's talked into letting the friend join in.'

He sounded like a TV producer putting ideas into words in a brainstorming session. I'm thinking rape, no, that's too violent, I'm thinking gangbang – marvellous, darling ...

'Have you brought your dressing-up clothes?' asked Robbie.

'Some things.' Carlos nodded. 'So? Are we on?'

I was most definitely on, even if it meant I had to swap roles and help the other two tie the reluctant Red to the tent frame and rape him, no sorry, gangbang him. But finally he nodded agreement, and before everyone started shuffling around wondering how to start I sent the guys down to the stream with the dirty pots and dishes while I snatched some quality time with Carlos.

'Is this for me? Or you?' I asked as soon as the others were out of earshot. 'Or is there another agenda here?'

'It's for both of us. It's because you'll be going home in a couple of weeks' time. It's because I might never see you again. It's because I really had nothing to do for Christmas. And not least, just for the hell of it.'

He drew me inside the tent and we kissed. His tongue explored my mouth insistently but tenderly, redolent of the lover he had been after the Maria incident. Strange really, when you consider he'd just asked me to play at being tied up and gangbanged by two other men while he watched.

'Heard from Susie?'

'Of course. She's running the office.' His face clouded over. 'I'll be back in Lima within a month. I guess we'll make up, but I'll never forget what she did to you.'

'Well, maybe it wasn't such a big deal.'

He snorted. 'She doesn't know where to draw the line, or rather she takes a sadistic delight in ignoring it. Power is one thing. Using it cruelly is another.'

'Pretend cruelty's different, though.'

Carlos picked up a black bag from the top of his rucksack. 'Talking of which . . .'

Ten minutes later I was dancing close – I mean *very* close – to Red, who was playing my boyfriend. He got into the spirit of the thing by feeling me up as I rubbed myself around him and he then undid the buttons of my shirt. I pulled it back to expose the front-lacing black basque that Carlos had brought for me, running my hands over my tits and offering them to Red. Robbie and Carlos looked on and, feeling like a stripper, I tossed off my shirt and unzipped my trousers. Wiggling my hips I pulled them down and stepped out of them, now wearing only the basque and a black G-string.

Although it was Red's hand I placed between my legs it was Robbie and Carlos I was gyrating for. I'd been worried that Red wasn't going to be able to perform with Carlos there but Red was facing away from him and as he fingered me, feeling my increasing wetness seeping on to the scrap of silk, I reckoned he was going to be fine.

I unzipped him and his penis sprang out, almost ready for me. Stroking it gently I coaxed it to its normal hugeness, luxuriating in showing off the length and circumference of it to Carlos. Did he feel jealous? As Red got his combats off completely I kneeled and took him in my mouth, licking up the shaft and then opening my mouth wide to take him in. His hands kneaded my shoulders and reached down to my nipples.

Partly because I wanted that huge cock inside me again and partly because I wanted to get on with the show, I lay on my back and undid the bows on each side of the G-string so that it fell off me.

'Fuck me.'

As Red rubbered up I turned towards Robbie and Carlos, drawing my knees up and showing them my cunt. It had started to twitch in anticipation and I wondered if they could see. It also occurred to me that as Robbie hadn't come on set yet, as it were, Carlos might appreciate a bit of commentary from me. And let's face it, I would appreciate it myself.

'Get your big cock inside me,' I said lazily, stroking my clit, but before he could get down to it I turned sideways so that Carlos and Robbie would have more than Red's arse and my waving legs to watch.

My moan as he entered me wasn't faked. He was so big that I couldn't help it: every time was the same. He moved slowly at first then as I expanded around the huge girth of his cock I raised my legs and put them over his shoulders.

'You're so bloody big. You fill me right up,' I breathed. 'Oh Christ. What do I feel like?'

'Bloody wonderful,' he said, his face on my tits as I teased my nipples for him.

'Do my tits look nice in this?'

He nodded. Red wasn't one for verbal intercourse, but then as he had Robbie for that side of things I guess it wasn't important.

His thrusts got deeper and faster and I guessed he was going to come soon. I wondered when Robbie would make his appearance as the 'friend'; we'd hardly had time to rehearse. I looked sideways and could see him, absorbed in watching me roll my nipples between my fingers.

Red's hand moved to my clitoris but I stopped him. 'Not yet. I want you to concentrate on coming.' Moving my hands away from my breasts I reached down to his balls. Because of his size it wasn't easy to reach but I stroked him a few times as he upped the rhythm and came with what almost sounded like a sob in his throat. After he had finished I put my legs down and held him.

'Maybe I've chosen the wrong moment to interrupt.'

Robbie came towards us and stood looking down, his face amused. I was quite impressed by his script.

Red looked up and smiled. 'G'day, mate. No worries, I've just finished.'

He lifted himself off me and sat back, legs crossed, and yawned. 'I've got to finish Bliss off, but that can wait.'

Robbie looked me over almost clinically. 'Let her do it for herself. I wouldn't mind watching.'

'Piss off,' I retorted. 'I don't need to do it for myself,

thanks very much. Anyway, I definitely wouldn't do it in front of you.'

'Why not?' He sat down and smiled at me impudently and complicitly. 'Go on, I've never seen a girl wank herself off before. He won't mind – will you, mate?'

Red grinned. 'Wouldn't mind seeing it myself. You've got a perverted mind, Rob.'

'Don't you really care if he watches?' I asked, realising I should stop acting so hammily; my voice sounded like I was auditioning for *Eastenders*.

Red shook his head.

'Doesn't look like you're that important to him,' said Robbie insolently. 'Just another slut, eh, Red?'

'Shut it,' I said, trying to put conviction into my voice.

'Go on, slut. Get your fingers down there and let's see how fast you can make yourself come. Or do you want me to do it for you?'

'No,' I said as positively as I could.

'So do it for yourself. Here, I'll help you.'

He pulled my legs apart and, after running his eyes up and down my gaping sex, shook his head and laughed. 'God, you're soaking wet down there. You really are a horny little bitch, aren't you?'

Yes, yes, yes! everything in me cried out, especially when he motioned Red round to hold one of my legs. Their hands sent jolts of electricity straight upwards as they grasped my thighs.

'Go on,' ordered Robbie. 'Or I will.' He looked at his watch. 'Ready, steady, go. See how fast you can do it.'

My sex muscles were already twitching and if it wasn't for the fact that I felt weak with desire and my hands were trembling slightly I reckon it would have been about thirty seconds flat. As it was I took him literally and rubbed myself in what you could describe as a workmanlike fashion. Their restraining hands and their eyes on me meant that it really didn't take long, and although I couldn't see Carlos I knew he was watching. I moaned as the orgasm tore through me.

'Jesus, you know how to come,' Robbie said, his voice rough and intimate. 'I wouldn't mind feeling that round my prick. Is she always like that, mate?'

'For sure,' said Red. 'Go on, have her if you like.'

'Excuse me!' I was in indignant mode again. 'It's up to me.'

Robbie sighed. 'You know you want it. You're a dirty little tramp, aren't you? The way you did that; don't tell me you don't make a habit of it. You'd fuck anything. You're just putting on an act because you think lover boy won't like it. Aren't you?'

'Don't mind me, Bliss,' said Red.

'I'll tell you what, if it makes you feel better, I'll tie you up and you can pretend you don't want it. How about that?'

Now I could think straight again after my relief I was full of admiration for Robbie. Not only was he acting like a pro, he'd scripted a play within a play. I decided that my next line was silence, which could be taken for acquiescence or otherwise, and waited motionless while Robbie picked something from the floor. I sighed as I saw the black leather ties, not with desire, because after my orgasm I felt temporarily sated, but with longing for the freedom of the chains.

Had he taken a quick lesson from Carlos? First he bound my wrists and then, lifting my arms above my head, wrapped the leather methodically round them as far as it would reach. I didn't see how else he could tie me, as there was nothing to attach me to in the tent apart from the thin wire of the frame. The basque was already moulded round my breasts, and it would hardly serve his purpose to tie my legs together. But instead he wrapped it twice around my belly, just above my pubes, and knotting it behind he ran it down the crease of my arse and tied it round my left thigh. I could feel it rub against my anus as he laid me down and wrapped the last leather band around my ankle several times, knotting it and then tying it around the only heavy item in the tent, Carlos's rucksack.

His face had been lost in concentration as he went methodically about his work but, having finished, he looked at me and smiled. The smile was a mask, part of the role he was playing, but I could see that beneath the smile his face was heavy with wanting. My sex muscles started to throb and I felt my own eyes narrowing with desire. I heard, or maybe imagined, Carlos breathing heavily and Red stirred, maybe slightly uneasily but also infected by the almost oppressive atmosphere that suddenly pervaded the tent.

'It's not up to you any more, Bliss,' said Robbie, his voice seeming rougher and louder in the steamy silence. 'I'm going to do exactly what I want. And you know what? I want to fuck you. Is that OK?'

'You just said I can't stop you,' I breathed.

'I don't think you understand what I mean. I wanted you to say that it was OK. That it was very OK, in fact that you want me to.' His voice was almost menacing.

'I do,' I said faintly. 'I do want you to.'

He was taking his jeans off. 'Please.'

'Please,' I repeated. 'Please fuck me.'

He rolled the condom over his hard cock. I remembered the taste of it so well and how good it had felt in my mouth. At last I was going to feel it inside me, and without prompting I repeated my plea.

'I want you to screw me. Please.'

His face was close to mine; I felt us breathe the same atoms of air that was already moist from the condensation that was building up inside the tent. I knew Red and Carlos were also affected by the electricity between us and as Robbie pulled my body forward so that my bound leg bent at the knee I raised my hips, offering myself to him, and symbolically to all three of them.

'Do you really want me, or would anybody do?' he asked.

I guessed at my line. 'Anybody.'

'Slut.'

My muscles quivered at the word. We smiled at each other; we were still playing our parts despite the haze of desire that engulfed us. I sighed as he entered me.

At last. He moved slowly but deeply inside me. I looked at his face and wished I could see myself, my arms raised supplicatingly above my head, my sex outlined in black, my ankle chained to the heavy bag. He had finally got his wish to see me bound and I wondered how he felt now.

'Do you like being tied up?' he asked me.

'Yes. Do you like having me tied up?' I countered.

'Yeah. You're helpless. I can do whatever I want with you.'

'I don't care: you can anyway.'

'Even a slag like you must have some limits.'

Slag, that's me. I felt my sex start to swell.

'No limits.'

I deliberately repeated Red's words of only two weeks before. Robbie pushed faster inside me and I was sure he remembered them too. His fingers reached down and stroked my clitoris softly while he watched my face. I nodded my approval and his fingers rubbed firmly and surely and he watched me as I came. I saw the surprise on his face and realised that though they'd both teased me about how violently my muscles contracted in orgasm, it was the first time he'd felt it with his cock. As he came he whispered my name and I managed to keep it going for as long as he lasted, feeling like a virgin.

Robbie sat back breathlessly. I knew we had to continue with the show but I was in no state for anything. He squeezed my mons just as I had finished, trying to suck the last faint vibrations from my orgasm, setting off that tingling afterglow feeling.

'Must be your turn again, mate,' he said to Red. Funny, the thought of Red fucking me again seemed like a violation, whereas we'd started off with him as the legitimate one. Still, this was Carlos's treat. I had been the first to agree to it and I could hardly pull out now.

'I'll have her from behind this time,' said Red. He turned me over, detaching my foot from the rucksack first and carefully tying it again after moving it to the other side. I couldn't judge what he had thought about the last scene. I just hoped he hadn't chosen that position because he couldn't bear to face me.

He moved me on to my knees and elbows and positioned himself behind me. 'Nice one,' he said, rubbing his hand along the leather band in the crease of my arse. Without any further preliminaries or even his usual tentative thrusts he pushed his thick length straight inside me.

'You've got to admit I'm bigger than him,' he said as he rode me hard.

'You are big. So thick, it almost hurts.'

'Do you want to be hurt?' asked Robbie from just behind my left shoulder. I guessed he was watching Red's prick stretch me open just as he had so many times before.

'No,' I said with emphasis. 'I just want to be fucked.'

I felt Red's hands round my hips, pulling me back on to his thrusts by the black leather. Sliding my arms forward I dropped my head to the ground submissively, abandoning myself to the big hands that pulled me on to the big cock, enjoying the passivity and anonymity of the position. I wondered what Carlos was thinking and whether he was as turned on as he had obviously expected to be.

'Get her to make you hard again,' Red suggested, nodding to Robbie. 'Let's watch her suck you.'

I wondered if Robbie also had déjà vu as he moved round in front of me and offered his cock to my mouth. Red gave me room to lift my head slightly so that I could start to coax Robbie's prick back to stiffness with my tongue. I was surprised to feel that it had already started to rise and was quickly hardening.

'Want to change places, mate?' asked Red, just as he had before. Again Robbie refused. Red seemed to be lasting forever but he'd come once already.

Carlos came closer; I suppose this was what he had wanted to see, me with both the guys at once.

Red had scooped up some of my moisture and, moving aside the leather band, started rotating his little finger gently in my arse. I wriggled with pleasure.

'Why don't I take her up the arse? You could fuck her cunt at the same time. How about that for closeness, mate?'

'No!' I spluttered, though as Robbie's now ramrod stiff prick was halfway down my throat nobody heard. Red's finger pushed in further and I squirmed again.

'She's loving my finger there. What do you think?'

Fortunately Robbie withdrew his cock to watch Red's finger at work.

'I said no,' I repeated firmly.

'You said no limits,' Robbie reminded me.

'But I didn't mean *that.*'

'You said I could do anything to you. Admit it, you're loving it, you little whore.'

Shit. He was playing the stupid bloody game again

214

and I was about to be anally raped. Of course, he didn't know that I really meant no this time, but Red knew only too well I wasn't into that. If he was so carried away with his desires he was going to go through with it regardless, Robbie and Carlos would assume my complaints were merely play-acting. In short, I'd be both literally and metaphorically buggered.

Red's huge prick was still thrusting into me and now he had his index finger in my anus. I felt slightly sick; Red had objected to the rape scenario and now he seemed to be on the verge of really raping me.

Once again I'd gone ahead with something impetuously only to find myself in trouble. With Robbie watching the action from behind I couldn't make eye contact. I was going to have to stop this.

But before I could formulate my words Red slowed his rhythm and pulled out of me. For one awful moment I thought he was going to carry out his threat but instead he untied my foot from the rucksack and turned me on to my back.

'Did I scare you?' he said intimately, reaching out to rub my clit. 'You thought I was serious?'

'Yes, I did, you bastard,' I gasped. 'I was really afraid you meant it.'

His blue eyes looked at me thoughtfully as he continued to manipulate me the way he knew I liked.

'I thought you'd like a frisson of fear. I wondered if you'd think I'd really go through with it.'

He ran his fingers gently and then firmly from my clit down to my arse alternately. My body started to shudder. Now I was out of danger I was enjoying the fear retrospectively.

'Come on, Bliss. I think we all like watching you come more than anything.' His fingers slowed and kept me hovering on the brink of my climax. I was afraid that I'd lose it if he didn't move faster but he was concentrating on unrolling the johnny with his other hand. It fell to the floor and he changed hands, putting his slippery wet one round his cock and the other on me. As he upped the speed on my clit he moved his other hand fast. His come felt hot as it splashed on my face and a split second later the muscles of my pussy heaved and rearranged themselves like mountains being thrown up by rock shifts during the Ice Age. My gasping mouth got its fill of his semen and I opened it wider and licked round my lips to take down as much as I could. I never swallow, but somehow I felt I owed him one.

I'd almost forgotten Carlos, but Robbie hadn't. Hard again, he sat on the ground just in front of Carlos, lifting me on to his cock. I felt like a rag doll, hardly over the sensation of my orgasm at Red's hands before I was hauled on to another prick. I guessed that Robbie was giving Carlos what he thought he wanted; but also he was putting Carlos in the position he was himself accustomed to, that of the one in the line of vision rather than the one with the penis. Personally I was sated, but Carlos was close enough for me to read his expression and I knew he was pleased. As Robbie slammed me down on to his reawakened hardness I wet my lips like a page three girl and after rising up on his shaft I wriggled my hips for Carlos, not that Robbie didn't appreciate it by the sound he made in his throat.

'Can I have one more request? I'd like Bliss to sleep with me tonight,' asked Carlos, addressing his question to Robbie but looking into my eyes.

'Sure,' said Robbie. 'OK, Bliss?'

'Fine by me,' I said, still lost in those dark brown eyes. Were we going to have one last screw?

Robbie came but I was more interested in the face in front of me, and I knew that was exactly how I treated

Red when Robbie was watching. My body was welded to one guy but my mind was being fucked by another.

The boys went to our tent shortly after and fetched back my mat and sleeping bag. It had started raining, and they were gloomy about our prospects for seeing the towers the next morning but set their alarm for six just in case. Carlos did the same and promised to wake me; my hands were tied.

Once they'd left Carlos came over and took off my basque and untied my wrists and arms.

'I wasn't expecting that,' I said, disappointed. Surely he'd been turned on watching? I *knew* he had been, for God's sake. Despite his predilection for postponing his satisfaction, I couldn't believe he could wait after what he'd just witnessed. Not that I wanted him for my own sake, you understand, but I wanted him to want me.

He laughed softly and gave me my T-shirt to put on, then refastened my wrists across my chest, just like he had on our first night together. Leaving the straps around my pubes and thigh he unwound the leather from my ankle and bound it round both. I thought I'd been mistaken in thinking he was going to postpone his pleasure, but no.

'I want to watch you sleep like this,' he said, half covering me with my sleeping bag. 'In the morning, we'll see.'

'We're going up the bloody mountain in the morning,' I said miserably. I suddenly felt I'd had enough of being watched.

'I doubt it,' he said drily. 'The rain's going to get worse. I'll set the alarm but I bet we'll get a lie-in. Then in the morning it might be my turn. If you want.'

He stroked my hair. 'You did enjoy it, didn't you?'

'You know I did. You did too.'

'Yes. Thanks.'

He was still watching over me when I fell asleep.

Like a guardian angel, I thought drowsily just before I dropped off.

The alarm shattered my peace at six in the morning.

'It's hopeless,' Carlos whispered after he turned it off. 'It's been raining all night. Go back to sleep and I'll tell the others.'

I did as I was told, still only half awake but drowsily remembering that Carlos was going to give me some attention when we woke properly.

In my dream Carlos was lashing out at Susie again, his voice steely and angry, but when Susie answered her voice sounded like Robbie's. He was shouting, and suddenly so was Red. I came to with the realisation that the argument wasn't inside my head but outside the tent and it was real. Carlos snapped something in a contemptuous tone and Robbie answered in fury. What the hell was going on?

Chapter Ten

Getting out of the sleeping bag with my arms tied across my chest and my ankles laced together wasn't easy. Luckily the zip was only done up half way so I managed to get my little fingernail in and pull it down.

I tried not to panic but once properly awake I could hear what they were saying and it wasn't pleasant. Carlos was mocking the guys' efforts at sabotaging his work in Chiloe.

'Your sort ought to realise what you're doing is a waste of time. Grungy kids and homeless New Agers trying to take on the real world? You'd make me laugh if it wasn't for the fact that you make me sick. Why don't you grow up, find jobs and get a proper life rather than interfere with decent people trying to do an honest day's work to feed their families?'

'Don't give me that decent shit,' said Robbie angrily. 'As you'll see now you've stolen our papers we know damn well how your clients are planning to staff their bloody holiday camp. Bringing in managers from the States and only offering menial jobs at criminal rates of pay for the locals; how decent is that?'

'Well, you haven't got the papers now, friend,' replied Carlos. 'And even if you had, what do you think you could do with information like that? It's not illegal. It's just the way the world works.'

'Only because it's perpetuated by conniving brokers like you,' sneered Robbie. 'And legal doesn't mean the same thing as moral. Not that I suppose you'd be able to tell the difference.'

I'd managed to get my legs out of the bag but realised that standing up with hands and feet bound was impossible. I rocked forward a few times but my attempts to stand on my feet were hopeless. For the hundredth time I wished I'd done my preparation for the trip in the gym rather than the hairdressers.

Giving up I started shuffling forward on my side. At least my experience as a slug was coming in handy.

'What do you think you were doing last night?' asked Carlos. 'Do you think that was moral?'

'Don't you even think about trying to make us feel guilty about that,' snapped Red. 'We did it for Bliss because she wanted to do it for you. It was your idea. And how you can accuse us of immorality while you're holding a gun on us beats me.'

I stopped wriggling towards the door. In fact, everything stopped, like my breathing, and I wondered if that thump in my chest could have been a heart attack.

Fortunately I managed to restart both my breathing and my brain function. So: Carlos was holding a gun on Red and Robbie. He knew about their investigation and had stolen their papers. I was bound hand and foot. It didn't take a genius to work out that we were up shit creek. And when Carlos spoke again it seemed like it was going to get worse.

'By the time the ranger gets back you could be in serious trouble. Without shelter, clothes, food and water, you might not last very long. He won't think there's any reason to get back here, so he'll be busy launching the search for Bliss.'

Great. The boys were going to die of hypothermia and starvation, but at least I knew what their prospects were. What was that bit about searching for me? Where was he going to take me?

But even more puzzling, what about the other campers? Were they all up the mountain, or did they think it was street theatre?

Suddenly the tent door opened and Carlos came in, or as far as he could without stepping on me. He had a sheaf of papers and films in his hands and through the door I could see why he was talking about not lasting long without clothes. The ground was white with snow and it was still falling.

'Carlos, what's going on?' I pleaded.

'I suppose I should have asked you that question before,' he said cynically. 'I know you know what they were up to. There were a couple of times in our relationship when I might have expected you to confess, but obviously the relationship I thought we had was just another way of keeping me under surveillance.'

My mouth opened to protest but he crushed his lips on to mine in a brief kiss. Before I could decide whether I should try to bite him or seduce him he moved away.

'I don't think we've really got time for that,' he said blandly. 'I've got to get on, I'm afraid. The park ranger thinks you wandered off in the early hours so he's gone down to raise the alarm and get a search party going. I don't expect he'll be back for some time, as nobody's going to think of looking here, but I'd really rather get out of the park as quickly as possible.'

He stuffed Robbie's file and the films into his rucksack.

'What's this about a gun?'

'Thanks for reminding me.'

It was true. He took a pistol from inside his jacket and placed that too in the rucksack, then picked up everything else in the tent.

'What happened to everyone else?' I asked faintly, half imagining a massacre.

He shrugged. 'They woke up at the crack of dawn to the white-out. The ranger was advising people to get down the mountain as quickly as possible in case it got worse. The last ones left about an hour ago.'

'But you can't have planned this,' I said, half to myself.

'I could hardly have organised a blizzard,' he said, amused. 'Of course I came to get the files, but I really was hoping to spend Christmas with you first. However, this opportunity was too good to miss.'

He started detaching the tent lining. 'I think you'd better get outside.' His voice was almost apologetic. 'I'm afraid I may need the tent again.'

'I'm having trouble moving,' I hissed.

His eyes moved down to my ankles as though he'd forgotten. 'Oh, I'm sorry. If it hadn't been for the snow I was going to enjoy you this morning. Still, you know how it is, Bliss, strike while the iron's hot and all that.'

Bending to my feet he picked at the knots in the leather and set my feet free. I aimed a kick at his head but he caught my foot in his hand. I wish I'd made better preparations for the trip, etc., though let's face it; even if I'd tried harder to get fit kickboxing wouldn't have been high on the list of techniques.

He was laughing at my efforts at self-defence.

'I'm not sure exactly what's so funny,' I said as haughtily as I could. Let's not forget here, I've got my arms crossed like a corpse and I'm wearing a leather belt up my bum. 'You're taking the tent down around me and leaving us to die in the snow with no shelter or clothes or food, is that right? And you're laughing?'

He sobered up. 'I'm not leaving you to die, Bliss. That was just a threat to get them going. Of course I wouldn't harm you. Or them, either. Come on, I'll get your clothes for you.'

Leading me by the straps around my arm he pulled me through the tent flap. Red and Robbie were tied back to back to each other and they were sitting in the doorway of their own tent. Carlos left me shivering at the door too and went inside the tent, coming out with my clothes. He put my trousers on for me and untied first one hand then another as he put my arms in my sweater and fleece, and then put socks and trainers on my feet. It was surreal; I was being dressed gently, like a child, by someone who had threatened to leave me for dead.

'The only thing I'm taking is your boots.' He was talking to all of us. 'You can try walking down if you like, but the snow's already deep and with only sandals and trainers I'm afraid you might not make it. My advice is to get back in the tent and keep warm till the ranger comes back. He'll come to the tent to tell you to leave because of the snow, so he won't miss you.'

Three pairs of boots were also stuffed into his rucksack. No wonder he'd been pleased to get rid of two cartons of wine and some food. He knew he'd be needing the space.

'Thanks for last night, guys,' he said airily as he shouldered his sack. 'And, Bliss, thanks for everything. You were pretty hot.'

We watched him walk through the campsite to the path. It was lucky we were under the trees; I could see the snow was much worse out in the open, falling thickly and horizontally across the mountainside opposite.

I looked at the boys. 'Not the best position to find ourselves in, eh?'

Robbie shrugged, a little smile at the corner of his mouth. 'Oh well. Shit happens.'

'You're very calm,' I observed acidly. 'Did you train at the feet of Houdini? Or have you suddenly discovered the appeal of submitting to bondage?'

His smile grew into a grin and then a laugh. 'There is a funny side, but I won't tell you until we're free. Now I've got pretty strong teeth and that leather round your wrist isn't that well knotted. Come over here and let me get my teeth into you.'

Two hours later we were romping down the mountain-side in high spirits. Or rather, we were tottering down the path with our inadequate footwear covered with plastic bags for insulation and socks for grip on the smooth snow. At least I had trainers; Red and Robbie's Tevas weren't ideal snowshoes, but our improvisation meant that at least our feet were dry.

I had started off extremely pissed off, despite Robbie managing to undo my ties with his teeth, leaving me able to untie the guys. He finally admitted that Carlos hadn't left their investigation with as many holes in it as he'd thought.

For one thing, the papers had already been copied and faxed to Red and Robbie's group in Australia, who had begun the process of trying to get media coverage of the plan to spoil Chiloe and the corruption it involved. Plus Carlos didn't even know about the tapes they'd made, which were already in the mail.

'But he's got your films,' I objected.

'Yes. Well – I don't really know how to tell you this.'

'What?' I asked crossly. 'I saw them. Three rolls of film.'

'Yep. Three rolls of what I expect is Bliss in Peru, Bliss in Bolivia and Bliss in San Pedro.'

The guys had been worried that Carlos might somehow get their spare gear out of store while we were away, which was why Robbie had the papers with him. Then at the last minute he had a brainwave and instead of taking his films he swapped them for three of mine.

'Sorry. Your holiday pics are going to be a bit disappointing.'

'Oh well. I did think they might launch me on a new career as a photographer, but perhaps that wasn't meant to be.'

So as I said, we were in reasonably high spirits, although I kept remembering with trepidation the steep, exposed section of the path that was some way ahead. Let's face it, I had already slid down one snowy mountainside on this trip, and that was wearing crampons and carrying an ice axe. Added to that I was starting to get pretty cold. The time we had sat immobile trying to free each other had meant the cold had seeped right into my bones. Thermal underwear hadn't been such a laughable idea as I'd thought. Still I kept my fears to myself, suspecting also that Red and Robbie weren't as carefree as they pretended to be.

The snow didn't seem to be easing up at all. We estimated it would take another two or three hours to get down to the refuge in the valley, hampered as we were by our footwear and the heavy going. Just as we consoled ourselves that the ranger might just return to his hut at the campsite after raising the alarm for the presumed-missing me, we saw a man walking swiftly up the path towards us.

'It's him!' I cried excitedly. 'He is going back! Thank God for that!'

We started waving at the advancing figure, who just carried on towards us at a brisk pace. As he reached us we saw that it wasn't the ranger at all, just a walker with a pack on his back.

'Hey! We've had our boots stolen! Can you help us?'

He stopped in his tracks and walked slowly towards us. 'Had your boots stolen? By whom?'

Amazingly he was English, a fit-looking middle-aged man with an alert expression and a public school drawl. Which may not actually have been a great advantage, because with inbred British scepticism he was eyeing us as though we were loonies. Maybe I forgot to mention that as I hadn't brought a woolly hat Red had given me his, and instead wrapped a spare T-shirt round his head under his hood, and Robbie hadn't had spare socks so had fastened underpants around his feet with the black leather ties. I guess it was also hard to believe that someone would be able to steal the boots from three strapping people like us, let alone why, and to be frank I felt quite embarrassed as Robbie explained that we were the victim of a multinational company's attempt to take over half an island.

As luck would have it when we explained about the ranger's wild goose chase he knew we weren't having him on. Earlier he had met a couple who had been at our campsite. On their way down to the valley they had been passed by the ranger, who had told them that an Englishwoman had gone missing.

'Look, we need boots and warmer clothes. I'm getting really cold. I know you've just walked up here, but you could get down much quicker than us; please ask the rangers to bring some warmer clothes,' I pleaded.

He nodded and then, having decided to help, organised the whole operation. Oh, the advantage of an English public school education.

'Right-oh. I'll leave my rucksack here while I raise the alarm; I'll move faster without it. Help yourselves to my spare clothes and any food you like. There's no point you walking any further without proper foot-wear, and walking downhill you'll only lose heat. Your best bet is to get over in that clump of trees and make yourselves a hot drink. You can use my stove and coffee.'

'Good idea, mate,' said Robbie. 'We've got our own gear. I reckon you're right: it'll warm us up. The speed you were walking at with your pack was pretty impres-sive, so I guess you'll be back before we know it.'

The Englishman smiled faintly. 'Hopefully. I'll enjoy the challenge. Wrap up and get some hot coffee down you and I'll be as quick as I can.'

Red and Robbie set up the stove while I pulled a sweater out of the Englishman's rucksack. It was a bit scratchy and overdue for a wash but what the hell. Taking off my fleece I was about to don it over my own sweater when two hands sneaked round and cupped themselves around my breasts.

'I bet Carlos didn't realise how sexy you'd look without a bra under that lambswool,' said Robbie in my ear. 'Let me keep you warm for a bit first.'

He unzipped his jacket and pulled me back on to his chest. It was the first time he had taken the initiative to touch me and despite our predicament I was instantly aroused. I was still chilled though and removed his hands and put on the Englishman's sweater, then pulled Robbie's hands back around me and pushed them up between the scratchy wool of the borrowed jumper and the contrasting softness of my own. The softness felt good on my tits and the odour of the stranger's sweater, a mingling of slight greasiness, damp wool and male sweat, stirred me for some reason. Red was looking up from the stove and watching the outline of Robbie's hands mashing my breasts, his fingers gently rubbing my hardening nipples.

I raised my arms in invitation. 'I'd be warmer if I had one of you on each side.'

Red undid his jacket too and put his arms around me. The fact that Robbie's busy hands were now pressed against his friend's chest excited me even more, and when Red put his hands round my arse and started kneading my buttocks I knew they were almost touching Robbie's cock. I could feel both of them hardening against me, Robbie pressed against the leather band we hadn't bothered to move from my arse and Red against my mons.

'If it weren't for the snow I'd like to fuck both of you,' I said softly. 'But in the circumstances I guess we'll have to wait.'

Robbie moved one hand down and sneaked it inside my trousers, still massaging my tits with the other.

'At least I can give you some pleasure. It might warm you up even more.'

He probed delicately until he found out how wet I had suddenly become and then moved his thumb to my clit. As he rubbed me gently and teasingly, as if we had all the time in the world, I knew his hand was rubbing against Red's cock. With Red's hands moving against his own I imagined the two guys rubbing each other off and my excitement increased. My mind saw Red and Robbie realising that their hands were exciting each other and after giving me my satisfaction masturbating each other, still with me in between them, coming simultaneously. I moved my hands, one forwards and one back, so that I could pull them closer towards me and so towards each other, circling their buttocks hard as Robbie's finger rubbed more roughly at my clit and Red's played on the leather string.

The thought of two men together has often piqued my curiosity, and I've always envied the decadence of dark rooms where anonymous mouths and hands offered pure satisfaction in a steamy atmosphere of random desire. Possibly it was even more perverse to imagine two friends, both overwhelmingly masculine, making out but the three of us had grown so close in our shared lust it seemed almost logical that Red and Robbie would want to satisfy each other as much as I wanted to satisfy both of them.

I remembered Kip telling me a story about two men who started off being forced to fuck each other but became absorbed with their mutual satisfaction. I imagined Red and Robbie in their place. The fantasy triggered the amber light in my sex muscles and I bucked against Robbie's hand and Red's cock, waiting to get to green. As I tensed on the edge of coming my rigid hands clawed round their arses and I pulled them both close to me. Picturing them going down on each other I went over the edge, riding the waves of my orgasm with shouts and gasps, muffled by the blanket of snow.

We stayed wrapped together as I recovered, my legs weak. Our silence seemed pregnant with possibilities until Red loosened his grip on my arse, kissing me on the nose as he did so.

'That should have warmed you up a bit. After some coffee you'll be fine.' His voice was affectionate but contained a slightly strained note, or maybe my fancy put it there. Realistically I knew that even if they might feel some desire for each other, nothing would come of it. Having stupidly gone to bed with a male flatmate once and having the whole friendship end in tears I knew well enough that it would be a disaster. Regretfully I filed my fantasy in the same drawer as the ones involving whips, rape, etc., to be called upon another day in imagination only.

Red made the coffee and we sat round the stove and tucked into the Christmas cake. We discussed the possibility of breaking the park rules and making a proper fire, but as help was on its way and we'd warmed up with sex and cake and coffee it didn't seem worth it. Hopefully we'd be rescued in less time that it would take to get a fire going.

Once I felt warmer I considered asking if the guys wanted their share of attention. They'd both been as solid as the tree trunk I was now leaning on while I had been the filling in their sandwich, but I reckoned they had probably calmed down by now. Not that I would have been unwilling to pass the time waiting for the return of our good Samaritan with a couple of blow jobs or hand jobs. Indeed, the exercise might well have produced a few more calories but, if they wanted, they knew they only had to ask.

We each drank two cups of coffee and after we'd rinsed the mugs in a stream and packed up the stove I beckoned both guys to me for a hug. As my fantasy had subsided as well as their hard-ons we just cuddled like old friends. I doubted that I would ever be part of such a close threesome again.

Suddenly we were hailed from down the path.

'Good, you're OK. I was afraid you were drowsy with cold huddled up there,' said the Englishman, who seemed to be alone. 'Thought maybe I'd underestimated how cold you were, in which case I shouldn't have told you to sit down.'

'No, it's OK, mate, we were just snuggling together for warmth,' explained Robbie insouciantly. 'We had some coffee as you suggested and thought it was the best way to keep warm.'

Our rescuer had acquired another rucksack from which he drew clean socks and three pairs of boots.

'Might not fit, of course, but better than nothing, and the socks will help. Got some spare sweaters as well.'

'Are you alone?' I asked incredulously. It was hard to believe that he'd alerted someone to our plight and got the boots and sweaters but they'd just let him get on with it.

He snorted. 'No, but I couldn't walk at their pace. Decided I might as well get up here, give you these and get on, if I can have my pullover back. The other chaps have got some food and hot water bottles, though by the time they get here I don't suppose you'll get much heat out of them.'

I suppressed a laugh as I returned the sweater and put on yet another man's woolly. Odd the things you suddenly find yourself doing twice in one day that you've never done in your life before. Idly I wondered if I might get stuck into a pattern of only feeling aroused while wearing a sweaty jumper. In reality it would probably be an easier peccadillo to maintain than either bondage or exhibitionism, the other new tastes I'd picked up on my travels.

The Englishman waved away our thanks, saying he wanted to get on. Red's reiteration of the warden's warnings to leave the campsite met with a tolerant smile; he was obviously hardy enough to look after himself. With no slackening of his swift pace despite his descent and re-ascent of the mountainside, he shook our hands and set off.

'I bet he'll go right up to the viewpoint and back to the valley today,' said Robbie with admiration.

'But what for?' I asked curiously. 'He won't see anything.'

'Because it's there,' said the guys almost simultaneously. Well, I guess it's just a boy thing.

As we toasted each other and our hosts and fellow guests with wine that evening the events of the day seemed surreal. To go from being tied up halfway up a mountain in a blizzard to eating a Christmas Eve dinner in a warm and cosy guesthouse was too great a contrast to be believable. I half wondered if I had dreamed the events of the day, or conversely if the celebratory meal was a hallucination brought on by hypothermia.

The rearguard of the rescue party arrived just as Robbie and I had laced on the boots; Red's feet were too large for the biggest pair. The two men were from the hut in the valley and decidedly pleased to see us. I guessed they suspected the Englishman was a complete fruitcake leading them on a wild goose chase, especially as he had run on ahead with their boots and sweaters. They did indeed have hot water bottles, which were still warm enough to be a delight to hold and, even better, a bag of empanadas, South America's version of a Cornish pasty. I let Red and Robbie do the explanations, as their Spanish was so much better than mine.

We followed the men down to the valley, ironically moving below the snow line, to find two park wardens waiting for us at the hut, one of whom was the one from the campsite. Robbie followed up my announcement of myself as the woman who'd been reported missing with something more cogent in Spanish. They sniggered at our story – well, God knows it was unbelievable stuff – but clearly they had no choice but to accept that we had definitely had our boots stolen and could not stay in the park. After a rapid-fire conversation that I don't think even Robbie could understand they gave us a lift to the park gates, where we caught the last bus out before Christmas.

The landlady was surprised to see us back in town only the day after we'd left. Robbie answered her briefly, smiling. Obviously the true story sounded too far-fetched; he had merely said that the snow had been very heavy and we realised we were ill-equipped. We were in luck. She had a room for us, and invited us to join her family and the other guests for Christmas Eve dinner.

It was only as we were going to bed that I thought we should have gone to the police.

'Or did the park wardens call them? I suppose they must have done.'

'No, they wouldn't have done,' said Red neutrally.

I was puzzled. 'Why not? Someone holds up three people at gunpoint and the authorities do nothing about it! That's a great advertisement for hiking in the national park, I don't think.'

Red and Robbie exchanged one of those private glances that meant, shall I tell her, or shall you?

'We couldn't tell them the truth,' said Red. 'Remember the look that Englishman gave us when we tried to tell him. Anyway, no harm was done, apart from losing our boots.'

'No harm?' I repeated incredulously. 'You two had a gun pulled on you; we could have frozen to death and he's stolen your papers, not to mention my films. How can we let him get away with it? We've got to tell the police.'

Red pulled me on to the bed. It was big enough for three, but none of us had any energy left.

'In the eyes of the police Carlos is a respectable Peruvian businessman. We're foreign backpackers; two of us are students. If we filed a complaint against Carlos don't you think they might believe him rather than us? Particularly if he tells them we tried to get in the way of a perfectly legitimate business opportunity he's trying to pull off, just because we're violent anti-capitalists?'

'But he lied to the warden about me being missing,' I said stubbornly. 'We can get him there.'

'The park warden wouldn't even remember what he

looked like,' said Robbie gently. 'And I'd put money on Carlos having an alibi. Like he spent all of the Christmas holiday tied up with your mate Susie.'

'Ha ha.' I wasn't amused. 'I bet the warden would remember him. I think you're wrong.'

That bloody look again. 'What is it?' I shouted. 'Tell me or I'll shout the house down.'

'Well, I had to say something. I told them you'd cheated on Carlos with us so he'd pinched our gear, but then must have been afraid we'd die and so reported you missing.'

'Great,' I said grimly. 'I thought they were giving me funny looks. They must have put me down as a real slut.'

Red burst out laughing. 'Well, it's not too far from the truth, is it? Anyway, you like being a slut.'

Very funny, I thought sourly as I stripped and threw my clothes on the floor. I barely heard Red get in next to me, or was it Robbie? It didn't matter.

Three days later we were on the road again, this time to cross the final border into Argentina. I had less than two weeks left and still hadn't seen everything I had planned.

Christmas Day was a non-event, the town being closed and our celebration having taken place the evening before. We lay in bed, got up to watch some TV, had a walk around the windy town and went back to bed. Robbie spent most of the next day at the internet café on line to friends at home and in the States and, despite my usual distaste for communicating with home while travelling, I sent an e-mail to Kip telling him exactly what he'd got me into.

We spent a brilliant week sightseeing on the Argentine side of Patagonia, but time was running out. In less than a week I had to get my plane from Buenos Aires.

Even though Red and Robbie hadn't planned to go that far north at this stage of the trip they didn't want to leave me. Not that they were exactly emotional about it – they were still Australians after all – so they merely said that Buenos Aires would be the best place to replace the missing boots so they could do the walks they'd planned. In reality I knew that after all we'd been through together they didn't just want to wave me off at the bus station and never see me again, so they decided to come with me and maybe return south later.

After a stop-off by the sea to break the long, monotonous bus journey, we reached the capital with four days to go before my flight back home. For the first time in ages it was actually hot, about thirty degrees, and after checking into a hotel as a treat for our last few nights we put our shorts on again and strolled around the noisy city streets, revelling in the bustle and life.

Apart from the sights I'd planned to see in the city I most definitely wanted to go to a tango class. Red and Robbie told me I was alone in that one, but I managed to drag them along to a lesson on our first night. Of course they were hopeless but I was thrilled. Most types of dancing seem banal, boring or just plain embarrassing to me, but there's something about the tango. I spent as much time as I could hogging the instructor, Luis. Although he wasn't attractive, being rather short and slightly podgy, he – or rather his dancing – made me feel that I was the most desirable woman in the world. As he bent me backwards and looked into my eyes I melted.

The streets were thronged with people when we left the class, mainly couples, women in revealing tops and short tight skirts, dark handsome men in white T-shirts and jeans, cruising languidly in the sultry heat. The neon-lit night throbbed with energy and possibilities and my body was still pulsing with the erotic rhythms of the tango. We sat in a restaurant and ate steak and drank red wine but the guys knew my mind was on other appetites. Our conversation dwindled to a minimum as we substituted eye contact and half-smiles for words; we didn't need to discuss what we were going to do next.

We skipped coffee and went back to our room. Though we had a fan we opened the balcony doors to let in the cacophony of the non-stop traffic and the all-night record shop over the road. In the glow of one bedside lamp Red stripped me while Robbie's coarse voice murmured appreciation of my body and suggestions as to what they should do with it. The heat and sensuality of the dance and the couples on the street who I knew were coupling themselves by now pervaded me with languor and I lay back as though drugged. Red and Robbie seemed to understand my passivity and slowly, with infinite patience, touched every pore of my body, inflaming every nerve end until I almost fainted with pleasure and longing, though they didn't allow me release.

'It's too hot to sleep tonight. We're going to make love to you till dawn,' said Robbie's disembodied voice, as he kneeled on the floor at the foot of the bed to caress the soft skin of my inner thigh, slippery not just with sweat but with the molten liquid that trickled uncontrollably from my sex. 'This is all for you, Bliss. We want to cover every inch of you with virtual tattoos that you'll always remember us by.'

I shivered as his fingers feathered my thigh, moving to make sure no tiny morsel of skin was untouched, like an artist meticulously dotting my body with a pointillist technique, his touch as gentle as the stroke of the finest paintbrush. But I couldn't concentrate on it fully as on the other side of me Red was running his fingers up my arm from my wrist right up to the curls that I had allowed to grow in my armpit, running his fingers around them as if flexing them for later, when he would wind them through my other, more luxuriant hairs.

They followed their caressing with kissing, retracing their fingers' movements all over me, then jointly sucking insistently at my nipples like babies, until finally their tongues penetrated me simultaneously. I kissed Red back with my mouth, not hard but with swollen parted lips that received his tongue fleshily and moistly in imitation of the wetness and softness Robbie was probing below.

I wanted to ask him to let me come now, to move his tongue to my clit and let it flicker over it just a few times, which was all it would take to make my cunt flicker and flare in response, but my mouth was still engaged with Red's tongue. Unable to articulate what I wanted, my body started to quiver. As though it had communicated its needs to Robbie he put his hands under my buttocks and lifted my hips, slanting me towards Red who moved his head downwards. As Robbie's tongue lapped at my moisture and gently rimmed my anus Red's tongue skitted almost imperceptibly over my clit and unbearably gradually licked me harder and harder until I exploded.

It was almost dawn.

I woke around eight thirty with Robbie's stiff cock nudging me behind. In contrast to the lovemaking of the hours of darkness, as I turned towards him he pulled me on top and entered me without preamble. Almost sardonically he made his excuses for his forwardness as he presumed I was already satisfied. Amused by his straightness and unable to refute his statement I shagged him quickly and energetically, enjoying the functional fuck for its own sake. Red slept despite the bouncing bedsprings and after Robbie came we too sank back to sleep. The next time I woke up Robbie was in the shower and I gave Red a similar efficient fuck, so we were all ready to face the day.

Despite the intensity of the night before Red and Robbie turned me down flat when I suggested another tango class. Although I felt almost achingly tender towards them both I was frankly relieved. I wasn't going to succumb to the lure of the tango with Red hauling me around like a sack of coal, a ludicrous parody of the beauty he had given me the night before. It only lasted an hour and a half anyway, so I agreed to meet them in a bar later. Part of me also knew that they had to re-establish themselves as a twosome again once I had gone, and bonding over a few beers seemed to be the Australian way of going about it.

Once again I loved the dancing and was on a high when I joined the guys in the bar. They had probably already had more than enough already but we got some tapas and I had wine while they continued to down the beers. We drank and joked like three best mates and fell into bed with all thoughts of sex erased from our minds. It seemed to be the perfect arrangement and so we agreed to do the same the next night.

Except that the next night, after the boys had gone to the bar early claiming dehydration, the room phone rang to say I had a visitor. I took the lift downstairs, part of me pretending to wonder who it was, but knowing deep down there was only one person it could be. Deep down I was right. Carlos was at reception, dressed in his cool cream business suit flashing a big smile at me.

Chapter Eleven

'*B*liss. I've missed you. You look beautiful.'

His tone was tender and he put his arm around me caressingly. What on earth the desk clerk thought I couldn't imagine. After all I was already sharing a room with two other men. Maybe he too thought we were brothers and sister.

'Well, I expect I look a bit better than I did last time you saw me,' I said tersely.

He laughed and held out a bag. 'I found some belongings of yours and the boys. Oh, and I had your photos developed for you.'

There was a glint of humour in his eyes, which took me aback. Surely disappointment should be his reaction to finding he had my films instead of Red and Robbie's, not amusement.

'Thanks,' I said abruptly, taking the bag from him. I peered in; three pairs of boots and three lots of holiday snaps. Plus a wodge of papers.

'You've left some papers in here,' I said sarcastically.

'No, they belong to the guys. Do tell them I'm sorry that I seemed to have run off with them.'

'Not a worry,' I said, consciously adopting the Australianism to demonstrate where my solidarity lay. 'They already had copies of them. And in any case they'd faxed them to their friends so they could get to work on them straight away.'

I faced him triumphantly as I told him that he was already on the verge of being rumbled in his crooked dealings. Worryingly he didn't look at all put out.

'I had assumed they would have done, but I was interested to read them all the same. Anyway, take that bag upstairs and I'll take you out to dinner.'

I couldn't believe his cheek. Exasperated, I took the bag from him and half turned away. 'Actually, I have dinner plans, not to mention a class beforehand, so I'm afraid you've had a wasted journey.'

'Oh, what sort of class?' he asked as if genuinely interested. 'Spanish?'

I glared at him. 'Tango, as it goes. So if you'll forgive me, I have to get ready and cross town.'

'Bliss, get off your high horse. Just take that bag to your room and I'll drive you wherever you want to go. I want to talk to you before you go home. Even if not for long.'

Yes, I know, I should have told him to fuck off out of my face before I called the police. But I couldn't help but be disarmed by how easily he took the news about the papers, not to mention his amusement at finding himself with my pictures instead of Red and Robbie's. As I stomped towards the lift I had to accept that the turbulence he had stirred up in my body wasn't due to indignation; if the guys could accept that he hadn't planned to harm us I certainly could.

Besides, it was very nice to look into his espresso eyes as a change from blue and grey. And I liked the idea of driving through BA with a man in a cream suit. Who wore just a splash of a rather sexy cologne.

His eyes widened appreciatively when I returned to the lobby dressed for the lesson. OK, it was extravagant, but after the first night I'd been shopping for a tango outfit: a short strapless red dress with a boned bra top and a pair of black kitten-heel sandals. It didn't have class but it was cheap and sexy, which was just how I felt when I put it on. As soon as I'd checked myself in the mirror before I left the room I knew that although Carlos wasn't completely forgiven I wasn't going to deny myself the pleasure of flirting with him.

He drove quickly and aggressively in his hire car to the address I gave him and stopped outside looking at his watch. 'Seven thirty. Have you got time for a quick drink?'

It was my turn to laugh. As I'd planned to either walk or take the subway it was fairly clear that the class wasn't about to start immediately.

'Lovely.'

We sat in a corner of an old-fashioned bar panelled in dark wood, with stained glass-windows diffusing the evening sunlight. I ordered a vodka tonic and threw Carlos a challenging look.

'Just out of interest, did you come all this way just to see me?'

'And return your things,' he teased. 'No. I had a bit of business to attend to.'

'I bet. What are you up to here? Buenos Aires seems quite developed enough to me.'

His mouth twitched. 'There's always room for more development. Actually, you might be interested, as the client is a Dutch company. They're test-marketing a new soft drink all over the continent and we're sorting out some possible factory sites for them on the outskirts of town.'

That déjà vu feeling again!

'Hang on a minute, is that the drink that's a bit like a fizzy milkshake?'

'So I'm told. I haven't tried it.'

He looked puzzled as I laughed out loud. I decided not to tell him that his client, or rather one of their marketing men, was my plane fuck, especially as I doubted he would remember my story anyway. I had a vision of international corporations criss-crossing the world with the various strands of their businesses, like a global spider's web. I ran my hand over my fringe as if to brush the thought, or the spider's web, away.

Carlos put his hand on my bare arm and drew his chair closer.

'Bliss, you do know I wouldn't have let anything happen to you.'

I believed him, but didn't want to seem too much of a pushover.

'You must think I'm pretty stupid. How on earth could you have known that I would be all right after you'd made your getaway?'

'Fairly easily,' he said, smirking. 'I phoned to say I had news about the missing woman; I was going to pretend that someone had seen her back at the camp site with two men. The park officer misunderstood me, though, and thought instead that I was enquiring about the missing woman. Of course he told me that she'd been found with two others and help was on the way.'

'Hmm,' I sniffed. 'I don't know why I should believe you. What about pulling a gun on Red and Robbie?'

'It wasn't loaded. I just thought they needed to learn that if you play with fire you can get burned. Didn't you think I threw it into my rucksack rather carelessly? Your career as a spy doesn't seem to have taught you very much.'

'Stop laughing at me!' I snapped. 'You shouldn't wave guns around, loaded or not. I might have had a heart attack. In fact for a minute I thought I had had one.'

He did laugh then, out loud. 'I really am going to miss you,' he said affectionately. 'American girls just don't have your sense of humour.'

'How is Susie, by the way?' I asked drily.

'Fine. I'm sure she'd send her best if she knew I was seeing you. She's down in Santiago for a few days. Tying poor Jorge up in knots, no doubt.'

'I wondered if he swung both ways, or whatever you call it. Susie told me you weren't interested, though.'

'No way. I like to be the one in control.'

'You don't say.' I sipped my vodka tonic. 'So what are you going to do now? Now that Red and Robbie have foiled your plans in Chiloe?'

'I hope they don't really believe that.' He laughed. 'Surely they're not that naïve – are they?'

There I was thinking I was being smart not letting him know that even they thought it had probably all been a waste of time, and all I'd done was make him think they were gormless innocents.

'They might get a bit of publicity in the left-wing press but nothing much will come of it,' he explained, as if to a child. 'That's if the plans go ahead after all.'

'Why wouldn't they?' I was confused. 'You're not saying that despite bribing the planning people and Susie prostituting herself and working out all the plans for staffing and sourcing the whole project might be ditched?'

He grinned. 'Gosh, you must have read all those papers. No, very possibly it won't get off the ground. These things often fall at the last fence. It happens all the time.'

I was definitely out of my depth. 'You're not telling me that all this subterfuge and corruption and planning go on all the time for *nothing*? It must cost a fortune! How can anyone waste that sort of money?'

'Bliss, you don't understand the real world, do you? We're talking about massive corporations with huge turnovers that think nothing of spending thousands on plans that may not bear fruit. It's better to go ahead with a feasibility study and then pull out than throw good money after bad, or even worse not to even investigate the possibilities and find the competition moving in.'

I was confused. 'But I thought one of the arguments against global capitalism is that they cut costs by employing slave labour in the third world; how can they do that when they throw money away like this?'

Carlos shrugged. 'Well, I expect your friends will tell you that's a good example of what's wrong with the way they work. But whatever they think, or do, nothing's going to change.'

It seemed to me that it was all a game. The multinationals played at setting up shop somewhere but then decided they'd go off and do it somewhere else. The activists played at trying to stop them but realised they didn't have much hope of doing so. The companies flexed their muscles just to emphasise who had the power, like Carlos pointing an empty gun at Red and Robbie's heads.

It was time for my class.

'Can I come with you? I know how to tango.'

I shook my head but I knew he was coming anyway. I couldn't stop him, any more than Red and Robbie could prevent the relentless takeover by the multinationals. Really, I thought, I just want to get my head back in the sand again as far as business and politics are concerned.

* * *

244

Carlos was dynamite. I rarely dance with men; as I explained I usually find dancing banal, etc. In fact this was the first time I'd danced with a lover, especially one who'd dressed me in black leather and chains and given me such exquisite agonies of anticipation, fear and shame. Despite the events of the last few weeks I still found him as sexy as hell and he pressed me close and manoeuvred me as intimately on the dance floor as he did in bed. By the end of the first dance it wasn't just the thirty degrees that were making me sweat, and it wasn't just on my back that a slick of moisture had appeared.

To my slight irritation Luis came and partnered me for the next dance to show me some finer points but I wasn't concentrating, instead watching Carlos with another woman. She was obviously a local and they laughed and rattled on easily in Spanish. He would have had no trouble getting her to go back to his hotel afterwards and I felt a stab of jealousy combined with a wobble in my reserve not to do just that.

We danced together for the rest of the class and left silently. My mind was whirling with possibilities. Should I escape from Carlos and scuttle off to the bar? Would Red and Robbie be interested in performing a replay of the scene at the campsite? Or would Carlos capture me and take me to his hotel for a final torrid night in chains, ignoring my protests? Would I, in fact, protest?

He opened the car door for me like a chauffeur and got in with a smile. 'Where to, madam?'

That rather unsettled me. Did he expect me to ask him to take me with him, or did he assume that I wasn't interested? Shrugging mentally I gave him the name and street of the bar I was meeting the boys in. He started the car and without further conversation drove back the way we came, almost driving past the bar but braking sharply just in front of it. Again he opened the car door for me and helped me out.

'Shall I pick you up at the same time tomorrow?'

'What for?' I asked, bewildered.

'For the class, of course. I enjoyed it, didn't you? We dance well together, don't you think? And of course a drink first. It's your last night, after all. Please let me say goodbye.'

Completely wrong-footed I nodded and he kissed my cheek briefly, got back in the car and drove off. As I turned towards the bar I saw Red and Robbie watching from the window.

'Nice time?' Red asked lightly. 'Thought you were going to your tango class.'

'I did. He turned up at the hotel before I left.'

I described the events of the evening, apart from my own indecision as to who to spend the night with, or at least who I might have spent the night with if I'd had another offer. They seemed completely unfazed by Carlos's reappearance, and were instead pleased that the Chiloe project might not get off the ground and delighted to get their boots back. Either they didn't think I could be interested in Carlos again or they were playing it cool, as they exhibited no sign of jealousy or even curiosity as to whether he had tried it on. I felt a bit piqued all round; didn't Carlos want me any more? Didn't Red and Robbie care if he did or not? I guessed that they'd all started to detach themselves from me as I'd soon be gone, and felt depressed.

For the second night running I drank too much and fell asleep as soon as I got into bed. Three hours later I woke dripping with sweat and with a raging thirst. Red was snoring next to me and Robbie was pressed against him. Pitying myself, I felt left out. I drank one litre of water and splashed another over my already damp body and crawled back into bed.

The next evening followed the same pattern, up to a point. Carlos picked me up and we had a drink in the same bar and went to the class. I concentrated as hard as I could on the dance steps, wishing I had longer in the city to learn them. Then halfway through the class Carlos pulled me close to him and murmured, 'Come back with me tonight. I can't let you go without making love to you one more time.'

'No,' I whispered, executing the turn clumsily as his words unsettled me. 'I can't. The boys are expecting me.'

'But you want to?' His voice was low and commanding.

'Yes. But I can't trust you. Look what happened last time I let you tie me up.'

Carlos laughed aloud, earning a glance of disapproval from Luis. We exchanged a guilty look at disrupting the mood of the class.

'You can stay free,' he persisted quietly. 'I want to touch your body again.'

'You're touching quite a lot of it now,' I pointed out as I wound my leg around his. 'It's not that I don't want to have sex with you, Carlos. It's just bad timing.'

'More like *Last Tango in Paris*,' he quipped. 'Seriously, Bliss. I want you badly.'

I nodded towards the girl he'd been dancing with the previous evening. 'Ask her, I'm sure she fancies you.'

'You'd be jealous.'

Shit, of course I would. But after all we'd been through I wasn't going to spend the last night without Red and Robbie.

He pulled me back and leaned over me, his face almost on mine. 'Let's leave now. There's a hotel next door. We'll get a room for half an hour.'

The sleaziness of the idea took my breath away. Almost numbly I nodded, and regardless of what Luis

247

or anyone else thought we stopped mid-dance and left the ballroom.

He handed over a few dollar bills to the desk clerk and we walked up the stairs; there was no lift. The paintwork was peeling and the stair carpet threadbare, though the dingy bulb cast little light on it. Room 212 was dark and musty and smelled of the last occupant's cigarette smoke but I didn't care, in fact the seedier the better. Carlos kicked the door to and turned round and grabbed me, kissing me with a dizzying intensity that took my breath away. His hands were on my breasts, pushing down inside the bra-style cups to lift them out and display them, his fingers playing with my nipples. Still with his mouth on mine he pushed me back against the wall and ran his hands up my legs, pulling my knickers down. I stepped out of them and he lifted my dress and surveyed me, his eyes sweeping from my cunt to my tits, with the cheap red imitation silk in between. Standing tall in my heels I revelled in his undisguised lust and took my dress from his hands so that he could undress while still looking at my swollen sex.

The door creaked and swung half open. In his haste he hadn't closed it properly. His hands were busy removing his trousers and he gave me a half smile and continued to undress without closing the door. Not wanting to lower my dress I too let the door hang ajar; if anyone should pass they would have seen me exhibiting myself like a wanton slut begging for attention, but in a place like this they would be hurrying to get into similar positions. I took a dark delight in the thought that it might add an edge to their excitement. Standing displaying myself like a whore in a cheap dress and shoes in a shabby hotel room rented by the hour gave me as much of a charge as being blindfolded and gagged.

Carlos pressed his body into mine, crushing me against the wall, and his hardness pressed desperately into me. His hands propelled me to the bed and I sank on to the grubby bedspread and opened my legs, not needing any stimulation and frankly not wanting it, just wanting to feel his cock push inside me and fuck me as hard as I knew he could.

We only had half an hour but he didn't rush it. It was the last time and I understood why he wanted to turn me over and thrust into me from behind, and then turn on to his back and let me fuck him. I finally lifted my dress off so that he could watch me play with my breasts as I rode his cock. The door was still half open and, though I had heard nobody pass, in my mind we were being quietly watched. As I mashed my clitoris hard against his bone I knew I was nearly there. He was too, and his hands moved to my clit to make sure we came together on this last time.

There were five minutes left for a quick shower in the bathroom down the hall before our half hour was up. We got into the car and he drove me to the bar in silence but unlike the previous day there were no unspoken questions between us. The loose ends had been tied; our game was over.

Like the night before he almost overshot the bar, screeching to a halt just in time. Again he came round and opened the door for me, and when I stepped out he bent formally to kiss my hand. I waited with a smile of affection and regret at our farewell on my face but instead of saying goodbye in the same vein he suddenly pulled me towards him and once again kissed my mouth with passion. Taken by surprise I responded almost automatically. His questing tongue forced my head back and his other hand pulled my arse towards him; my back arched as if we were still dancing a tango. He hadn't showered and smelled of sweat and sex and me.

Suddenly he stopped and straightened, hugged me briefly and got back in the car and drove away. Confused, I realised that people had stopped to watch us kiss; two of them were Red and Robbie, who were standing at the entrance to the bar.

'G'day,' said Robbie amiably. 'Good class?'

I nodded, suddenly feeling remorseful. 'Yes thanks. Don't suppose I'll get the chance to dance the tango again.'

'He gave you a good send-off,' observed Red nonchalantly. 'Shame he didn't hang around, we could have had a last drink together. We were going to say if he wanted you before us tonight we wouldn't have minded.'

'Excuse me! I thought we'd agreed that your opinion doesn't come into it.'

'No, Bliss, you've got it wrong,' said Robbie, his voice grating as he held my arm firmly and started walking down the street. Obviously we weren't going to the bar. 'You're the one who doesn't count any more, now you've proved just what a slut you are.'

I held my breath. Was this for real, or was it the last final game?

'We know what sort of dancing you've been doing for the last hour,' said Red. 'Did you do a special dance for him, or just open your legs?'

My legs that had opened for him were now trembling slightly. 'Both. We danced for a bit and then went to a hotel.'

'Sounds sleazy,' said Robbie. 'But that suits you just fine. Anyway, in case you're wondering what we think about it, we think you owe us. After the nice time we gave you the other night, we reckon it's our turn, especially as you've just had yours with Carlos.' His smile was almost sinister. 'We won't tie you up as long as you promise you'll do everything we tell you.'

'That's OK.' I hoped it would be.

'Good, because you don't really have much choice.'

'Dinner first?' I asked hopefully.

Red grinned broadly. 'We've had ours. If you're very good we might go out later for a drink and you can get something to eat then, but don't count on it.'

'Fine.'

My voice was a whisper and I walked through the humid streets of Buenos Aires with my two lovely boys on either side, knowing that my last night in South America was going to be no disappointment. I wondered if they had known that Carlos and I had fucked or whether they just guessed, but knew that they didn't really care.

Compared to Buenos Aires London was a freezing, dull, grey non-event. No vibrancy, no colour, no excitement. The people on the streets were uniformly drab; I could see how the tango started in the *barrios* of Buenos Aires, whereas all that the cockneys had come up with was the knees-up. The men I met socially seemed complete tossers compared to the sophistication of the Argentines. I couldn't believe I'd willingly left Carlos and Red and Robbie for the asinine lads I met everywhere I went. It was as though I'd traded in David Ginola and a pair of Mel Gibsons for a gaggle of David Beckhams and Robbie Williamses.

It was also clear that my career wasn't as easy to change as I'd airily supposed before I left. Nobody was interested in my photographs, though I thought some were pretty impressive. I had to accept that someone with a degree in fine art who'd spent the last five years designing dress materials wasn't likely to get any photographic work. I applied for a job in Nottingham, which would have had great prospects, but as bad as London was I knew I needed the big city. It seemed likely that I was going to have to go back to my old job, but I kept putting off the phone call to say I was back. Every day I wished I were still in South America.

Kip was entranced by my adventures and inspired by my introduction to bondage, although of course he wanted some reward for being immobilised, i.e. pain. We played around once or twice but I didn't enjoy the active role and being bound by a boringly image-conscious effete masochist just didn't do the trick for me. His friend Stevenson offered to experiment with both of us but I didn't fancy him, and anyway two men together would only make me miss Red and Robbie more.

Their postcards were the only bright spot in my life. Rather than go back to Patagonia they had gone up to northern Argentina and crossed the border into Brazil. They said they wished I were still with them; their second card consisted of nothing but WE MISS BLISS written over and over again by each of them alternately, and it almost made me cry. There wasn't much doubt that they'd be popular with sexy, brown-skinned, fabulous-bodied Brazilian women and I felt wistfully jealous.

I thought obsessively about our last night together, how they had started by making me tell them exactly what had happened with Carlos. When I got to the bit about the open door Red had smiled and raised the blinds and turned on the main light, musing that maybe the tenants of apartments over the road might be interested. He made me stand by the balcony door as I had stood for Carlos and turn in slow circles so both they and anyone glancing out of the block opposite would see me posing like a prostitute in an Amsterdam brothel. After that they had me dance for them, shimmying like a lap dancer, dressed in nothing but my black holdups and cheap shoes, and I undressed them and gave Red a hand job with my red dress sliding over his cock. His come spurted all over it. I still haven't washed it.

When I remembered that long night I would feel a quickening of the pulse in my cunt and was unable to resist sliding to the floor and slipping off my knickers, touching myself as I relived how Robbie had told me it was time I did the talking, and how I had described to them my deepest and darkest fantasies, except of course for the one about them together. While I talked I did whatever they wanted, stroking Robbie's still hard prick and pausing in my narrative while I sucked Red gently to get him hard again, then continuing while I obediently fingered myself and masturbated with everything they handed to me, from the famous torches to my hairbrush handle and even a pair of tooth-brushes, rubbing my clit – carefully – with the bristles of one while rotating another inside me.

Back in Stratford I pressed the flat of one hand over my mons while my finger stroked my clit and thought about the way they had lain on the bed with their legs interlaced, their pricks inches apart, while I sank on to first one and then the other of them with alternate strokes. As I slid down the length of Red's massive shaft I felt Robbie's just slightly smaller one press against my clit, and as I lifted myself and pushed down on to Robbie's cock Red's rubbed my buttocks. My thigh muscles started to scream at me but I was more interested in my tense and ready sex muscles and kept going until Robbie came inside me. I stayed with his cock until his groans subsided and then went back to Red. He too was nearly there and while I rode him to his climax Robbie's hand reached out and rubbed my engorged clit with my own wetness until I came too, my cunt muscles shouting and spasming loud enough to drown out the cry of my aching legs.

Back home I came at the same time as I remembered our last almost-simultaneous orgasm, but it was a pale imitation of that tremendous explosion, and afterwards I wasn't enveloped in the lovely, loving arms of Red and Robbie.

After a few weeks I pulled myself together. Life was passing me by – I couldn't sit in my flat having solitary sex for ever. I had to get out and meet people; it was time to get back to work. I phoned my old firm and agreed to start the following week. Then I had a call from Marcus Livingston.

He was a friend of Red and Robbie, he said. He knew the part I played with them in Chile, and wanted to meet me. Any friend of theirs is a friend of mine, I said, and we made a date for the following night.

The next day I had an e-mail from the guys, telling me I was going to be contacted by Marcus Livingston, who was a friend of theirs, etc. They went on to say that he had similar interests to theirs and thought I might be able to lend him a hand with a project he was involved in.

I assumed the similar interests were political rather than sexual, but you never know. I dressed carefully for my meeting with Marcus in a Hackney pub: my short Liquorice Allsorts skirt and black top and, just because Red liked them so much, my black holdups. He turned out to be short and hirsute and his passion was for politics, so we talked globalism. Despite my on-the-job rôle he told me more than I already knew about the Chiloe deal; he was a leading member of what he called a mirror group to Red and Robbie's. He offered me a job.

'Spying again?'

'Sort of. I'm afraid I don't mean a job with the group;

we don't have any money. We're looking for someone to work as a waitress.'

I won't tell the name of the restaurant chain as I can't risk blowing my cover. But let me tell you that it's not only in the third world where employees are exploited. Hopefully you'll read my shock horror report in a national newspaper one day, but I've become as accustomed as Red and Robbie to the apathy of the media, or indeed the public, so I'm not holding my breath.

Everyone thinks I'm crazy slaving away as a waitress for a bare minimum wage when I already had the offer of my old job back. Sometimes I think I should be doing this for a TV network, where I'd be pulling in a journalist's salary as well. But, hey, it's only money. My trip cost less than I expected, thanks to spending so much time under canvas, so I had some left over. That had to go; having spare cash around makes me nervous. If I'm not on the brink of financial ruin by the end of the month I feel like I'm not really living. Money just gives you an illusion of security, and who wants security anyway?

What's more, apart from the fact that I adore the thrill of espionage, I've found out what a mirror group means. We share all our information with the groups in Australia and the States. The boys are back in Perth now and once a week we meet at Marcus's house and download any information the other groups have and send ours. After the others have gone Marcus and I have a special on-line session with the guys. This week Robbie started by stripping me down to my underwear, though of course Marcus had to provide the hands and type out exactly what I looked like. Robbie then used Marcus's finger to stroke my clit while the screen filled with his words of profane encouragement.

This week was pretty special because though I've asked for this before it was the first time that Red allowed me to use Robbie's hand round his dick. I bent over the keyboard to tell Robbie how his finger was probing and stroking me, though I lost it as I came, so Red took over and told me how well I was pumping him. When his message read *fuck fuck fuck fuck fuck fuck fuck* I guessed he'd come too. Marcus seemed keen on the image of Robbie and Red wanking each other, even only as proxies. I think he hero worships them and though he's not gay I bet he wouldn't mind one of their hands round him, virtual or otherwise. He doesn't get much else out of the session, though I guess he jerks off after I've gone. There's always the possibility that Red or Robbie will ask him to fuck me for them, though I somehow don't think they will.

Of course, now Red and Robbie have sort of acted out my fantasy of the two of them together, I might have to reciprocate by letting Red into the inner sanctum of my arse, via a slimline vibrator in Marcus's hands. That possibility can stay in my head for the time being, though.

My political education hasn't come on as well as you might expect considering my new career, but the more I learn the more committed I become. Working for a big company in a menial position would open anyone's eyes to the outrages they get away with. I don't know if there'll be another assignment for me when I've got enough information from this job, but I don't care. One thing I've definitely decided is that I'm not going back to my old job. I'll be thirty-one in a couple of months' time and I'm not going to risk suddenly realising I'm fifty-one and have just wasted twenty years of my life going through the same routines day after day, week after week.

Mum was pissed off with me because she thinks I won't get very far in life without a good employment record. I had to laugh, as her own is abysmal. Surely, I asked her incredulously, she doesn't really want me to work hard, play hard, keep my nose clean and generally live by all those tenets of the faith of Willem van Bon? She had to agree that that's going too far.

I'm not worried about the future, anyway, as Red and Robbie are contemplating a trip to Vietnam after they graduate; not on any mission, but just for a holiday. They want me to go with them and I just might. They've promised that they're going to spend next week's on-line session forcing me to agree. Marcus is looking forward to it, but not as much as I am.

Visit the *Black Lace* website at

www.blacklace-books.co.uk

Find out the latest information and take advantage of our fantastic **free** book offer! Also visit the site for . . .

- All *Black Lace* titles currently available and how to order online
- Great new offers
- Writers' guidelines
- Author interviews
- An erotica newsletter
- Features
- Cool links

Black Lace – the leading imprint of women's sexy fiction.

Taking your erotic reading pleasure to new horizons

BLACK LACE NEW BOOKS

Published in November

THE ORDER
Dee Kelly
£6.99

Margaret Dempsey is an Irish Catholic girl who discovers sexual freedom in London but is racked with guilt – until, with the help of Richard Dalbeny, a failed priest, she sets up The Compassionate Order for Relief – where sexual pleasure is seen as Heaven-sent. Through sharing their fantasies they learn to shed their inhibitions, and to dispense their alms to those in sexual need. Through The Order, Margaret learns that the only sin is self-denial, and that to err is divine!

An unusual and highly entertaining story of forbidden lusts and religious transgressions.

ISBN 0 352 33652 8

PLAYING WITH STARS
Jan Hunter
£6.99

Mariella, like her father before her, is an astrologer. Before she can inherit his fortune, she must fulfil the terms of his will. He wants her to write a *very* true-to-life book about the male sexual habits of the twelve star signs. Mariella's only too happy to oblige, but she has her work cut out: she has only one year to complete the book and must sleep with each sign during the month of their birth. As she sets about her task with enthusiastic abandon, which sign will she rate the highest?

A sizzling, fun story of astrology and sexual adventure.

ISBN 0 352 33653 6

THE GIFT OF SHAME
Sara Hope-Walker
£6.99

Jeffery is no more than a stranger to Helen when he tells her to do things no other man has even hinted at. He likes to play games of master and servant. In the secrecy of a London apartment, in the debauched opulence of a Parisian retreat, they become partners in obsession, given to the pleasures of perversity and shame.

This is a Black Lace special reprint of a sophisticated erotic novel of extreme desires and shameful secrets.

ISBN 0 352 32935 1

Published in December

GOING TOO FAR
Laura Hamilton
£6.99

Spirited adventurer Bliss van Bon is set for three months' travelling around South America. When her travelling partner breaks her leg, she must begin her journey alone. Along the way, there's no shortage of company. From flirting on the plane to being tied up in Peru; from sex on snowy mountain peaks to finding herself out of her depth with local crooks, Bliss doesn't have time to miss her original companion one bit. And when brawny Australians Red and Robbie are happy to share their tent and their gorgeous bodies with her, she's spoiled for choice.

An exciting, topical adventure of a young woman caught up in sexual intrigue and global politics.

ISBN 0 352 33657 9

COMING UP ROSES
Crystalle Valentino
£6.99

Rosie Cooper, landscape gardener, is fired from her job by an over-fussy client. Although it's unprofessional, she decides to visit the woman a few days later, to contest her dismissal. She arrives to find a rugged, male replacement behaving even more unprofessionally by having sex with the client in the back garden! It seems she's got competition – a rival firm of fit, good-looking men are targeting single well-off women in West London. When the competition's this unfair, Rosie will need all her sexual skills to level the playing field.

A fun, sexy story of lust and rivalry . . . and landscape gardening!

ISBN 0 352 33658 7

THE STALLION
Georgina Brown
£6.99

Ambitious young horse rider Penny Bennett intends to gain the sponsorship and the very personal attention of showjumping's biggest impresario, Alistair Beaumont. The prize is a thoroughbred stallion, guaranteed to bring her money and success. Beaumont's riding school is not all it seems, however. Firstly there's the weird relationship between Alistair and his cigar-smoking sister. Then the bizarre clothes they want Penny to wear. In an atmosphere of unbridled kinkiness, Penny is determined to discover the truth about Beaumont's strange hobbies.

Sexual jealousy, bizarre hi-jinks and very unsporting behaviour in this Black Lace special reprint.

ISBN 0 352 33005 8

Published in January

DOWN UNDER
Juliet Hastings
£6.99

Fliss and David, 30-something best friends, are taking the holiday of a lifetime in New Zealand. After a spell of relaxation they approach the week-long 'mountain trek', brimming with energy and dangerously horny. It's Fliss's idea to see if, in the course of one week, they can involve every member of the 12-person trek in their raunchy adventures. Some are pushovers but others present more of a challenge!

A sexual relay race set against a rugged landscape.

ISBN 0 352 33663 3

THE BITCH AND THE BASTARD
Wendy Harris
£6.99

Pam and Janice, bitter rivals since schooldays, now work alongside each other for the same employer. Pam's having an affair with the boss, but this doesn't stop Janice from flirting outrageously with him. There are plenty of hot and horny men around to fight over, however, including bad-boy Flynn who is after Pam, big time! Whatever each of them has, the other wants, and things come to a head in an uproar of cat-fighting and sexual bravado.

Outrageously filthy sex and wild, wanton behaviour.

ISBN 0 352 33664 1

ODALISQUE
Fleur Reynolds
£6.99

Beautiful but ruthless designer Auralie plots to bring about the downfall of her more virtuous cousin, Jeanine. Recently widowed but still
young, wealthy and glamorous, Jeanine's passions are rekindled by
Auralie's husband. But she is playing into Auralie's hands. Why are
these cousins locked into this sexual feud? And what is the purpose of
Jeanine's mysterious Confessor and his sordid underground sect?

A Black Lace special reprint of a cult classic of the genre.

ISBN 0 352 32887 8

To find out the latest information about Black Lace titles,
check out the website: www.blacklace-books.co.uk or
send a stamped addressed envelope to:

Black Lace, Thames Wharf Studios,
Rainville Road, London W6 9HA

Please note only British stamps are valid.

BLACK LACE BOOKLIST

Information is correct at time of printing. To avoid disappointment check availability before ordering. Go to www.blacklace-books.co.uk

All books are priced £5.99 unless another price is given.

Black Lace books with a contemporary setting

THE TOP OF HER GAME	Emma Holly ISBN 0 352 33337 5	☐
IN THE FLESH	Emma Holly ISBN 0 352 33498 3	☐
SHAMELESS	Stella Black ISBN 0 352 33485 1	☐
TONGUE IN CHEEK	Tabitha Flyte ISBN 0 352 33484 3	☐
SAUCE FOR THE GOOSE	Mary Rose Maxwell ISBN 0 352 33492 4	☐
INTENSE BLUE	Lyn Wood ISBN 0 352 33496 7	☐
THE NAKED TRUTH	Natasha Rostova ISBN 0 352 33497 5	☐
A SPORTING CHANCE	Susie Raymond ISBN 0 352 33501 7	☐
TAKING LIBERTIES	Susie Raymond ISBN 0 352 33357 X	☐
A SCANDALOUS AFFAIR	Holly Graham ISBN 0 352 33523 8	☐
THE NAKED FLAME	Crystalle Valentino ISBN 0 352 33528 9	☐
CRASH COURSE	Juliet Hastings ISBN 0 352 33018 X	☐
ON THE EDGE	Laura Hamilton ISBN 0 352 33534 3	☐
LURED BY LUST	Tania Picarda ISBN 0 352 33533 5	☐
LEARNING TO LOVE IT	Alison Tyler ISBN 0 352 33535 1	☐